D0956080

THE ONE

THE ONE

a novel

Julia Argy

G. P. Putnam's Sons
New York

PUTNAM
— EST. 1838 —
G. P. Putnam's Sons
Publishers Since 1838
An imprint of Penguin Random House LLC
penguinrandomhouse.com

Library of Congress Cataloging-in-Publication Data

Names: Argy, Julia, author.
Title: The one: a novel / Julia Argy.
Description: New York: G. P. Putnam's Sons, [2023] |
Summary: "A razor-sharp and seductively hypnotic debut novel about the very fantasy of falling in love"—Provided by publisher.
Identifiers: LCCN 2022049215 (print) | LCCN 2022049216 (ebook) |
ISBN 9780593542781 (hardcover) | ISBN 9780593542798 (ebook)
Subjects: LCGFT: Romance fiction. | Black humor. | Novels.
Classification: LCC PS3601.R478 O54 2023 (print) |
LCC PS3601.R478 (ebook) | DDC 813/.6—dc23/eng/20221024
LC record available at https://lccn.loc.gov/2022049215
LC ebook record available at https://lccn.loc.gov/2022049216

Printed in the United States of America
1st Printing

Book design by Alison Cnockaert

Men act and women appear. Men look at women. Women watch themselves being looked at. This determines not only most relations between men and women but also the relation of women to themselves. The surveyor of woman in herself is male: the surveyed is female. Thus she turns herself into an object of vision: a sight.

—JOHN BERGER, *WAYS OF SEEING*

THE ONE

NIGHT ONE

MIRANDA WANTS ME to act like I'm about to meet my husband. She says I should walk toward him like I'm walking down the aisle. Through the dark tinted window of the limousine, Dylan looks like the model in a Folgers commercial, so blandly hot that he could be anyone's husband, which is exactly why he was picked for the role. Miranda starts counting down for the woman across from me to exit the car first. The next time she gets to one, it will be my turn. I'll step out of the limo and make my debut on national television. The first woman seems composed as she greets him, her cornflower blue silk dress flowing over her thin frame, and her skin like the skin of a regal baby in a painting. They hug, talk back and forth a bit, laugh, and hug again.

I want him to look at me the way he's looking at her already, his eyes crinkling at the edges with a smile. I can be desirable if I try hard enough. In my regular life, I do it all the time, pouting about the heat so my downstairs neighbor will install my window A/C unit for me, laughing too hard at barely a joke from a man on the phone to get a discount on my renter's insurance. It's never come naturally to me, not that it needs to. I learned how the world works by being a quick study. When the tall double doors of the mansion close behind the first woman, Miranda starts counting again.

On the ride over, all of us took tequila shots. I sweated through each curve of the desert road, up the scrubby hills toward my potential future husband. We bit down on pristine wedges of lime from the minifridge, careful to not smudge our lipstick on the rinds, and then we screamed. I tried not to think about what I was getting myself into. Earlier today, when I modeled different outfits for Miranda, she said it was an asset that I never watched the show.

"What's he going to be like?" I asked her for what felt like the hundredth time. I was in a ribbed butter yellow dress, so cheaply made that it pilled beneath my armpits within fifteen minutes of wear, as though it was only ever supposed to be looked at and never used.

"Tall," Miranda said. I spun, and Miranda shook her head no, vetoing the dress. "Stop overthinking. He's going to like you."

"And if he doesn't?"

"Then eventually you'll go home, and then three months from

now, you'll see yourself on TV and think, 'My whole life is different now. Better. Thanks, Miranda.' Trust me," she said.

"I do trust you," I said.

"Good. You'll need to."

When Miranda gets to one, the driver opens the door and the damp skin on my thighs, exposed through the slits of my jumpsuit, shears off from the leather seat. In my peripherals, there's an encampment of tents, travel trailers, filming equipment, and porta-potties. Two women dressed in black sit on a grassy slope behind the limousine, staring at a phone. The blue light illuminates their faces. My own phone was taken away as soon as I landed at LAX, and I miss its pretty, sedative glow. I had trouble falling asleep the first few nights at the hotel away from it, my brain unable to slow down without the anonymous lull of my Instagram suggested page, filling in square after square of lithe dancing teens and reports of dogs elected as small-town mayors. Next to the women on the grass, a cameraperson sits behind a rig the size of a medieval catapult and turns the camera toward me.

"Thank you," I say to the driver as he shuts the door behind me, a habit ironed into me by my mother. Thank the bus driver when you leave. Thank the men who hold doors for you at church. Thank the cashier at 7-Eleven for giving you free coffee every morning for being pretty, sixteen, and in a Catholic school uniform. Thank as many people as possible, and then, every morning and night, thank God for all your blessings. The driver nods and backs away. When I feel brave enough to look up at Dylan, he's focused on Miranda, who has slunk out from the passenger door.

"Again," she calls out. The catapult camera swings back toward the fountain to recapture my entrance. "Don't thank the driver. I thought I told you that."

"Oh, sorry," I say. I apologize more loudly to Dylan, who's smiling at me across the driveway.

"Think of them as moving furniture." He gestures to the vast number of people responsible for creating the atmosphere for us to fall in love, which seems at least a little ungrateful. Dylan tries to ask my name, but Miranda yells at him from inside the limo to cut it out.

"Patience is a virtue," I respond, and I know it's a good line, that I'm being alluring. Back in the limo, Miranda starts counting as soon as the door shuts and the other women stay silent. As we drove here, I tried to think about what made me stand out from them, but we're all slim and beautiful, dressed up like it's an adult prom. I've heard that in the dank corners of boys' locker rooms women are ranked by two factors: tits and ass. Whatever television executives chose Dylan to be the One would pick someone more evolved, surely, but as each of us parades in front of him for ninety seconds max, he can't rank us on much else. My assets on both counts seem to be lacking. I'll have to make a go of it based on a sugar-sweet personality.

When I get out the second time, I stare at his hair, parted down the middle. It's almost unfashionable, but for some reason it looks good, so precisely tousled that he must have his own hairstylist. He may even be wearing makeup. Later tonight, I could touch his hair and find out if it's stiff with gel or crispy with mousse. Now that

I'm here, I could press my lips, coated in a dry cupcake-flavored liquid lipstick, against his and see if any of his balm comes off on my own. The makeup artist kept referring to the color as "your lips, but better." This seems to be the general perspective of the show. I'm going to date, but better. I'll showcase my personality, but better. If I do a good enough job, my life, too, will end up being better.

"Hi, I'm Emily," I say.

"Dylan," he answers. "You look great in that dress."

For a second, I go to correct him, but decide against it. I'm not even sure if men like him understand what a jumpsuit is and, further, I'm not sure how I would explain it. It's a dress, but it has legs. It's supposed to be sexy, as the entirety of my naked back is visible, but cool, in that I'm in the minority of women not wearing sequins tonight. Because I'm trying to show that I have independent thoughts: I'm supposed to wear a formal dress to this event, but instead I'm wearing something that only looks like a formal dress. It's meant to be subversive.

"Oh, thanks," I say. "I've been looking forward to meeting you and to beginning this adventure."

Miranda told me to call my time on the show an adventure or a journey, and never a process, situation, or circumstance. She kept telling me I needed a hook for when I introduced myself to Dylan. I tried to make a pirate joke and she didn't laugh. She offered up ideas about costumes, fancy transportation, animal sidekicks, special gifts from home, and musical performances. She said I should show him that I'm down-to-earth. She asked if I had any cute photos of me and livestock that I could share with him, or if I had a sweet old granny who lived on a farm who could write an encouraging note for me to carry around. If it happened to slip out of my pocket and fall directly at Dylan's feet, then so be it. I failed to answer a series of probing questions about what I liked. "I don't know," I kept saying. "I like everything." Eventually, she told me to say my name and something flattering.

The day before I auditioned for the show back in Boston, I had been fired from my job as an administrative assistant at a biotech start-up. My boss told me that, as I could probably guess, it wasn't working out. I nodded, though I hadn't expected it. I had been working there for almost two years with the same total lack of skill and enthusiasm. I didn't know why he'd decided he no longer wanted me. Whenever my semiannual reviews approached and I got worried about my nonexistent deliverables beyond refilling the staplers, I googled whether or not I would be terminated. The forums said as long as I had a cheery disposition, I would be fine, so I baked treats for the office every week and had extended chats with the annoying men from the research unit as they walked by my desk. I kept a special calendar of staff birthdays and wrote handwritten notes to celebrate them. In a generous estimate, I spent about 10 percent of my time each day doing my actual job, which involved organizing detailed meeting agendas and the endless scheduling for said meetings. The professional advice columns told me that managers hate firing people. It's such a hassle for them, I've read, so I apologized to my boss for the inconvenience.

The next morning during rush hour, I took the bus into the

city wearing business casual. I wanted the semblance of a commute, though I was only going to a coffee shop to trawl through job boards all day and drink cup after cup of frothy matcha lattes that cost $6.50 including tip. A woman stopped me on the street, and I looked at the ground, thinking I had dropped something. She was dressed like the kind of young professional I wanted to be, pretty in a loose geometric-printed top and white pants. She asked me if I had heard of *The One* and I said that I had. I'd never seen it but knew about it in the way that everyone did: each season alternating between helicopter rides and women sobbing, then switching to giant jacuzzis and men shedding a single tear. The woman was a casting associate in town for a general recruitment day at the hotel ballroom down the street. She showed me her badge for the event and pointed to the sign outside the hotel's wide automatic doors. It featured a woman with a beatific smile and floating script above her head reading, "Are you ready to find *The One*?" The hotel was fancy enough to have red carpeting extending out toward the street, with bellhops and their gleaming golden carts in front.

"I love your look. You'd be a fresh face. A breath of fresh air," the casting assistant said, and then asked if I would be interested in learning more. She was heading there now, and if I had a few minutes, they could do a short screen test before the throngs of other women arrived. The event was to ensure they had a backlog of willowy young singles at their disposal, but there was a last-minute opening for the season that was about to start filming. The whole thing felt like a happy coincidence, a pot of gold dropped in my lap if only I had the gall to take it, and I had no reason to say no. I told myself I could be done applying for jobs that day, postponing the hours of reformatting my résumé, pressing the space key again and again to make sure all my life experiences were perfectly aligned. If I got a callback, I would be even more pleased. I didn't have any memorable experiences to share at dinner parties, and it would be a quirky story to tell if I ended up on the show.

"I'm actually in the market for a new opportunity," I answered, and thus my journey to find love began.

Four days later, as I slept on my flight to LA, Dylan was announced as the lead. Miranda, having already taken my phone, flipped through hers to show me photos of him. One was a screenshot of him at a tropical dais from last season, looking sweaty and upset. I assumed it was a photo of when he got dumped after proposing to the lead, a woman named Suzanne. I felt bad that millions of people had watched him perspire. Miranda said it was an ounce of sweat and tears for a whole lot of reward. She told me he was a fourth grade teacher, which was a good sign—not just a teacher but an elementary school teacher—because it meant he probably didn't have major issues with his masculinity. That, or he wanted a career surrounded by women where any semblance of caring behavior toward children would be celebrated as an astronomical feat, skyrocketing his hotness through the stratosphere.

I thought about these scant facts for the next three days as Miranda shuttled me to meetings with other producers, a primary care doctor, a psychiatrist, and a cast therapist. Each night, I ended up back at my hotel room, where I filled out a five-hundred-question personality test. Trapped, I had to order room service for every meal with a hundred-dollar per diem, but the hotel food was so overpriced that I only ate appetizers. I watched the four channels of cable news for hours on end, the first time doing so since I was in middle school. It reminded me of my parents' house. I had nothing to click, nothing to do.

Outside the mansion, Dylan tells me he's looking forward to talking to me more later tonight. As we hug goodbye, his breath skitters by my ear, warms my neck, and his eyes crinkle for me, too. I sway my hips as I walk away since I know he's watching me. Another cameraperson tracks me as I go through the doors. I'm desperate to hear that I'm doing a good job, to ask what Miranda has said into their earpiece, but I keep walking down a set of short steps that opens to a large living room. The prick of my heels on the tile echoes from my ankles to the walls and I can feel the reverberations in my rib cage. The first woman to enter, Winna, sits on the couch alone. Trays of crudités, dips, cold cuts, and crackers that look like fancy Ritz line a side table near her.

"We're the first ones here," Winna says as though to welcome me. She has a thin flute of champagne in her hand and a stick of celery in the other. She's so thin that I can see her ribs through her dress like rungs in a ladder, making their way up to her long collarbones. "My friends back home made me watch the last season with Dylan after I applied. They wanted me to see the group of men the producers were going to pick from for the next One. They said the order of the limo exits matters, like the first ones and the last ones are the people who are wife material."

"Oh, wow. I didn't know that. I'm Emily." We already exchanged names in the car, but I don't know what else to say. I try to think about what makes us both wife material, but all that I can latch onto is that we were the only two women in the limousine who weren't blond. For a second, I try to suss out whether she is prettier than I am, and hope she is doing the same to me.

"Winna. You should sit down," she says, gesturing next to her. "I was feeling like a social pariah all alone in here." This is the kind of thing an actual social pariah would never admit to, which reassures me. I pick up a butter cracker and take a bite, caking my mouth with dry, salty dust. I have trouble forming an appropriate next sentence. The feeling of Dylan's breath on my neck still tingles there and my cheeks flush.

"Did you know Dylan was the first out of the limo last season?" she asks into the silence.

"Oh, wow," I repeat. "Well, this is looking good for you then."

"I didn't mean it like that," Winna says. "I'm nervous. I'm just saying things. I'll feel better soon."

"I'm nervous, too."

The ceilings are tall and vaulted. A large bronze statue that could be a vagina or a peapod takes up an enormous corner of the room. Out the window, twinkling lights dangle from the house to a gazebo. The circular pool shimmers blue like one of those tropical coves from the show's previews. The whole house and outdoors are alit, the studio lighting creating a false, bright daylight against the dark sky.

"I'm glad it's him, though. Dylan seems too mature for drama. He never got in a single fight last season," Winna says. I file this information away, hoping it will help me at a nebulous point in the future.

"Hi, ladies," a woman says, wearing a fanny pack full of wiring and black rectangles. She hands me a glass of champagne. "The bartender is over in the kitchen and he'll be here all night. How many girls do you think are going to come?"

"I don't know, at least two dozen more," Winna says.

"Can you say it in a full sentence? And look at Emily." The production assistant knows my name, but I don't recognize her. She must have seen the mortifying headshot they made me take plastered up somewhere in the staff break room, my face on an index card, flipped over and shuffled before I arrived. At the shoot, the photographer kept telling me I needed to work my angles. "Tilt your head, tilt your head," he said, as though he wanted me to pose like a mangled corpse in a horror film. It felt like school picture day, when I would look panicked no matter how hard I tried to look my best. I would prepare for days in advance, picking an outfit and flipping through a girls' magazine for intricate braids and piecey updos I could never pull off. I would enter the classroom, the marbled blue screen behind me that you could pay extra to get photoshopped as another color, and feel confident. Weeks later, when I would open the set of two-by-three prints my mother bought in bulk, I was disappointed. How I looked in my mind was never how I looked on camera. I listened to the photographer against my better judgment, tilting my head. "Hands on your hips," he said. "Girl power!" And I tried to listen to that, too.

"At least two dozen more women must be coming tonight. Can you imagine?" Winna says. I grimace.

"Thanks, great," the woman says. She pulls the cameraperson toward the door before I have time to answer. One of the blond women from the limo walks in, now donning a cowboy hat.

"Hi, ladies!" she says with a thick Southern accent. It sounds so strong that for a second I wonder if it's a ploy to make herself memorable. Then I regret my mean impulses. Her dress is cinnamon red and barely hits her legs. Folded fabric around the neckline creates an optical illusion that her already large breasts are impossibly larger, like one of those Elizabethan corsets that hoist your boobs up to your neck, nearly choking you. Maybe the first set of contestants are meant to showcase the vast scope of women who desire Dylan, like going to a big-box store where at the head of each aisle is a sample stand, enticing you down to the rest of the similar wares. I need to figure out what brand of woman I'm supposed to be. The production assistant somehow has more champagne, having disappeared for a mere moment, and places it into the new woman's hand.

As more women arrive, I count things to pass the time, starting with the number of individual false eyelashes. Each of the women here, myself included, has them glued to her eyes, heavy and trembling like fuzzy, poisonous caterpillars. The sparser ones must have at least fifty threads per eye, nearly doubling the count of actual eyelashes, but the thicker ones go above 150. The crew slithers around with cameras perched on their shoulders or strapped and stabilized against their abdomens like precious swaddled babies. I melt into the corner of a dimpled leather sofa, chatting, chatting, and chatting. Booms arc above us like waving trees in a windstorm. I try to keep track of who is who, but I had one glass of champagne and two of white wine, so my eyes are trimmed with a grainy cast of tipsiness. At one point, a woman comes in with a large koala mask on, the size of a beach ball.

"Hi, ladies!" she says. I regret not saying "Hi, lady!" to Winna as I walked in.

"A koala," a woman proclaims, but the koala is obviously another gorgeous woman. I turn to Winna, hoping to make eye contact. Behind her, a camera tracks me. Look nice, look nice all the time. Look happy, but also extremely sultry and hot. My face neutralizes. The woman places the mask on the floor and begins chatting to a group of women who all look like adult babies. Their wide doe eyes sparkle, hundreds of eyelashes among them. A production assistant hands her champagne, makes sure everyone has a glass, and then hands me two flutes.

"Give this to Dylan," the assistant says. "He'll come in from that door."

Before I can say anything, the assistant walks away, sheltering in a far corner of the room as an additional fleet of cameras arrives. A drop of condensation from the cool glass drips onto my wrist. I straighten my spine, thinking of my mother's parting words: "Don't slouch on TV."

"Hi, ladies," Dylan says. I slink forward and hand him the glass. We have the height differential where if he was to lift his arm up, I'd be able to huddle underneath him like an awning. This always seemed like an attractive quality in men: shelter.

"Thanks, Emily," he says with so much intensity that the interaction suddenly seems fraught. My throat closes up a little at the women's collective gaze on us. "Thank you all for coming tonight. I know you sacrificed a lot to be here and I'm excited to get to know all of you. This adventure can be hard at times, but I know that it will be worth it in the end. If there's anything that I learned when I was in your shoes, it's that you can't get through this without being honest. Be honest with yourself and be honest with me . . ."

An oil painting of the desert hangs behind Dylan's head. The summer when I was twelve, my parents rented an RV. That year, we went to northern Michigan. On a hike up a giant sand dune that crested above Lake Michigan, there was a sign that said if you walked down and had an emergency, you would be charged rescue fees, so my father waited at the top. He would never do anything that constituted a risk. I took off my flip-flops before descending with my mother, though the sand burned my feet. When I reached the crystalline shore, I waded in and splashed my face. The fresh water spilled into my open, panting mouth, and I swished it around to cool myself down from the inside out. I asked my mother to take off her sneakers and join me. She said no, that she couldn't because she had two unsightly bunions, so eventually we turned around. There was no one else around. I never was sure who she was hiding the image of her feet from, her daughter or herself.

"Cheers," Dylan says. The room twinkles with the sound of the thirty of us clinking our glasses. It's finally the full group, and the night begins.

A cameraman tracks a brunette woman with a pale pink dress as she invites Dylan for a private chat. They walk out of the room holding hands. I've never held hands with someone in our fourth minute of conversation, but I guess this is a place for expanding my horizons. The host of the show glides into the room before we can resume our conversations. She has the type of taut, angular face that could be any age. Winna whispers to me that she used to be a race car driver or maybe one of the women who wave checkered flags at NASCAR events. She sets down a tray on the coffee table at the center of our circle. A long golden necklace lies there, its delicate chain perfectly arranged. The host doesn't say anything, but smiles even more cheerily as the women frown.

"Already?" one woman says, breaking the silence. I take a sip of champagne. The cold, crisp bubbles explode on my tongue. I didn't even want to drink it. I only wanted to look like I had something to do. A frantic energy rattles through the room, as though we've all decided that in the presence of the necklace, we can size each other up without subtlety anymore. It's possible that I've descended into deeper circles of hell without realizing. There are no clocks anywhere and all the crackers have been eaten. There's nothing but alcohol and Dylan's potential presence looming around every corner. Miranda has my phone hidden in a vault somewhere, so I have nothing to make me look aloof and alluring. At parties when I feel overwhelmed, I excuse myself to stand in the corner, typing fast as though I have important dispatches to send. Usually, I'm writing notes about who I expect will hook up that night and time-stamping them so I have a record of my premonitory abilities the next morning, even if I don't remember them. My watch, which I normally never take off, is tucked away in my toiletries bag as Miranda said it looked like a middle schooler's calculator. She asked if I was planning on bringing my wheelie backpack, too. I put my half-drunk glass down. One thing that is nice about being on a reality TV show is I don't have to worry about being roofied.

To get away from the commotion, I skirt around the pool toward a potting shed at the far edge of the property. The driveway's pavers glimmer despite the fact we're in a desert and it hasn't rained in weeks. Some intern must have dumped buckets of water across the stones to add some romantic allure to the ground. Through a privet hedge, I can see Dylan and the woman who grabbed him first flipping steak on a small, rolling grill in matching aprons embroidered with Dylan's last name: the future Mr. and Mrs. Walter. The smell of char and blood wafts toward me, and I worry I might throw up.

The roar of a motor erupts from the side of the driveway and a woman in a dark green dress comes to a skidding stop on a dirt bike. Gleaming studio lights sparkle in the reflection of her helmet, obscuring her face. She swings her leg off the bike and latches the heel of her platform shoe around the kickstand to prop it up in one swift motion. As she takes the helmet off, blond curls swing out and tumble down her back. They look real: wide, frizzed corkscrews, unlike my own silky pressed hair. Her eyes are rimmed thick with black eyeliner.

"Hi there," Dylan says. "I wasn't expecting you." Dylan starts to triangulate between the two women, the brave one who grabbed him first seeming slight and awkward next to the new arrival. The woman's shoes clack toward him on the cobblestones, out of my view. I thought the world had run out of beautiful women by now, but it appears I was wrong. After my first interview with the psychologist, Miranda said that it's clear I have a fear-based mindset and that while I'm here, she's going to switch me over to an abundance mindset. If I believe I can have anything I want, she'll do her best to help me, but if I don't buy in, I'm on my own. I rub the leaves of a potted shrub between my fingers, trying to discern whether the plant is real or fake. They're so thick and leathery, it could be either. All the outdoor plants here are the succulents I keep potted at home now freed to their natural habitats, jade bushes and firesticks, turning red at the tips. I zone out in the way of a tipsy person, mesmerized by the feeling of my body existing, trying to keep still. I feel something's eye on my back. I drop the leaf to the ground and pivot. Instead of a camera, a cow plods toward me, leather leash dragging behind it. Its smooth caramel fur lightens around its eyes and nose. No one warned me about a cow.

"Are you real?" I ask it. I could be more drunk than I thought. "Where are your people? Do you live here?"

The cow comes up next to me and presses its face against the leaves covering the fence. I tell the cow to not eat them, that the leaves are plastic, or might be anyways. Closer up, its eyes are rimmed in black and its lashes are an inch long at least, curling up with a vigor that I wish my own possessed, as though production applied makeup to it, too. The cow snuffles through the mulchy earth on the corner of the yard. It must be hungry or thirsty. I don't know if it wandered over here from another property, or if it's part of the show.

"Don't move." I push open the door of the potting shed, looking for a bucket to fill from the house spigot. It's comforting in the shed, all sorts of rusty rakes hanging from the walls, hoses coiled like pythons, shears of all kinds, almost like a real shed for a real family. To get farther toward the back, I lift the edges of my jumpsuit and shimmy around a folded-up wheelchair and a rattan table puckered with holes. Something rustles outside and I skitter out, afraid of being admonished for trespassing. The cow is gone, and in its place is the dirt bike woman. Her dark green dress dips down to her sternum, the curves of her breasts flush against the seams. Her hair is now in a loose bun tied up in a knot with no elastic in sight. Fine blond hairs frame her face, catching the yellow porch lights behind her like a halo. Her eye makeup has smudged a bit, but it only suits her more.

"Hi," I say, thinking of the disappearing cow, wondering if it was real, wondering if everything here is a test I'm about to fail, like the woman in front of me.

"You don't look drunk," she says. Her breath smells sweet like lemon-lime soda.

"I'm not anymore," I say. Her long neck cranes over toward my ear and the capped sleeves of her dress flutter as she moves.

"Good," she says, voice in a half whisper. "For the rest of the night, you're in charge of telling me if my nipples pop out."

"Okay," I say. I do not look down to her breasts, despite the directions.

"I'm Sam," she says, sticking her hand out. I shake it, though the introduction feels oddly formal for the moment. "I've got it taped down pretty well, but I want someone to confirm the situation visually." Sam turns back to the pool and tells me she wants to dip her toes in. She slides her shoes off without needing to unbuckle them and is felled to my height in heels. I stare at her for a moment, her brown eyes ringed lighter yellow toward her pupils, before Sam hikes up the hem of her satin dress to her hips and sits at the pool's edge. Her calves look strong and tanned even through the warped perspective of the water. There are a few thin clouds above us, patterned like giraffe spots. The light pollution from the city and the set makes the sky dim and gray. I wonder again what time it is, how long I've been there, and when the night will be over.

"I've seen nearly every episode of this show," Sam says, stirring her ankles around the water. I brush dirt off my heels and line them up next to me as I sit down at the edge next to her. "That's, like, twelve weeks of life, nonstop, awake, eyes glued to this train wreck."

"Are you serious?"

"I used to watch with my mom growing up and I never could stop. It's like a competitive sport."

"Can you predict what's going to happen to us?"

She looks over to evaluate me, and I avert my eyes. The water is cooler than I expected, and the filter burbles from the far edge. It's a worse feeling than when I auditioned at that hotel conference room, waiting as Sam tries to figure out the kind of person I am, the kind of woman I want to be.

"I assume you were one of the first women out of the limo because I heard you handed Dylan the wineglass during the toast. You might get the Golden Necklace tonight if it swings your way. If not, you'll get yours at the ceremony, and then in a few days, you'll be on a date, maybe an individual one. You look cute, smart, and not like you'll try to blow up your life. You'll go far. Don't worry."

"And what about you?" I ask, feeling strange, as though she's spoken all my desires back to me. I'm not sure if it would have been worse for her to be completely wrong about me, or completely right.

"I'll stick around for as long as I can," she says. She plucks apart one of her curls. "I don't think I'm Dylan's type."

This can't possibly be true, as she seems like everyone's type. "Why were you late?"

"Oh, to sow discord, it seems," she says.

"Sam!" a man's voice says. I whip around, expecting Dylan. There aren't many men here, aside from Dylan and some of the camera and sound people.

"What the hell, Sam," he says. "Don't get your dress wet."

"Wyatt, Emily. Emily, Wyatt," Sam says, rising easily from the pool. Wyatt reaches for the hem of her dress and keeps it off her wet legs. "He's my bodyguard." She bounces on her toes, and chlorinated water slides in rivers down her shiny skin, which sparkles with some kind of iridescent lotion in the light. Wyatt is handsome and Asian with long hair pulled back into a bun and a sharp jawline.

"Producer. Hers is Miranda," he tells Sam. He turns to his radio. "Two towels, poolside. You"—he points to me—"stay in the pool until a PA comes. You," he says, looking up at Sam from where he's bent, still holding her skirts, "once we dry you off, it's showtime. Dylan's in the gazebo and needing a rescue from a cat lady. She brought taxidermy."

"If there's one thing I'm not, it's a cat lady," Sam says. She shivers a bit from the chill in the air. A production assistant comes with two fluffy towels. Sam takes one and pats herself dry while Wyatt gives me a hand out of the pool.

"See you on the other side," Sam says to me, and Wyatt whisks her away.

"Where should I put these?" I ask, grabbing Sam's towel off the ground.

"I'll take them back," the woman says. She looks to be my age, working the same type of stepping-stone job that I had only a few weeks ago. Before I can thank her, the assistant darts inside, her radio firing off more commands. I go back to the living room, hoping to find Winna, the only woman besides Sam who I've managed to keep concrete in my mind. Though I no longer feel drunk, so many hours have passed that a heavy fatigue has set across my limbs. A small woman with red hair in a pixie cut calls me over. She looks sympathetically at me, standing with nowhere to go, and introduces herself as Vivian. I feel a strong and sudden kinship with her, as we have the shortest hair in the house surrounded by twenty-eight other long manes. Mine isn't even that short, cropped straight across my shoulders. Vivian introduces me to two women, but as soon as she says their names, I forget them, using the pause in the conversation to plan what I'll say next. Vivian asks what I do.

"I was an administrative assistant at a biotech start-up." I hate every second of talking about my former place of employment. The shame from being fired roils hot in my stomach.

"That's nice," one woman says. "How'd you end up here?"

"Oh," I say, "it was pretty funny. Someone stopped me on the street last week."

"What?" Vivian says. The women look shocked. "Like a teen model at the mall?"

"You were recruited last week?"

"I guess," I say. I explain the process, my run-in with the casting associate, my day of answering questions and taking photos, the gift bag of teeth-whitening samples and microneedling coupons. I ask the women how they ended up on the show.

"Applied online."

"My sister nominated me," Vivian says. "She said that I needed to stop focusing on my kids, and focus on myself for once. She said that an empty cup can't pour water."

"Applied over social."

"Oh," I say, wanting to change the subject. "Do you know who brought the cow?" The three women look more confused.

"What cow?"

"Never mind," I say, embarrassed to keep blundering like this. When I started at my last job, I tried to do everything right, but it felt like everyone knew how to work in a corporate office without needing to be told the rules. I couldn't tell if I was allowed to use my lunch break, who I should say hello to and who to ignore. I read the employee handbook front to back multiple times, desperate for someone to tell me how to act. I tried to do what it instructed, but still, I got fired. It feels like that now with the cow, with being recruited for the show, that there are topics I shouldn't bring up, and that the other women know something that I don't. Vivian steers the conversation, asking where each woman is from, weaving in surrounding national parks, how they are going to miss most of a season of a thriller murder show that they all watch, and when they are going to try to talk to Dylan. A cameraperson comes over at the mention of Dylan like he has supersonic hearing only for mentions of the lead.

"I don't want to be too aggressive," the brunette woman says. "That's not who I am."

"Like, you saw how Brandi grabbed him before he even had a chance to sit down? That's not aggressive, that's desperate," the blond woman says.

Vivian nods. "We're all worried about getting time to talk to him tonight."

"I'd hate to leave before Dylan has a chance to get to know me," I say, hoping this will be vague and relatable enough. We are all talking past each other, our words blowing slightly askew as though moved by a breeze drifting through the house. Soon Dylan enters, and hope blooms in my throat.

"Hi there," Dylan says. He reaches down to pluck the Golden Necklace off the table and walks out of the room as the cameras soak in each moment of our reactions. I wish he had greeted me and said my name then like he did when I gave him the champagne glass. His voice even makes boring "Emily" sound like something precious. I can't see Sam anywhere and am tempted to follow Dylan out and see if she gets it. If I could watch her break into a luminescent grin, brimming with demure surprise, I could learn how to act when my time comes. Instead, Miranda comes in and pulls me to a side room filled with people and equipment.

"We need to talk about the necklace," Miranda says as if I'm unaware of its importance, but even I know the gist. I can almost feel the latent humiliation of leaving on the first night and returning home, jobless with no direction. Everyone, myself included, would wonder what is wrong with me. "Did you see how he looked at you when you botched that limo exit, when you gave him that champagne? All the other women saw it, too, I'm sure. Maybe you've got that sexy-librarian thing going on."

"I feel like that is code for you trying to tell me I look plain," I say, self-conscious enough already.

"I'm trying to tell you that you have a brain, sweetie, which, I don't know if you've noticed, is more than a lot of the other women here can say," Miranda says. I didn't know she could make jokes like that. "So, what are you going to talk to him about? Do you have a game, a fun fact?"

"No," I say. I think of the cheesy lines I prepared about doing 4-H as a child and growing exemplary cultivars of vegetables to pass the time. "I'm hoping to talk like regular people. A conversation, one could call it."

Miranda snorts at this prospect. She asks me about what makes me attractive. I tell her I am five foot two, 110 pounds, and that my face is symmetrical. "More," she says. I shrug. "Fine, I'll help you."

Miranda tells me that Dylan loves kids and loves his family. I, too, love kids, but don't want to talk to him about the children that I, his potential future wife, might carry in our first interaction. I love my family, but I get the sense I love my family in a different way than Dylan loves his, in that I am happy to see my parents once a season: Thanksgiving, Christmas, Easter, Fourth of July. During these visits, I skirt through the house during the day, eating cinnamon graham crackers and planning vacations I'll never go on, while my dad goes to his accounting job at a Tupperware factory and my mother sews quilts and volunteers as a crossing guard at the local elementary school. At dinner, we eat at a small circular table in the corner of the kitchen, and no one seems to know what to say to one another. Miranda tells me that Dylan lives an hour away from his parents and three other siblings, and that he visits them on weekends to sit in their Jeeps, sniff tree resin, and pray to the Lord. "You know, what people in Colorado do."

I could be close to his family, probably. In high school, many of my classmates had a smattering of siblings throughout the K–12 system, big families with a quick rotation of hand-me-downs and communal cell phones hoarded by the oldest children. The mothers drove cars with three rows of seats, steeped in the scent of old McDonald's fries and dog hair, going from boys' school to girls' school for pickup and dropoff. Sometimes, I imagined myself as the youngest in those families. I could've blended in, pale and freckled with brown eyes, but I felt like I still would be noticed as a brood parasite, the evil chick out of place in a nest, who the mother feeds resentfully.

Done with the planning session, Miranda pushes me toward the patio. I think of pirate movies where women hostages in flimsy chemises are made to walk the plank into a pitch-dark roiling ocean. "It's your time to shine," she tells me. "Say you're tired."

"What?"

"Do it."

The sound of my shoes and the looming shadow of a new camera make Dylan and a different blond woman perk up. He does seem happy to see me, but maybe that's just his nice-looking face. I follow the script Miranda gave me about being tired, and he takes my hand, saying he knows a place. His hands are smooth and large, with trimmed nails and pale hairs running up to his knuckles. He's the oldest man I've ever dated, almost a decade older than me at thirty-two, which is a comforting thought. No one is expecting me to be in charge. We descend to the lower portion of the yard where there is a tiny house with glass French doors shrouded by curtains. He pulls an old-looking key from his pocket and holds the door open for me. A giant California king bed covered in pink rose petals spans nearly the whole width of the room. The scent of artificial vanilla that wafts from an array of candles has reached a dangerous saturation point, and I stifle a cough. Dylan props himself up high on the excess of tasseled throw pillows in the middle of the bed. I worry that I smell like chardonnay, sweat, and chlorine from my partial dip into the pool with Sam. I can imagine her smooth palms, not clammy like my own, as she slides into bed with a stranger, unbothered by the league of cameras. Dylan crosses his legs, loafers shining with the dotted reflection of the holiday lights that are draped across the ceiling. I stay at the far edge, teetering off the end of the hard mattress. There is no skin-to-skin contact, and I'm tempted to scoot closer to him, picturing the weight of Miranda's glare, but I can't manage it.

"Good night, honey!" I say cheerily, and turn to face away from him. I pretend to fall asleep, all the while wiping my damp hands on the comforter out of view of the camera.

"I see how it is," he says, laughing. I sit up and shake out my hair, preening for a moment before I edge closer to him. He watches me with his fingers interlaced on his lap, his face patient and open.

"Just giving you a taste of what our future could be like together," I say.

"I'm liking what I've seen so far."

"Do you want to take a nap?" I ask, voice lingering on the question. Sensing tension, the cameraperson moves to the foot of the bed, and I can make out the faint screech of the lens zooming in. They're so close to us, the moving furniture. It's like I live in a haunted house and have learned how to coexist with the ghosts. Dylan puts his arm around me, and I rest my temple on his chest, a pose I've learned from movies. I close my eyes and hope he doesn't speak to me. I'm on my own now, no Miranda coaching me, no lines prepared, no mythical Sam to imagine myself into. My body thrums, moving hot blood to the tips of my ears. I picture us for a moment, five years from now, playing a rousing match of doubles badminton at his parents' house. I'll be so devoted to him and in love that I'll finally be able to hit the birdie in an elegant way, the racket an effortless extension of my arm. Maybe I'll be ten weeks pregnant, keeping it a secret from everyone but him. I never imagined I would get to have a life like that, the kind that other women would be jealous of, but this could be my chance. At a press event after the season ends, I could laugh about finding my husband on a reality show and say that my experience, genuinely, is one in a million. Everyone would tell me how beautiful our love story is. The proof of my success would be available for anyone to consume, popping episode after episode like candies from an ornate tin. Dylan's heartbeat, like an ancient drum, is so slow and ominous that it almost scares me. It seems unnatural: all his hard work and exercise, only to make it seem like he's barely even alive. I squeeze his hand and he squeezes mine back. When we reemerge into the night air, his eyes are bleary, and for a second, neither of us moves. A woman calls his name far above us, and I hide behind him, bashful.

"It's a jumpsuit," he says as he hugs me goodbye.

"What?"

"I said I liked your dress earlier, but it's not a dress." He pinches the fabric of its wide legs. "Correct me next time," he says, and follows the woman toward the pool.

Miranda beams at me from her perch on a short rock wall nearby. She grabs my shoulders and shakes me. "Gold," she says. "That was pure gold."

For the rest of the night, I glow. I talk to the women and don't worry about remembering their names. In the library, the producers line us up on a low set of steps that circle around the room vaguely according to height. Dylan calls me up first, widening the ends of a necklace for me. I walk toward him slowly, smiling, as I was supposed to do when I got out of the limousine. It's my wedding and I'm walking toward my husband. The cameras bear down on me, but I don't care. His fingers brush away the ends of my hair. The pressure from his hands is so acute that it's as though I can feel the ridges of his fingerprints. The faces of the women in front of me are blurred, though I haven't had a drink in hours. The arches of my feet ache from my new high heels, and small blisters have erupted on both of my Achilles tendons. I hear the faint click of the necklace as he latches it around my neck. I press against the rough skin of his jaw as we hug. After, he calls up a couple more women and leaves the room. I can't tell how much time passes while he's gone before the cycle repeats again. The understanding that I'm going to fall in love here dawns on me. I shift into a dream logic, having been awake for nearly twenty-four hours. Five women get sent home, pushed out into the predawn light with tears in their eyes, like a handful of Eves evicted from Eden.

In a vast tent outside, our luggage is labeled and sorted. A producer tells us we should haul our belongings upstairs and pick a room to sleep in. I take off my heels, letting my toes curl over the cool cobblestones. Yellow spots stain the interior satin lining of my shoes where my blisters popped. The driveway is dry now, no longer needing to impress anyone. In the light of day, the tent city is fully visible, a mansion on one side of the property, a line of porta-potties on the other. Sam finds me in the crowd. Against all reason, I can still smell the chlorine on her skin.

"I knew you'd make it through the night," Sam says, wrapping me into a hug. All the women congratulate each other. "Let's go to bed. We can deal with this shit tomorrow."

I nod, eyes trained on the necklace swinging across her collarbone. She notices and runs the chain between her thumb and forefinger. It's not the first golden chain that was laid out for a special woman. She was called up after me. As we start toward the staircase, Winna and Vivian wait in line to grab their suitcases. Vivian's eyes are so red that it looks like she could have been crying.

"Get them, too," I say, and Sam grabs their wrists. Sam leads us upstairs and picks the room at the end of the hallway. Vivian shuts the door. I turn in a circle to inspect the three bunk beds and see Sam's naked back and lace thong scaling a ladder.

"Good night," Sam says, and moves a pillow to cover her head. Winna slides the blackout shades down, twisting the string back and forth to get them to cooperate. I sit on the bed underneath Sam and fiddle with the buckles on my shoes. Vivian unzips Winna from her dress. Her waist is imprinted with fine red lines from the cinched fabric, like fresh stretch marks. When I turn over onto my stomach, the sharp prongs of the pendant's setting dig into my chest.

Raised Catholic, I grew up obsessed with resurrection. There are so many stories about things rising from the ashes: phoenixes, wildflowers and seedlings, Jesus. It was nice to think that any suffering I experienced would lead me to a better, purer life. Even if all I ever experienced was misfortune, as long as I remained humble and gracious, I would still end up in eternal paradise. Like an app where all the bugs get fixed with automatic updates, I could improve myself without needing to be ambitious, to make decisions about what I wanted. I only needed to be docile enough. When I walked into the casting call, I realized I might need to work a little harder for my opportunity to be reborn. So, I moved the boulder from the tomb I was trapped in. I signed the papers and stepped out of the limo.

CANDLES

OUTSIDE, MIRANDA BEGINS to blow out the candles. It's the art department's responsibility to maintain them throughout the night, skirting behind shots to relight a taper or shift a candelabra bumped too close to a curtain by a drunk woman. However, when the sun comes up and the contestants are in their bunks sleeping themselves into tomorrow's hangover, each department gets roped in: sound, lighting, handlers, story editors, production assistants, field managers, camera assistants, the electricians, even senior producers like her—everyone but security, but they are contracted out anyways. It's almost a ritual after a quarter century doing this. The staff spread themselves thin from the entryway and, flicker by flicker, sunlight replaces candlelight.

She wanders to the various spots outside the house where Dylan talked to the women: the firepit with the promising Winna; the champagne bucket with Lauren K, so average that she was one of three Laurens present. The season is off to a good start. She can already envision the web of drama and romance being twisted around Dylan like perfect pink cotton candy around a white paper cone. Sometimes she wonders if, in any other field, she would be considered a visionary. She got one of her girls into the Casita, an unprecedented move for the first night. The girl, Emily, is a total catch. When they called her friends for references, everyone said she's a good girl. Even her former boss who fired her a week ago called her sweet. Her parents believe she's above going on the show, which is always the best type of contestant. She's never seen a full episode, never had a serious boyfriend. When Miranda got her as one of her ten girls in the production lottery, it was like being handed a fresh package of Model Magic, the airy white foam clay for kids. From reading her application, Miranda knew she could make her into anything.

Someone buzzes in her ear, Wyatt or Andrea probably, wanting to talk about the girls. She takes her earpiece out and stuffs it into her pocket. The morning desert air is dry and thick in her nostrils. Behind the mansion is the travel trailer she'll stay at during the rare hours she can sleep. Behind that, somewhere farther away, is her husband waking up and getting ready for work. She'll see him off and on for the next month, but then, once they've started traveling, it'll be a full month away. She knows she's supposed to feel guilty about it, but she doesn't. A few candles float in the pool water, drifting with the flow of the circulating currents. No one is around, all back in the tent village or the basement, so Miranda strips off her shirt. She unbuttons the fly of her black jeans and pulls the taut fabric over her ankles. She used to buy the polyester blends that slackened as she worked, drooping in unseemly places over the course of her long hours, but she's old enough and rich enough now to buy jeans that cost hundreds of dollars, jeans that actresses wear while running errands: slow fashion, organic denim, button fly, handmade, double-stitched. The pool water is warm as it reaches up toward her knees. She wades to the first candle and blows it out, cupping it in her hands like a drowning mouse and placing it at the edge of the pool.

She dips her mouth and nose underwater, keeping her eyes on the house. She shouldn't be here, but her pulse still thrums through her veins after the long night fueled by dark-chocolate-covered espresso beans. No one outside of this place knows how good she is at this. It doesn't matter that Wyatt got the double bonus last season for producing both the guy who Suzanne selected and Dylan, the fan favorite who became this season's One. It doesn't matter that Frank, the showrunner, might at any moment latch onto the idea that she's aging out from the industry entirely. He already wondered in passing whether the girls would relate better to someone a bit younger. Of course, he never mentioned age. *Fresh* was the word he used, as opposed to Miranda, a stale box of crackers everyone is too lazy to even throw out, let alone eat.

She knows it's not her time to leave yet, that she has a well of genius left within her. When people talk about *Frankenstein*, snobs always like to correct laypeople that Frankenstein is the doctor and not the corpse monster, though Frankenstein is the true monster of the text. It's called dramatic irony. She's never understood that reading. However perverse his methods, Frankenstein delivers on something that everyone asks for, for death to not be so final. When Miranda works with the girls, it's a bit like that: people faulting her merely for giving life to their desires. She offers a little escapism from a hard world, something indulgent to consume while slumping in front of a smudgy laptop screen. She wants the viewers to let their brains numb out, fingers thick with Cheeto dust and minds fizzy from white wine. She wants a sea of viewers enthralled by the composition of her siren's song. Nothing from past seasons matters now. Nothing at home matters either. It's just the girls and her skills and their bright futures blooming before her. That's the mindset it takes to win. She blows out the final candle and goes inside.

WEEK ONE

WITHIN HOURS OF being awake, a tacit agreement formed among the twenty-five of us that as long as you're not on the toilet, the doors to the four bathrooms should be open. Women drift through the hallway behind me in blurs of athleisure sets. Their perfumes and shower scents float into the bathroom, like the traces of spirits. I wash my face again and again. As I slept, my makeup seeped into my pores and congealed into a range of painful pimples in the middle of my forehead, with a stray peak on my chin. I used to take pride in the simplicity of my feminine habits, my bulk vats of moisturizer and unthreaded eyebrows. That was before I was on TV, where all the women seem to have cheeks as plump and bouncy as beach balls despite getting four hours of sleep.

The only other time I stayed up all night was first semester of my first year at college when I had a paper due the next morning. It was in passable shape by midnight, but I wanted to see how it felt not to sleep, to build a schedule based on frivolous desires. At home, my parents ate dinner at 5:30 p.m. and were in bed by 9 p.m. In my dorm common room, I ate mozzarella sticks from the twenty-four-hour snack bar, crisp malt balls from the vending machine, and drank a liter of Diet Coke. The next day, I got mononucleosis. I was sick for two months, sleeping all the time, awake only in a heady trance. During that time, I exclusively consumed miso soup and peach smoothies from the cafeteria snack bar. I guess I learned that everything you deprive yourself of catches up with you in the end, so I never did it again until now. Winna comes in, thready wisps escaping from her bun, and pulls out a large crocodile-skin bag from underneath the sink.

"Here," she says, "use this." She shakes a glass bottle of separated oil and water and pumps it onto a pillowy reusable cotton pad. All the makeup in her bag is in cloudy glass packaging or thick metal tubes, purchased annually in Korea when she visits her grandmother, Winna says as I admire the collection.

"Thank you," I say. "This stuff I brought from home isn't doing anything."

Winna looks at me with a horrified expression as I wipe at the mascara. "Don't tug at your under-eyes!" she says, taking the cotton pad from my hand. "It causes wrinkles." She whispers the word *wrinkles* as though, if she says it three times in the bathroom mirror, she will age instantaneously. Winna cannot be older than twenty-six, with nary a wrinkle in sight. Like most of the other women, she seems mature and driven, but still open to helping me. Around the house, no one whispers of the competitive aspect to the show, though I can't be the only one who thinks about it. Miranda told me to consider it a competition with myself. Winna pumps more tonic on the cotton pad. "Close your eyes," she says, and presses it to my eyelid, holding it there as the formula sinks into my skin. I take shallow breaths, trying not to let my exhalations reach Winna's hands.

"That's better," she says. She puts the blackened cotton pads in a small silicone bag, also reusable. I can't imagine being diligent enough to launder my makeup-remover cloths. "You know, Viv's an aesthetician. She could probably do an extraction for you."

"She'd pop my pimples?"

This idea horrifies me a bit, but it seems better than my original strategy of washing my face with great care twice a day in penance for my one night of negligence. Downstairs, we make breakfast. The eggs I crack have bright golden yolks, the kind of extra-cage-free eggs that cost ten dollars a dozen at an organic market. A handler told us we could add whatever we wanted to a grocery list, but we had to do our own cooking, cleaning, and laundry. If we have dry cleaning, they'll send it out for us, but we'll pay using the credit card information they have on file for us. I write down all the expensive items I can think of: extra-cage-free heritage chicken breast, crème fraîche, pine nuts, 80 percent ethically sourced dark chocolate, and any type of mushrooms that aren't button. I don't even know what I'll cook, but I want to have luxury at my fingertips.

"Can I get in on this?" Sam says, eyeing our breakfast. Her skin is shiny with sweat from working out, and her hair is in a ponytail, the ends tucked in the neck of a ratty T-shirt. "I can make us cappuccinos."

"You can make a real cappuccino?" Winna asks, looking delighted at the prospect. She reaches over to free Sam's hair. I marvel at the natural ease Winna has, her hands near my eyes, her fingers on Sam's neck. Being here is like being back at Our Lady of Heavenly Virtue Academy, a place with so much chaotic feminine energy that, senior year, our class of thirty girls tried to sync our periods up for graduation. The nun who doubled as a health and chemistry teacher caught wind of our plan and sat us down in the gymnasium during lunchtime. She told us there was no such thing as syncing up. She called in Sister Alexandria, our math teacher, who calculated on a rolling chalkboard the likelihood that in a group of thirty women with menstruations lasting five days each twenty-eight days, there would be some overlap, but never complete. As we watched the tally of permutations become increasingly complex, we didn't believe them. Fifteen of us were already bleeding into our pads.

"I'm basically a career barista at this point," Sam says, riffling through the drawers for the portafilter for the mansion's fancy espresso machine. Jazmin comes in, the woman who got the first necklace last night. She has big brown eyes, shoulder-length natural hair, and a small ugly dog underneath her arm. She tells us that the espresso machine doesn't work. She points us toward the drip machine, the hot plate sizzling underneath a dark vat, saying it tastes worse than diner coffee. Sam steams milk for us nonetheless and pours it into our mugs.

"They're too busy funding all the hidden cameras to pay for working appliances," Jazmin says.

"How many are there?" I ask, looking toward Sam. She explains there are cameras everywhere in the mansion, even in the bedrooms, and outside by the pool and yard. The only place we're not filmed is the bathrooms, but if we get far enough to travel, it won't be like that. We'll have a bit more privacy. Jazmin and Winna don't seem disturbed by this. When I was thirteen, a news story went viral about some creep rigging up cameras at a club in a city nowhere near rural Ohio. Still, I worried that I would be filmed in every public restroom I entered. I would walk in and press my index finger on the dingy reflective squares above each sink to make sure the mirror didn't go both ways. Now at least I don't have to worry. I know for sure.

"They try to get your weak points," Sam says.

"That's why we had to fill out all those freaking personality tests," Winna says. "What was the point of asking us the same thing twenty times? 'I am important. Agree, disagree. My thoughts are important. Agree, disagree. What I think is important. Agree, disagree.'"

"Have you ever wanted to murder someone? Has killing someone ever crossed your mind? Have you ever wished to send someone else to the afterlife?" Sam parodies.

When I filled out the personality test, I took great care to be consistent. I answered questions about whether I liked gardening, whether I feared windstorms, whether I become possessed by evil spirits, whether I'm attracted to women, and whether I'm often constipated. I wrote I had been an accomplished Girl Scout, which was true and also seemed like a good trait for a wife, and that the worst thing that ever happened to me on a date was that I got food poisoning, which wasn't true, but I couldn't think of anything else to write down. Nothing either particularly good or particularly bad had ever happened to me on a date. I felt like I was trying to invent myself from thin air. At home, the only child of older parents, I would listen to my dad's plans to reroof the shed and my mother's project of organizing a community cookbook with her weekly dominoes group. With my high school friends, I loved college football and would go to tailgates on Thanksgiving weekend, where I drank beer at 8 a.m. and ate soft pretzels until I puked. Barhopping with girls from college, we'd buy drinks that tasted like juice and talk about how messed up the world is that we have to spend all day wearing business casual instead of living on a Mediterranean catamaran. We'd hatch plans to find husbands who were in business school. I've told people at parties that I love EDM or am thinking of going vegan, not even men I'm trying to impress, just anyone I'm talking to so that we have something to bond over.

"You have something on your nose," Sam says. My hands are soapy from the dishes, but before I can dry them, she swishes the milk foam away with a brush of her thumb. "There, saved your life."

"What?"

"It's something my mom used to say, like after wiping an eyelash away."

"Oh, thanks." The feeling of her thumb on the bridge of my nose lingers, almost an itch. Sometimes, I can't stop staring at women like Sam, women who don't have to summon their personalities like curses from a cauldron. Wyatt, Sam's producer, comes in and tells us to be ready for the first date announcement in the living room in five minutes. Sam and I bound up to the bedrooms to put on slightly nicer loungewear than we had been wearing before, but Winna goes straight to the couches, already looking beautiful. She wears the wardrobe of a rich mom: cashmere shawls and shearling slippers. The packing list said I needed to dress for below freezing to over a hundred degrees, black-tie dresses, loungewear and athletic gear, all in two suitcases. There was, of course, no stipend attached to these demands. I used half my severance money to express order all the formal wear from Amazon. I throw on a white T-shirt and denim shorts, clothes no one can complain about. Downstairs, Miranda arranges us in a semicircle. She hands Sam and me each an empty mug.

"Look casual," she says, so I cross my arms. Sam stares at one of the four cameras, smiles, and takes a pretend sip. The host walks in with a note on a brass tray covered in flower petals. Something about her gives me the creeps, and I'm pretty sure it's her blatant veneers, one size too big. I can picture her real teeth before the procedure was finished, filed down to small stubs like an eel's, the husk of whatever undesirable shape they were before.

"I got this note from Dylan, but before you read it, there is something you should know. Dylan has decided that each week, one of you will receive the Golden Necklace. It can be given at any time, on any date. The woman who receives the Golden Necklace will be safe for the rest of the week. Remember, Dylan thinks that his wife could be in the room here. That's how seriously he takes this. Have fun, ladies."

"Anna Mae," says the third senior producer, younger than Miranda by several years, "you can read the card." I've started to question the secret meanings of who the producers pick for things like this, like when I gave Dylan the champagne glass for the toast. Sam told me that she didn't even know she was coming in late; she thought she was arriving with everyone else. There's a larger plan taking shape around me, and if I pay attention enough, I might be able to figure out what it is.

"'Winna, true love is in surround sound. Love, Dylan,'" Anna Mae reads, and her accent jogs my memory. She is the cowgirl. Winna covers her mouth with her hands, and we all congratulate her. I give her a thumbs-up from across the room when we make eye contact. I snap a glance at the camera, hoping the gesture seemed authentic.

An associate producer steps forward. "Now, we're going to

have a quick girl chat. What do people think about Winna getting the first date?"

"I'm a bit surprised that Dylan would give the first solo date to a stripper," a woman named Morgan says, as though the show has permitted our gossipy underbellies to rise, brazenly, to the surface.

"I'm not a stripper," Winna says, "not that there's anything wrong with that profession. Who told you that?"

"Someone said you were a dancer," Morgan answers, her confidence unrattled, though she throws a glance toward the production assistant.

"I am. I'm a ballerina." Winna's face reddens, though her voice remains remarkably calm.

"You know, you have a great body. It's not a wild assumption."

"I injured my ankle and had to take the season off. My mom nominated me." She takes a deep breath and tucks her hair back behind her ears, like a newscaster ready to go live. "She wanted me to relax for once, to do something that had less to do with my body and more to do with my heart."

"It was an honest mistake. Why is everyone looking at me like I'm a criminal?" Morgan says, realizing something has gone wrong.

"I don't think you know how criminals are treated," Sam says. In a matter of seconds, the discourse rises into a fight, one of silent and not-so-silent retorts and glances across the room. It's the kind of fighting that I thought only happened on the internet.

Gossip is a sin. Gossip is an empowering network of connections for women to share information about dangerous men. If you don't want people to get mad at you, don't share rumors like they're fact. Dylan doesn't seem like the type of man who would date a stripper. Strippers aren't prostitutes. You're not supposed to say the word *prostitute* anymore. Please explain what's exotic about St. Louis. Someone suggests that Winna do a pirouette in front of us to prove that she's a ballerina. I stay quiet, taking in the allegiances as they percolate to the surface, hoping that a general consensus will be reached and then I'll know what to say. Production keeps insisting that only one woman speak at a time.

"They want clear audio," Sam whispers to me. "That's why they're trying to do the talking-stick thing."

"It's such a shame that there's so much disrespect in the house already," a blond woman says. "Like you, Emily, when you interrupted my time with Dylan last night after five minutes, then took him for way longer."

I clench the mug in my hands, surprised the spotlight has been cast in my direction. For a second, I wonder if there is another Emily in the room. My mind flips like a Rolodex through last night's interactions. "Sorry, I don't remember what you're talking about."

"So now I'm not even worth remembering, that's nice," Leigh says. "Making your priorities clear."

"I thought Dylan was supposed to be my priority. Like, isn't he all our priority? Isn't that the point?"

"Are you saying you're not here to make friends?" Leigh asks. Without makeup and studio lights, I don't even recognize her as the woman I interrupted before Dylan took me to the Casita.

"That's a tired line. I want the house to be about women supporting women."

Leigh spins my phrases into a nasty knot. She's making me sound mean, but she could be right—I can't seem to tell the difference anymore. None of the other women are standing up for me, unlike how they did for Winna, and I simmer in the silence. The idea that spending time with Dylan could be unsupportive doesn't make sense. Should I be supporting the other women by falling behind, a kind of meek lamb as they excel? Leigh stares at me, waiting for me to relent.

The producer jumps in. "Emily, do you feel like spending that much time with him at the Casita last night made your connection stronger?"

"You went to the Casita on the first night?" Leigh says. The women go quiet for a moment, taken aback.

"Um," I say, having no idea what answer will make this situation go away. "We went to that cottage in the backyard."

"No one goes to the Casita on the first night," Sam says. She looks at me, impressed, as though I've surprised her. The idea that I've done something noteworthy fizzes through me. It seems like all the reasons I came here—for a little attention, to stand out a bit—might be happening. I want Sam to see me as a competitor here, not a background character. I want everyone to think of me like that.

"What did you say to him to get there?" another woman asks.

"I didn't say anything. He suggested it." As I say this, Miranda slips out of the room. I remember her telling me to say I was tired. She might be the person I have to thank for my notoriety this morning, so the least she could do is help guide me through it now. "I'm excited to keep growing our connection in a respectful way going forward."

Sam snorts in laughter at my PR statement and takes a fake sip of coffee to cover it up. The producer shifts to questioning Jazmin about the Golden Necklace. When the cameras shut off, Wyatt pulls Sam aside for an appointment with Dr. C, the cast therapist, who we all meet with weekly in an effort to reduce the show's liability for our bad behavior. Using my tried-and-true ability to repent with grace, I apologize to Leigh in private and tell her I've never watched the show, that I didn't understand what interrupting might do. I'm allergic to people being mad at me and am terrified of further confrontation. It's the reason I got fired. I was so afraid of disappointing people that I never told anyone when I was confused or behind on making a team lunch invitation or couldn't track down an email that I should have had. I would become late on things, embarrassed to say I was late, and then would never do them. I hoped that my tasks disappeared into the ether of other people's minds as they did in mine.

"Did you sleep with him?" Leigh asks me.

"What?"

"The Casita is where people go to have sex. Everyone here thinks you slept with him."

"Well, I didn't."

Upstairs, as Winna picks out her outfit for tomorrow, I tell her and Vivian that all Dylan and I did was talk. I should've known it was a sex room with the candlelight and rose petals, but the idea that Dylan wanted to have sex with me last night didn't even cross my mind. The room had all the trappings of a seduction, but part of me was always cognizant that none of it was about me, that the gesture was in service of something else. Each time a couple goes in, the candles are replaced and relit, the crusty petals disposed of and fresh ones strewn artfully about. Dylan didn't want my organic emotion, but wanted just a fast pass toward intimacy. Upon entering the Casita, I was able to tune in to a standardized frequency: this is where you fall in love and this is how you do it. Vivian asks about how Winna is feeling after what Morgan said.

"I feel like a wrung-out sponge," she says. "Do I look it?"

No, we assure her, she looks lovely.

That afternoon, every hour on the dot, a woman goes into the bathroom to recurl her eyelashes, squashing the thick black mass of mascara in the evil-looking clamp. She releases it, then flutters her eyes in the mirror, and steps back outside to the pool, or kitchen, or library, or scrubby desert grounds. When Dylan is gone, being in the mansion is like being at my job or at my apartment, always waiting for something to happen to me. After dinner, Brandi and Melanie, the fifth and sixth girls in our room, sit on the floor, showing each other the cocktail dresses they packed. Jazmin pushes open the door, holding her dog in one arm and a dog bed in the other.

"Can I swap rooms with someone?" she says. The dog cranes its neck to lick my hand. "Anna Mae doesn't want Guava to 'chew her shoelaces.'"

"Isn't Anna Mae a cowgirl? Hasn't she, like, met a dog before?" Brandi asks while Melanie volunteers to switch. Jazmin goes to get the rest of her stuff, leaving the dog bed embroidered with his full name, Guava Alfonso Archibald Lock, at my feet. I squat on the floor to pet him, and he rolls to give me full access to his belly. He's a strange-looking dog, wiry fur and an underbite, but it's nice to have a living creature to dote on in the house, another thing to do to pass the time. Jazmin argued to her producer, Andrea, that having the dog past the first night would be on brand, given her professional title of "Dog Person" for the show. She got him from work, an animal rescue where she drives vans of dogs from Houston to Chicago. I can picture her, disco on the radio and eyes on the road, as the creatures in the back howl, whine, and sleep, the raucous sounds of a changing life. When she returns, Jazmin admits that she also has been building out his influencer presence and thought the show could be good exposure for him and, thus, the rescue. He already has 150,000 followers and brand deals with a bespoke leash company.

Vivian comes up from the kitchen and takes a large plastic case from one of her suitcases. "Okay, let's do it," she says, crooking a finger at me.

"Do what?" Sam asks, popping her head out from the top bunk.

"Extractions," Vivian says.

"On me." I gesture to my pimples.

"That's fun," Jazmin says, though that can't possibly be true. We follow Vivian into the bathroom, which is miraculously empty of other women. "I watch videos of pimple poppers on Instagram sometimes. I can't stand the big cyst ones, though. I hate the pus. They call it 'cheesy.' Blackheads, though, that's the shit I like."

"Cheesy?" Sam says, disgusted. As I lie down, the tile of the bathroom floor cools my exposed skin. Vivian turns the shower on, letting the steam fill up the enclosed space. She says this will help open my pores. The warm recessed light lingers in the clouds of condensation. I close my eyes and listen to the sound of rushing water.

Someone puts the toilet seat down. "Isn't California undergoing a drought?" Sam asks.

"No ethical consumption under capitalism," Jazmin says, shrugging it off. She shakes three dark blue glass bottles of essential oils around. Pastel droplets flick against the marble tiles, making the room smell like orange zest and ylang-ylang.

"Ugh," Sam says. "Does anyone else walk into a bathroom and need to pee regardless of the circumstance? My eyes see a toilet and my bladder is like Pavlov's dog."

"That happens to me," Vivian says. "And after my second kid, my bladder has never recovered. I basically became incontinent and had to stop drinking coffee. People think I only drink tea as some kind of artisanal statement, but it's me and my dysfunctional bladder fighting against caffeine."

Sam pulls her pants down, and I look away from the crease where the tops of her thighs meet her hips. Vivian sits on the rim of the bathtub above me, her calves on either side of my face. I stare up at her, her upside-down face clownish in the thin fog, as though I'm her third child, emerging from her crotch. She is one of the two women older than Dylan here: thirty-three with sons, ten and eight, from a previous relationship. When she was my age, she toted around a one-year-old baby on her chest, waxing women's pubic hair and the backs of hairy men. She says she's worried that people will judge her, say she's a bad mother to do something so superficial at her boys' expense. I'm jealous, though. At least she has someone to go back to.

Jazmin plays with the long row of light switches on the wall. A heat lamp turns on above me, radiating warmth across the room. Vivian slaps fragrant lotion across my face, rubbing her fingers upwards from my jawline to my temples. Guava curls up at the bath mat beneath her feet. Occasionally, Vivian asks Jazmin to pass her a different product or tool: essence, toner, cleanser, the hot washcloth, tweezers. I feel the sharp prick as she pulls out an eyebrow hair straying toward my forehead. She moves a pink quartz roller in precise strokes across my face. Sam attempts to juggle the crystals that Jazmin brought into the room, but is quickly stopped. My jaw slackens, and I almost emit a groan. It feels so good that I am tempted to pay her, but the producers have my wallet. Someone opens the door. I open my eyes, afraid it's production coming to film our bacchanal. Vivian's extraction tool, which looks like a dentist's pick, nearly skewers my eyeball.

"No moving," Vivian scolds me, pushing my head down into the pillow again.

"What are you doing in here?" Winna says, squinting in the

steam and red light. She is wearing a silk slip dress, black and faded as though she truly wears it every night to sleep.

"We made a spa," Sam says, shushing her. "Here, you have a big day tomorrow. Sit in front of me and I'll give you a massage."

Winna rests her back against the toilet, and I close my eyes again. "Who do you think said that about me to Morgan?" she asks.

"Maybe it was one of the girls from the limo," I say.

"Ha, I think Morgan started the whole thing herself and that's why she's not saying names," Jazmin says.

"Who's her producer?" Sam asks. "I don't think she's with Wyatt."

"You think it was Andrea?" Jazmin says.

"Why would Andrea think that about Winna?" I ask. "They have all our information. We had to fill out all those quizzes."

"Emily," Sam says. She looks at me like I'm a kindergartener who asked why war exists when people could just get along. "She doesn't really think that. She knows Winna's job."

"Miranda says I should do a 'private performance' to show what kind of dancer I am on the date. Tomorrow has gone topsy-turvy already. I don't want to talk about this anymore. Can you press harder?" Winna asks Sam. Vivian adds more pressure to my pimple. The first one gives way and I feel as though I can almost hear the pop.

"Gnarly," Jazmin whispers.

"Harder, still," Winna says.

"Jesus, you're a beast," Sam says, and I picture her brutally thumbing Winna's neck.

"Are any of you worried that the show isn't going to work?" Jazmin asks. "Like it was created with a hypothesis that has been proven to fail season after season."

"Oh, bring on the blasphemy," Vivian says. She runs a thin metal plate across the contours of my nose, passing over the enlarged pores in the crevices and squeezing out whatever debris is there.

"It's, like, my entire lifetime the show has been running, and there are ten surviving couples from the forty combined seasons," Jazmin says.

"That seems like better odds for marriage than dating someone for six weeks in the real world," I say.

"Yes," Winna says, patting my shoulder. "A believer like me."

"Fair point," Jazmin says. "It feels riskier than everyone is talking about, though. Andrea keeps saying she knows this could work for me, and I'm like, really? Because I don't."

"What do you think, Sam?" Winna asks.

"I disagree with the premise of the question." Maybe, Sam concedes, the show has proven that, when under enough pressure, most people will agree to a quick engagement with someone they're incredibly horny for. At the base level, this is all a psychological experiment with a desired economic outcome: trap thirty people together as they fight for a limited quantity of the same thing, something everyone wants, true love, and the results will be scintillating enough to attract millions of viewers to sell advertising. And that, the real hypothesis, has proven true, season after season. "I'm with Winna and Emily, though," she says. "Our odds are better here. Last date I went on, before the waitress took our drink order, the guy told me he wasn't looking for anything serious, then asked if I would be able to give him a ride home."

"It's also, like, say you're engaged and stay together for five or ten years in a loving relationship. You travel the world together, rent an apartment in San Diego, adopt an elderly cat, then down the line something breaks. Is that so bad?" Vivian asks. "Is all we can ever hope for to be with someone for the rest of our lives, and anything else is a failure?"

A loud knock rattles through the room, and a woman calls out from the hallway that she needs to pee.

"Can you not tell we're busy?" Sam says back.

"We should let her in," Winna says.

"What if it's someone we don't like?" Jazmin says.

"Who don't we like?" I ask. "Besides Morgan."

"Oh, I'm sure we'll find out soon enough," Sam says. Vivian pops the last of my pimples, and we turn the fan on to suck away the steam. The air clears, leaving the faintest smell of orange. In the hallway, Miranda intercepts me on the way to the bedroom and tells me to get into my Night One outfit and makeup.

"We need to do pickups," she says. "What's wrong with your face? You look like a steamed beet."

"What?"

"An interview. Come on. Meet me downstairs in fifteen."

"It's almost midnight," I say. "I'm tired."

"Fifteen," Miranda sings out, and goes back downstairs. "Don't worry too much about the makeup. No one will care what you look like. They'll only care about what you say."

This is the opposite view to how I have understood the show so far, but Miranda has yet to steer me wrong. In the interview room, more weird fake-or-real plants dot the corners. My hair is limper than last night, and skin less dewy despite the facial. Vivian assured me my skin will show the benefits of the procedure in a couple days. An assistant attaches the mic pack to my back, winding up the straps on my jumpsuit. Miranda has a glass of wine in one hand and passes me another. The dim lighting creates the atmosphere of a fancy bar, and Miranda looks like she could be the notorious sommelier, dressed in all black with her hair in a sleek ponytail. Japanese blinds sit in the corner of the room, blocking off technical material. I try to summon memories of the video screen test for my audition. They asked me to describe my ideal man while being loose and conversational. My mind went blank as I tried to picture him. The only man I could think of was Woody from *Toy Story*, so I described him: tall, loyal, resourceful, flexible, passionate, committed, down-to-earth. I thought it sounded pretty convincing, and apparently, they did, too.

"Good?" I ask, adjusting myself to be inside the frame of the tripod camera.

"Full sentences," Miranda answers.

"Is this good?" I repeat.

"No, when you answer. And use present tense." Miranda stands to the side of the lens. "What are your feelings for Dylan so far?"

"Dylan and I have good chemistry, and I'm excited to get to know him more."

"Look at the camera, not me," she says. I take a sip of the wine and look into the lens. "What did you think of what happened with Kendra?"

"Who is Kendra?"

"She cried all night and got sent home. Were you even at the party? What about Leigh and Morgan this morning? Nuts, right?"

"I don't know what to think about all that. It was so stressful."

"Have you ever heard of the truth test?" Miranda asks. When I shake my head, she goes on to tell me that whenever she came home from high school and was mad about something that Katie or Becky or Lisa did, Miranda's mother would make her do the truth test. She would say aloud her darkest, most sinister feelings about the other girls and see whether, after uttering them, they felt true. Miranda's mother said that it casts away the taboo nature of women's anger and allows you to see what you believe in.

"I'll start," she says. "What Morgan said seemed like a genuine misunderstanding. You try."

"I don't know," I say.

"Oh, come on," Miranda says. "It's just for fun. How about 'Morgan's a bigot and Leigh is a bitch.'"

"Leigh is definitely bitchy," I say, trying to muster Miranda's exacting coldness. I've never been the type of person who can be blunt, but sometimes, I wish I were. She waits, seeing how I feel, but I don't believe myself. "Nope. Here," I offer. "Morgan shouldn't start rumors about things she knows nothing about."

"True?" Miranda asks. I nod. "What about 'I'm the hottest woman here, I deserve to be with Dylan'?"

I laugh, the statement so outlandish it has never crossed my mind. I've never considered that I could deserve to be with anyone. Miranda tells me I need to work on my self-confidence. She insists, "You deserve to be with Dylan."

"I deserve to be with Dylan," I repeat. She clinks her glass of wine with mine as though I've accomplished a great feat in personal growth.

"Does it worry you that he's dating all of them at the same time he's dating you?"

"I think we're in a unique circumstance. I think—" I stumble. "I think the person I'll marry one day ultimately is choosing to pick me despite having the option to date the other women in his life that he meets. This situation—"

"Journey," Miranda corrects.

"This journey is a more explicit version of that choice."

"Better," she says, and continues to drill into me. "So do you think this journey won't work for you?"

"I have every hope that I will come out of here with a strong, long-term relationship," I say, despite the conversation from the bathroom lingering in my mind. I wanted the other women to say something encouraging about the show, something trite and sweet that I could latch onto, and instead, all it did was lodge shrapnel of doubt into the folds of my brain. "I am certainly ready to be engaged. I'll have to see where love leads me."

"How do you know you're ready to be engaged?"

I didn't think Miranda would ask for specifics. It seemed like a general prerequisite that you come on the show ready to be engaged, since that's the whole point of being here. From time to time, I check on a few women my age, married with children, from my hometown on Instagram as their kids roam through pumpkin patches, or they pose for pregnancy announcements with a new stocking over a fireplace with artificial logs. These women work from home on intricate crafting projects to sell online or become passionate about a political cause that affects their children. If I moved back home, my mom would be happy to set me up with one of her church friend's sons, a Catholic guy who works in pharmaceutical sales and wants to have five kids before I turn thirty so he doesn't have to worry about my desiccated womb. When I left for college on the East Coast, the women I met scoffed at the idea of marrying young, and we all took up an interest in binge drinking. Instead of service projects on the weekends, I went to parties every Thursday, Friday, and Saturday night. The girls from private boarding schools taught me to keep Wonder Bread in my dorm room so I could roll the plain slices into tight wads to absorb the churn in my stomach. Once, I stole a shopping cart from a Star Market to push my blackout-drunk friend back to our dorm room since I couldn't carry her by myself. I got a dating app and I swiped yes on everyone, but never sent a single message. I wanted to see who would like me back. None of that prepared me for an engagement either.

"Do you know why the show is called *The One*?" Miranda asks.

"I don't know why the show is called *The One*."

Miranda swishes her hand in the air with frustration, and the rest of the crew leaves.

"Aristotle," she says. She takes a big drink of her wine and begins in earnest. "Aristotle said that people originally had four eyes, four arms, and four legs, but only one soul. Then they did something bad and Zeus chopped them in half, and now we're all bumbling around looking for the one, the other half of our soul."

"You're trying to tell me *The One* was modeled after the ideas of an ancient Greek philosopher?"

"Fifteen years ago, the night I first met my husband, I was a single, broke PA for an asshole executive producer, not this show but another reality one. I worked eighty hours a week and slept in a storage container most nights, like the ones out there. It didn't have heating, so I wore all my clothes to bed. I smelled like powdered deodorant and burnt Starbucks. One night, my friend dragged me to a party, free food and fancy drinks, celebrities. There he was. He was tall, imposing. That's the first thing I noticed about him, how big his hands were. Was it like that with you and Dylan? Anyways, we talked all night, kissed in the car after he drove me home. After that, I stopped taking shit from people. I moved out of the trailer. I had better things to do because I had my person to go home to. Don't you want that for yourself, to have your person? Don't you want to have a better place to be?"

"Yes," I say. "I want that."

I've heard that story about souls ripped apart before. In the Bible, it says the opposite, two flesh become one. People talk about both ideas all the time and think they're beautiful. I try to picture Miranda younger, her hair without the streaks of gray, still wearing all black and sleeping three hours a night on a cot. Even then,

I can't picture her flailing around her life like I'm doing with mine. I picture Dylan and me squashed together into one form, a monster tottering around. It doesn't seem particularly romantic. Then I picture us bound together, reunited after our soul got split apart, with him inside me. That's what I'm supposed to want. Sex is the only type of spiritual closeness I have access to now.

"Full sentence," she says. The camera's red light blinks at me.

"I want to fall in love. Dylan could be the one for me. He has every characteristic that I'm looking for in a life partner. I can picture our journey together lasting our whole lives."

And when I say it, it sounds true.

SOULMATE

"NICE WORK IN there," Wyatt says, watching the stream from his swivel chair in the production room.

"Thanks," Miranda says. Despite it being the middle of the night, his hair is coiffed perfectly, more impressive in its sleekness than Dylan's, who has a whole team of stylists at his disposal. She has never been able to figure out why Wyatt wanted to be on this side of the screen as opposed to the other. He's got the look and the magnetism; it's part of why he's such a good producer. The women want to trust him, and the men think he's one of their own. He watches the footage from the girl chat this morning on double speed, the slick, high voices of the women rattling through Miranda's ears.

"You're working hard this season. Are you gunning for the bonus?" he remarks without making eye contact. "Trying to renovate your house this summer or something? Baby on the way?"

She flips over the collar of his cashmere sweater to check the tag and lets her hand linger on the back of his neck as she stands over him. "Did you blow through yours already on Frank's favorite sweaters? Cute of you to try to match Daddy."

Wyatt pulls up the footage for Miranda. Emily's face, flushed by the end of the interview, becomes increasingly pale as he scans for the right moment to start the playback.

"I thought you met your husband at a gas station," Wyatt says.

"Come on, Wy, don't play dumb." He hates the nickname, so she uses it to bother him. "You know that's not the story she needs to hear."

FIRST DATE

THE NEXT MORNING, a production assistant wakes everyone at 7 a.m. to wait in the driveway as Dylan spirits Winna away on a date. The cameras watch our faces and scan our pajamas as they leave, some kind of cruel torture designed to make us increasingly bitter and unhinged. Another date card arrives for half the women, this time reading: ***All's fair in love and war. Love, Dylan.*** Sam says we're going to fight each other, but I tell her that's not romantic. Jazmin is worried because she's not going on a date this week, but Sam assures her that the person who gets the Golden Necklace before the Night One ceremony never gets a date in the first week.

"It'd be boring TV for someone to actually fall in love quickly. Then what would we do here, play in the pool together?"

Still, we pass the day by the pool, wondering what Winna and Dylan are doing, and what we will do tomorrow. Leaf detritus floats on its surface, as though it hasn't been cleaned in months, and the tiles where the water level laps have a scummy smooth surface. I apply a thick layer of zinc sunblock to my skin and pretend I'm on vacation, which is easy to do when Miranda is gone with Winna on the date. The water sputters like a puking woman, and we have to call in a production assistant to fish out twigs from the filter. In our room that night, Sam's index finger is tucked in the pages of a book. I was told we weren't allowed to bring any reading material with us. I stand at the end of my mattress on my tiptoes, hanging from the guardrail of her bunk to peek over.

"What're you reading?"

"The Word of the Lord," Sam says, waggling it in front of her face. "It's the only book they'd let me bring, and I'm trying to figure out what Dylan is all about. Great first line. 'In the beginning, God created the heavens and the earth.' No wonder this is a bestseller."

"It's sacrilege to mock the Bible, Sam," I chide.

"Isn't polygamy?" she says, gesturing around to the bunk beds. "You know, the sanctity of marriage and all."

"As far as I remember, that's still up for debate, and besides, he's only supposed to marry one of us."

"Are you religious?"

"Raised super Catholic," I say.

"No."

"It's true," I say. I quote the next lines: "'The earth was a formless void and darkness covered the face of the deep, while a wind from God swept over the face of the waters. Then God said, "Let there be light"; and there was light.'"

"I'm gobsmacked."

"I'm full of surprises."

When I called my parents to tell them I was going on the show and wouldn't be able to speak with them for two months or so, my mom said, "Television, sweetie?" "Yes," I told her. My parents only watch *American Ninja Warrior* and the news. I could picture my father stroking his white goatee. "Honey," my father said, "why?"

"I'm learning about myself."

Marriage is a sacred covenant with God, they said.

"I'm not getting married. That's a different show."

Then what's going to happen? they asked, and I told them I didn't know. They said they wouldn't watch and asked if people would find out my full name. Yes, people would probably find out my full name. Yes, I would have to wear a bikini at some point. I don't know if the man has family values. I don't even know who the man is, I said. This made it worse. "God leads us each down our own path," my mother said. "And the devil tempts you along the way," my father added. The cell phone crackled as they held my voice on speakerphone between their hands. Which call are you answering? they asked, and again, I told them I didn't know, but I said I would tell them if I found out. They told me they loved me and would pray for me. My father left the room and my mother stayed on the line for another moment. She said she would support me no matter what happened and that their neighbor Bethany watched the show and that she heard there are good people on it sometimes—that's the only reason she asked about family values. That's when she told me to watch my posture; then she hung up.

Being here, I'm glad to have grown up like that. It makes me sound wholesome. Miranda tells me that it gives Dylan and me something to bond over, even though he's Baptist. It seems like my parents' prayers that I would find godly people here, people interested in Scripture, were answered. Ask and it shall be given to you.

"Dylan's gonna wet himself, he'll be so pleased. I'm having trouble getting through it, though. He'll be disappointed in me."

"I can't say it's most people's pleasure reading."

"I'm also dyslexic, which doesn't help," she says. I consider offering to read to Sam if she's having trouble. It's what my parents do at night, read to each other to settle after their days, sometimes with the Bible and sometimes other classics, like *The Scarlet Letter*, "about the equal sins of premarital sex and gossip."

"Wyatt thinks I should tell Dylan about it tomorrow on the date," Sam says.

"Do you want to?"

Sam explains it to me: that tragedy acts as capital here. Each time you get him alone is an opportunity to explain yourself to him. The sadder your life story is, the less likely he is to send you home that week. No one wants to dump a person who bared their soul; it seems callous. Parental divorces are good fodder, broken engagements, too. Your own divorce is less sexy, since you could be flawed if you can't commit to a marriage. Widows are a hot commodity. Sam brings up earlier today, when one of the other women told us her plan to tell Dylan about her childhood home being burned down in a wildfire. Her family didn't live there anymore, but the idea of it being razed because of greenhouse gas emissions broke her heart.

"She's smart. Climate change," Sam says. "That's buzzy these days."

I laugh. "Yeah, I'll say."

"Have you got anything good?"

"No," I say. I feel like I barely have any backstory at all, like that movie about a secret agent who wakes up and has no idea who he is or how he got there.

"Bummer," she says. "I mean, I'm glad you're good and all, but that could be a tough sell. You'll have to keep being hot and happy, then." But this, I already knew.

The next morning, Sam comes in from the kitchen wearing a loose white blazer with a bralette underneath and matching trousers. She smiles, all teeth. My watch reads 6:15 a.m.

"Wake up, ladies. Today, the hens are flying the coop." We have only been stuck in the mansion for two days, but time stretches strangely here.

"I hate morning people. You're like my dad," Jazmin says, rubbing her eyes.

"Your dad must have a great ass," Vivian says.

"Thank you, Viv," Sam says. "I'm sure that's what Jazmin meant. I've made coffee."

"Winna, is that the Golden Necklace on your bag?" I ask.

"If I were you, I'd be wearing that necklace day and night,"

Brandi, our other roommate, says. On the date, Dylan and Winna went shopping for a formal gown that the designer let her keep for free. She tried on options for hours, radiant in luxury goods, as Dylan complimented each one. They walked the red carpet for a movie premiere. It was an animated kids movie about three sockeye salmon who need to lay eggs upstream, but keep encountering grizzlies and dams. Pretty bad, but whatever, she says. It seemed like the production company and the show had some kind of publicity deal. After, he took her for dinner in a botanical garden. She did end up dancing for him along the cobblestones, among the marjoram bushes, twirling in her gown until she collapsed, drunk and enchanting, into his arms.

"I thought that I would find it demeaning or something," she says, "being forced to parade my profession around because of these rumors in the house, but it felt so good to dance for someone who looks at me the way Dylan does."

Though it's 7 a.m., women line up in two rows to find a tiny slice of their reflection in the bathroom, leaving no space for me. We need to dress in formal-casual evening wear for our date tonight so we can spend the day in interviews. Vivian crouches in a corner, stretching her eyelids thin for her liner. In the bedroom, Winna lends me a portable stage mirror she brought, explaining to me that reflective surfaces are bad for filming. Catching a camera in the shot crosses the fourth wall and ruins it for the viewer. It's reality television, I say; the cameras are the point. I tie my hair back in a braid, trying to look elegant and mature. I tug on a black minidress I got at Forever 21 in college, with a hole in the center of my sternum, like an opening to stab me in the heart with a wooden stake. I stopper my plastic foundation bottle with the back of my hand and tip some out to smear across my face with my fingers.

"You look good," Sam says, entering the room. I wave my hands to fan air across the foundation until it becomes tacky.

"Thanks," I say. She leans over my shoulder to apply red lipstick from a small black bullet. The tip of the lipstick is a deep, well-worn curve the exact shape of her lips. As a girl, I used to read infographics in magazines in checkout lines about what the shape of your lipstick says about you. My mom would never let me buy them, and besides, I've never worn enough lipstick to make a noticeable dent.

"Do you want some?" she says. It's too bluish for my skin tone, but I take it anyways. I apply a bit to the center of my lips and blend it out because I heard that it looks like I've been newly kissed, which is enticing to men. A department store tag sticks out at the back of her blazer collar, marked full price at $348.

"What's that?" I ask.

"Just some budget hacking," she says. She turns away from me to tuck it back in place. At the door, Sam asks me if I'm ready for the night. I pose and smile at her.

"You have lipstick on your teeth," she tells me, and I lick the bottoms of my two front teeth and smile again. "Open your mouth." Instead of brushing off whatever lingered, she places her entire finger in my mouth. It's cool and heavy against my tongue. "Close." She pulls it out, knuckle by knuckle, and shows me the ring of red at the base.

"Thanks," I say. I feel like I have something crawling across my skin and we go downstairs in silence. Sam turns in front of a production assistant, letting them reach around her waist to get mic'd up. When it's my turn, the touch of the assistant's fingers on me, even though my clothes, feels feverish. Then, we laze around the house as the women get pulled one by one for interviews. In my pull-aside, Miranda asks me questions that seem to be designed to make me anxious: what I hope we'll do today, if I've ever been on a date with eleven other women, if I'm worried I won't get enough time with Dylan. She focuses in on the fact that Dylan and I might kiss today. I don't know if we'll kiss, I keep saying.

"Do you have a cast fortune-teller? You should ask her and not me."

Miranda doesn't laugh. By the time the bus pulls up, I've redone my makeup twice and it's nearly past dinner. The producers order barbecue chicken wings, salad, and pizza to a parking lot in a warehouse district area of LA while we wait some more. Morgan, who fought with Winna, is on some kind of fanatical diet where she picks up a slice of pizza, sniffs the pepperoni, and proclaims that that was all she needed. We speculate about what the date card means, what's taking so long. I munch on smoky almonds from the bottom of the salad, oily dressing dripping off the tips of my fingers. We talk about shaving versus waxing. Some girl brings up that she thinks a jackalope is a real animal, which devolves into a conversation about imaginary animals that could be real. Vivian says she hasn't totally suspended the childhood belief that there could be woodland fairies that live under toadstools.

"Why else would mushrooms look so freaking cute?" she says, and the jackalope woman nods in response. Eventually, Andrea, Wyatt, and Miranda come onto the bus.

"We've got bad news," Wyatt says. "Dylan's sick and won't be able to make it on a date today."

Some of the women switch to maternal-caring mode so quickly that it can't possibly be an act. Vivian asks if he has a temperature. I mostly think about how he wasted our time. He better have food poisoning or something terrible.

"But," Andrea says, "we feel bad for you ladies, getting all dressed up for nothing, so we're going to do something we've never done before and let you have a night out."

The bus erupts into cheers. We haven't had any kind of stimulation in days. A night of drinking and dancing could do us good, and besides, I'm already in the outfit. A group of production assistants come around the bus and remove our mic packs. The bus drives us to a hulking cement building with a blank facade, somewhere in Hollywood. It's early in the night for the club to be full, but there are enough people for it to not be embarrassing when we show up. Miranda opens a tab for us, and we do what we've done all day, chat in circles, but this time we have professionally mixed cocktails and small packs of men walking toward us. The producers tell us they'll be back in a few hours and to not make any trouble. They point to a bouncer in the corner watching us and tell us to contact him if issues arise.

A blond man with a cutting jawline comes over and stands next to me. His hair is long and tucked back behind his ears. He's slightly shorter than Dylan, but much stronger, with a rounded nose that would look cute on a baby.

"Hey," he says, "what are you drinking?"

"Oh," I say, "it's a gin and tonic." This is the drink I order under any circumstance, because it sounds sophisticated, even though I don't particularly like the taste.

"I love a G&T," he says.

"Yep," I say. "Me, too."

His name is Rob and he's here with his buddies for a college reunion weekend. I can't tell if I find him attractive, even though he's objectively handsome. Whenever I look at men my age, I start to wonder about what my life would be like if we were married. That could be why my disposition was primed to go on the show. Rob seems like the kind of guy who works in real estate, spends the whole day talking on the phone, and played college football, like he followed that trend where people add butter to black coffee in an effort to jumpstart their metabolism. His mother would want a big wedding for him because he's her only son, and he listens to everything his mother says, including what shower curtain to buy. I would have to wear a princess-style satin dress and be destined for a life of photo shoots: engagement, wedding, then maternity. I try to think about whether I could live like that and be happy.

When he slips behind me to get another drink, he places one hand on the small of my back and then both to grip my hips. He says, "Excuse me," with his pink lips close to my neck. Many of the women have split off with the men from the reunion group. Sam talks to an extremely tall man with buzzed hair and fashionably baggy clothes. I can't tell if she likes artsy guys like that. For all our talking, she has never mentioned her type. Winna usually dates other dancers, but the competition in the companies for the few straight men is worse than *The One*, she says. Jazmin dates "the kind of guy who is moderately active in the local DSA." Rob returns with another drink for me and gets me talking about Boston. He loves it, he says, loves all the bricks. Great hospitals, too. He's been there once. I agree with him that it's nice. He tells me he went there for a college football game with his buddies. I have never heard a person use the word *buddy* so much. He used to play as a fullback in school and loves the game. I knew I was right about that. He asks me if I like college football, and I tell him I'm generationally obligated to support the Buckeyes.

"Hell yeah. I love girls that aren't afraid to watch sports, who don't just do girly things. So many women are high-maintenance these days. I love that you're laid-back."

"That's me."

Part of the problem with going to bars or parties is that I feel bad whenever I try to end conversations, even if I'm desperate to leave. Once someone seems like they want to talk to me, I can't extricate myself. He says he likes my dress and his thumb presses a light stroke through the cutout on my sternum. I shiver. Men are so bizarre. He probably thinks it was sexy, or fun, or harmless, but it's not normal to caress strangers this way. I down the last cold gulp of my fourth drink of the night and set it on the table.

"I have to go," I say, pointing to the dance floor. "I've got pent-up energy." This is as close to honest as I can come, but I still feel shivery, like I've taken a risk. Some of the other women have started to dance together, extricated from their male counterparts, though some of the others are dancing with the men who chatted them up. "It was good talking to you."

On the dance floor, colored lights illuminate our limbs in shocks of neon. We aren't allowed to listen to music of any kind in the house, and it's cathartic to have something besides my own thoughts humming between my ears. I scream along with each song I know, watching the dance moves of the women and reflecting them back. The club fills with people, crowded and alive and fun. It's like the pulse of real life has returned to my body and I start to thrum. After a while, I drip sweat, darkening my black dress in half-moons by my armpits and under my boobs, but I don't stop dancing. I sling my arms over Vivian's shoulders for a bit, and she half shouts in my ear that she hasn't gone out like this in years. I smile at her, thinking of her sons, thinking of what it takes for women to get a little taste of wildness. The next song, someone puts their hands on my hips and I press back against their body, but the body isn't right, too big and too hard. I turn around and let out a sharp yelp. People turn and stare. Rob steps back and raises his hands in front of his chest in apology.

"I'm sorry," I say, knowing I was rude. "I thought you were someone else. I'm sorry."

He looks embarrassed as he merges back into the crowd. Sam grabs my hand and pulls me toward her.

"Are you okay?" she asks. "What'd that guy do to you?"

"I got spooked. I assumed it was you or Vivian. He didn't do anything."

"I'm glad to know you wouldn't scream if I tried to dance with you," she says with a snort. She takes my hand in hers and lifts it in the air, gesturing for me to spin, and I do. Her eyes flash in the changing lights, and the smell of her perfume and my shampoo and our sweat intermingles. When our eyes catch, looking at her feels better than looking in the mirror. The music shifts, and we dance together until the humidity is too much and the alcohol wanes. When it's time to load into the bus, one woman is passed out asleep on a bench and the others are scattered throughout the club, some saying farewells to the men from earlier in the night.

The producers don't let us sleep in the next morning, and in our pajamas, we circle up for another date card. A knock at the door comes, and a production assistant signals for me to get up and answer it. Instead of a card on a platter, Dylan stands in the doorway.

"It's Dylan," I yell back to the women, giving them a half second to redo their hair and look more presentable. He reaches down to give me a hug and kisses my cheek.

"How're you feeling?" I ask as we walk toward the sitting room.

"I'll fill you in later," he says, and squeezes my elbow twice in front of all the women, a code so secret I don't understand it.

"Good morning," Dylan says. He gets a deeper tone of voice

when he starts these speeches, like the rote recitation of a pilot at takeoff and landing. "Trust is something so important to me in relationships, and last night, we evaluated that trust. In reality, your night off was a night on. It was a way to see if you were serious about being here, and I'm sorry to say that some of you did not pass the test."

I should've known we would never be allowed to do anything fun. Now that he says it, it makes sense. It would've been a giant liability to let a group of unsupervised women with no wallets, no phones, and unlimited amounts of alcohol go to a real club. The date card even tried to warn us that everything is fair game. I look to Sam to see if she knew, but she looks surprised as well. I hope she didn't do anything bad last night.

"The men from last night were paid actors and were responsible for recording and reporting back to me on all the conversations you had. They were paired with each of you based on your personality types. Morgan and Wendy, based on your actions, I don't believe I can move forward with our relationships at this point." One by one, after hugs from the group, the two women apologize to Dylan. Winna looks on, neutral with the Golden Necklace around her neck, as Morgan and the other woman are escorted out.

"I'm here this morning to talk to the remaining women who went on the date last night and further our connections. Vivian, can I grab you first?" Dylan says, and they go off somewhere in the backyard. Jazmin, Winna, and I meet in the kitchen, and Sam joins a couple minutes later.

"What the hell happened last night?" Jazmin asks as she makes us a giant green smoothie.

"We went to a club and there were some guys who hit on us. I didn't think anything of it. Apparently Wendy was so drunk she made out with one of them, but Morgan said she was single and got too flirty," Sam says. "Wendy apparently got her guy shirtless and ran her hands up and down his bare chest. Very naughty."

"How'd you find out about that?" I asked.

"I asked Wyatt," she says. "Producers are such sneaks. I'm kind of pissed at Dylan, too. Like, if last night was about trust, you'd think Dylan would trust the women he thinks could be his wife."

"I've been cheated on before," Jazmin says. "Dylan could have that lingering fear, too."

Winna gives a lengthy summary about attachment styles and how they fit into our sun signs and enneagrams. She has an encyclopedic knowledge of these categories, having listened to podcast episode after episode about the stars, and the spirit world, and the self. Jazmin is a Virgo and an "investigative thinker," a 5 on the enneagram, which she resents.

"I don't know how you can stand to have these types put upon you," Jazmin says.

"What a classic 5 thing to say," Sam says, trying to annoy her.

"It's an order to the world that I can access," Winna says. "That's why I like being here—I mean, other than Dylan, of course. Every day for us, every season, it's the same thing."

I slip into the groove I'm used to, of being in a group of women dissecting each part of our relationships with men. If only we had phones with us so we could parse, word by word, straightforward text messages from guys we like. I sip on my smoothie. Unlike Sam, I think the night of dancing and relaxation, even as an illusion, was worth it. If I wasn't willing to give up my freedom for a bit of fun, I don't think I would have come here, but maybe I'm used to being powerless. Winna, after all, does diagnose me with an avoidant-dismissive attachment style.

"That doesn't sound like a compliment," I say.

"You don't like when people get too close to you," Winna says. "You can seem closed off."

"Hey," Sam says, nudging my shoulder with hers. "Don't go too hard on our girl. She's never been in love before. Someone's going to sweep her off her feet any day now and she'll blossom like a beautiful flower."

"I've never admitted that outright," I complain.

"Honey," Jazmin says, "you don't need to."

Soon, Miranda comes to bring me to the stone ledge of the outdoor fireplace to talk to Dylan.

"You're so loyal," Dylan says, reaching over to tuck a strand of hair behind my ear.

"Thanks," I say, but in reality, what I did or didn't do had nothing to do with Dylan. I hadn't even been thinking about him. I just didn't like the paid actor, Rob, or whatever his real name was, who they sent me.

"So you weren't sick?" I ask.

"No," he says, laughing, "I wasn't. I noticed you play hard to get with everyone. I was glad to see it wasn't only with me."

"Oh," I say. Dylan touches his knee against mine, and if a barometer were in the room, the mercury would have dropped flat. I hate kissing, especially first kisses, especially the moment before when I know it's going to happen and I'm waiting for it to be over. Men look at my lips, then my eyes, then back to my lips, then do a small smile. It's like they take a group class as teenagers on the technique. I'm not sure if it's supposed to be sultry or if it's genuine, but either way, it makes me itchy. Whenever it happens, the air gets heavy and a ringing sound starts in my ears and I have a violent urge to pull away and never see them again. I always leave the kiss feeling embarrassed for them and myself. Four women kissed Dylan on the first night, and Winna kissed him on their date. That's part of what we talk about all day at the mansion, tallying who does what and when. I lean away from him. Behind the cameraperson, Miranda's eyes burn in the morning sun. I'll have to explain myself later. I change the subject and ask about his students. He tells me about the subjects he likes to teach them. I tell him about my internship at college at the early childhood education center, the university preschool where I babysat for course credit.

"Do you play favorites?" I ask him. "I always did. There were some kids who I liked more than others."

"I try not to," he says. He smiles at me and looks down at my lips. "But sometimes, it's hard."

I smile back at him and think of Rob and his finger tracing across my ribs. If Dylan did that to me in the Casita, I could relax and let it happen. When Rob called me laid-back last night, maybe this is what he meant. Men find it easy to picture me pliant, expectant, seductive. Hot and happy, like Sam said. I can picture myself like that, too. I think of Winna, Jazmin, and Sam teasing me over not having been in love before. I'm not sure what I'm so scared of, what I'm trying to avoid. Dylan can teach me that, if I let him.

ORDER

IN THE SIDE room, Dylan selects the women's headshots as Miranda, Wyatt, and Andrea nod along. Terry, his personal producer, guides him through the process. Both women who got sent home after the club date were Miranda's, and two more women are on the chopping block tonight. She doesn't like for her numbers to dwindle this early. After tonight, three women will go home each week. An intern from the art department arranges the necklaces on the tree stand in the corner. It's not the real production room, where Miranda hoards tiny hundred-calorie snack bags of cheddar cheese popcorn in her desk drawer and each long night the recycling bins fill past the brim with Starbucks containers.

This one is sanitized and shrouded in red velvet drapes. When the lead cracks at the necklace ceremony and needs a private, filmable place to cry in, this is where the camera crew takes him.

Dylan points to Ashley's photograph. "Who's that one again?"

"Koala Head. Went to Columbia. You talked about deep-dish pizza with her this week, how she likes it even though she's a born-and-bred New Yorker," Wyatt answers. He's such a good actor, pretending that he's not gunning for Dylan's top pick.

"Oh, yeah, that was weird. Keep her."

She hates that Wyatt and Dylan have such a strong friendship since he produced the last season with Dylan as his contestant. She needs to redirect. "So, Emily's here to stay," Miranda says. "Who else?"

"Winna. And the blond one," he says, though half of the women are blond.

"Which blond one? Anna Mae, Southern accent?" Miranda says. It's her job, as it's the job of all the senior producers, to predict and react to Dylan's wishes before he even knows what they are. She worries sometimes about the number of people her actions shunt into a level of generic, low-tier fame that consists of shilling affiliate codes for modular wood pulp furniture to pay bills. The only thing that assuages her anxiety is that she, too, always wants more. At work, she wants to win, and at home, she wants to be at work. She was a great student early in life, knowing that perfection was always within her reach, so she reached for it with every strained ligament in her body. She craves that same feeling now, the sharp lick of the whip when, for a moment, she's without question the best. Her blood pulses at the end of a good season, and she signs back up for the next round.

"Cowgirl's cool and all, she can stay. I'm thinking of the one with the big eyes, like a hot bush baby." Andrea points to her girl, one of the Laurens, and Dylan nods.

"Yeah, keep her."

"We're going to ask that you keep Leigh and Brandi for another week," Terry says.

"Fine, fine."

"Come back after the first four," Terry says, handing him the final list. One more of her girls is getting cut and one of Andrea's. None of Wyatt's, of course. No one expects Dylan to remember all their names in the right order, especially when there are still twenty-three women left. Dylan studies the first names, tapping the girls' faces on the board as he visualizes them in his mind, perhaps trying to remember how good they are at kissing.

He's a good guy, better than some of the past seasons' male leads. Before him was a party boy whose engagement dissolved within six months, and then, six months later, he maimed someone while driving drunk. Disaster for the franchise. Dylan, though, could marry one of these women. That's why he was chosen, after all; they needed someone squeaky clean. She pictures her girls and the life they could lead with Dylan after here: God, romance, and a gaggle of kids roaming the mountains. She can sell her girls on that. After all, she's selling the whole country on it. That's where the real power comes, not the bonus she tallies up at the end of every season. She shaped what millions of people will see. People talk about influencers changing the perceptions of followers one subtly placed cannabis-infused seltzer at a time. If you want to talk about influence, she thinks, you should talk to her.

WEEK TWO

OUTSIDE THE MANSION, a dirt track encircles the house, forged over years by women and men bound to the grounds and eager to get their energy out. I'm never alone anymore and I can't stop sucking in the juices of every other woman's problems. Even my roommates, my last tether to sanity, have noticed I'm irritable. The midday heat elicits a kind of clean sweat like ocean water from my pores. Still, running beats my current pastime of waking early to hear about other women being invited on dates with my boyfriend and staying up late to hear about how those dates went. Except for when other people are actively on dates with him, I'm not sure I would actually consider him my boyfriend. I've only known him for five days, after all. The show lies about what a week is. In the world, it is seven days. Here, a week is the time between each Necklace Night: four days. If Dylan and I get married, it will seem to the world that we have fallen in love over the course of ten weeks—barely reasonable—when in reality, it will be only six—unhinged. For reference, the gestation period for a ferret is also six weeks. I made a production assistant google that for me.

The house is set on a hillside, and I sprint up by the driveway. By the pool, gravity drags my feet in long strides back downwards. A lizard skitters underneath a scraggly shrub and I think about a mountain lion slinking up behind me, waiting to tear me into shreds. There are times when I wish it would pounce sooner. I run by the shed where I met the cow and Sam. Apparently, the cow never meant anything. One of the women brought it to make a good first impression on Dylan, but it didn't work. She didn't even make it into the top twenty. Sweat stings my eyes. At a varying point on each loop, I pass Jazmin walking Guava, and Leigh running back and forth with a heavy vase that she grabbed from the house for strength training. She wasn't able to pack her weights because of the luggage restrictions, so she has to make do. She's a real estate agent/fitness model, and is jacked out of her mind. It seems like the only difference between a fitness model and a regular model is you have to be equally hot and skinny, but you also have to have biceps when you flex. As I run, the size of the track seems to collapse on itself, a spiral instead of a circle. I follow it until my watch beeps at forty-five minutes.

In high school, most of the girls in my class joined cross-country running, as it was our only coed sport besides golf. We got paired up with the boys from St. Anthony's Academy. We spent hours after school together, drinking orange juice from tiny boxes. Sometimes I would drink five cartons a day, jittery from the sugar, my teeth eroding from the acidity. All of us, girls and boys, arranged ourselves in a circle in the school parking lot, foam cylinders beneath our thighs, rolling back and forth. Sometimes, one of the boys would let out a loud moan, not from the pain of it, but a sexual sound meant to elicit giggles from the girls. Whenever it happened, I'd stare at the ground and press my palms farther into the pavement. Our coach, Sister Mariah, would smack the boy in the head with her roster clipboard. Once, a girl moaned instead of a boy. No one laughed, and Sister Mariah didn't even bother to hit her. We looked at our legs until we were told to switch sides. When we finished that day, tiny shards of granite were lodged so deep in my skin that the indentations lasted for hours.

When I do my laundry in the basement of the mansion, I pull a clump of hair from the rubber seal of the washing machine, a mat of different colors and textures. Drying racks have been opened and spread into a maze along the floor, layered with lace bras, shapewear, and thin hang-dry dresses dampening the air. There are holes in the wall with delicate piles of drywall dust accumulating below. When I came to the mansion, I didn't expect it to be falling apart. At night, when Sam climbs up to the bunk above me, the whole frame shakes so violently I dread to think about what would happen in the event of an actual earthquake. Jazmin keeps saying that California is meant for a whopper any day now. The washing machine rattles at a disturbing decibel, though none of the contents inside are spinning. On my run, I, too, felt like screaming and spinning in circles. I bang once on the washer door with my elbow since I have no idea how to fix anything, and this seems like as good an attempt as any. This must be why women want husbands. I could call Dylan's name from our basement and have him deal with this.

Upstairs, the women are frenzied. Winna tells me that Laura is going to Dylan's rented house nearby right now to talk with him.

"Who's Laura?" I ask.

"Are you serious?"

"Yeah, there's Lauren K, Lauren N, Laurie, and Leigh, no Laura."

"Laura, she's a middle school teacher." Isn't everyone here? I think, but keep this to myself. Winna tells me that Laura's grandmother has passed away, and she's returning home for a few days to attend the funeral. I only have one surviving grandfather and my two parents. I don't want them to die, but for a second I imagine how nice it would be to get a respite from this place, to hold my phone in my hand and scroll through my feeds instead of journaling about my feelings to pass the time. There's something to be said about looking at the pigs in farm sanctuaries and ads for overpriced, poor-quality clothing rather than mulling over my problems on loop.

"The laundry machine is broken," I say to the group as we wait for a producer to arrive. "People are going to have to start handwashing again."

Laura comes back, flanked by two camerapeople and Miranda, Wyatt, and the other producer, Andrea.

"Miranda," Winna calls out, "the washer is still broken."

"And the coffee always tastes burnt," another pipes in.

"I'm not going to rate this Airbnb highly until I see some changes around here," Jazmin says, and the women laugh in agreement.

"Wyatt, if it's broken, someone is going to need to send out my dresses and I don't want to be the one to pay for it," Ashley says. "I'm like Cinderella with all the hand-washing I have to do here. I'm laboring too much."

"Cinderella washed other people's clothes. You're only washing your own clothes. It's not the same," Jazmin points out.

"What's happening?" Laura says, sounding tired. Someone makes space for her on the couch, and she slides in next to them.

"She broke the laundry," Anna Mae says, pointing to me. The whole room looks at me, waiting on my word.

"I didn't. It doesn't spin. The water foams up and it makes this freaky squeaking noise, like ee-ee-ee. I swear the basement is haunted."

"I'll get someone to call the appliance guy. We need to film this all again," Andrea says, gesturing to the women. "No more chore talk, Cinderellas."

Only this time do I notice the Golden Necklace dripping across Laura's collarbone. So, this is what we were supposed to be reacting to, but on the reshoot, no one takes the bait, an impressive moment of solidarity in our otherwise disparate group. Laura grabs her packed bags, already waiting for her in the corner of the room.

One of her roommates says "I love you, sweetie!" as she leaves. Another tells Laura that her family is in all our prayers. She lists Laura's parents and siblings by name, like they've known each other for years instead of days.

"Laura got the necklace," Miranda says. They can't expect us to get jealous of Laura after her beloved Meemaw died. Disappointed, Miranda grabs me for an interview about last night's ceremony, and I slide onto the bench in the candlelit side room.

"So," Miranda says, "have you and Dylan kissed yet?"

"No. Dylan and I haven't kissed yet."

"Why not, do you think?"

"I'm shy." Miranda waits in silence as the camera is trained on me. Perhaps she went to graduate school to be a therapist. The control she exerts over me, my desire to please her as I reveal things about myself, seems clinically honed.

"When was the last time you kissed someone?"

It was near midnight at a New Year's Eve party, three months ago now, on my third date with a boy who I would never see again. He did some kind of computer math work at another biotech company in Kendall Square, and a coworker had set us up. He was handsome enough for me, in that I didn't care so much about looks and wanted someone who would listen to me. His sister's apartment steamed with packed bodies. We had been experiencing a cold snap, and with windchill, the temperatures were below zero. One room had been taken over by outerwear, identical black puffer jackets piled so high the bed was no longer visible. My back leaned on the outside of the bathroom door as people shimmied past me in the small corridor to get to the living room where the countdown was soon to start. Someone retched into the toilet on the other side and my stomach churned in sympathy. I had fled there a few minutes ago, not wanting to kiss my date and pretending to not be aware of the time. Before the party, I had assured myself that I wouldn't do this when the prospect of a kiss arose. He found me regardless as the countdown began. He looked at me in silence, then put his hands on my face as a preamble. His fingers smelled like hummus. I wished the person would come out of the bathroom. The door would open, and I would slip on their vomit, tumble backwards, and on the way down hit my head on the toilet bowl, crack my skull open, and be ushered to the emergency room, bleeding brain pulp all over him. Instead, the countdown got to one and the man leaned over to kiss me, staring straight into my eyes during the approach. The momentum caused our teeth to knock, and his breath from his nostrils was humid across my face. With that, the new year began.

"Oh, a few months ago," I say to Miranda.

"Have you ever been in a serious relationship before?"

"No," I say.

"Why is that?"

I want to say that I wasn't correctly made as a person and that it would have been better for me to be born into a time when I was shunted off to a husband who was at least three decades older than me who would soon die. Then I could have lived peacefully as a widow for the rest of my life, but instead, I say, "I'm looking for someone who understands me and I haven't found that person quite yet."

An hour later, I catch Vivian in the kitchen handing a phone in a mirrored case back to a production assistant. She's allowed to call her sons once a week as they wait for her return at her parents' house in Minneapolis. Her parents have shorn her towheaded kids' hair down so cropped that they look like newborn lambs, she says, looking like she has been crying.

"Do you think Dylan would be a good dad?" I ask. I've always wanted kids, and on every date, Dylan talks about being ready to settle down.

"Yes," she says, "or at least, it seems like it. I try to picture how Dylan will be meeting my boys, but they're so shy. This sounds bad, but I'm worried that if they don't act cute enough at the family date toward the end, Dylan won't pick me. I can't tell if I should be coaching them for it in advance during our phone calls, but then it's like, I'm producing my own children for a reality TV show. He can't be worth that, can he? I know this is like telling other people about your convoluted dreams," she says. "But I don't have anyone else to talk to about them."

"I'd love to hear about them whenever you want to talk," I say, and if there's one thing I can offer to people, it's a friendly face between two passive, listening ears. I can picture Vivian getting pregnant again with Dylan as the father and, nine months later, delivering a squalling gingery baby. They would create a picture-perfect blended family. She seems like a good mother, the kind of woman who has a spare granola bar in her purse and a fresh pack of tissues in her glove compartment, prepared for daily life in a way that I never am.

Sometimes, when I was bored at work, I filled out HR worksheets about crafting my own personal mission statement. One day, a professional affinity quiz churned out that I love rules and should consider becoming a prison guard. I switched tabs and started a new, more in-depth quiz. It took me an hour to complete and said that, since I enjoy working with my hands and animals, I should become a dairy technician and milk cows all day. I excused myself from my desk to a bathroom stall, where I breathed heavily on the toilet for five minutes. To stop picturing myself as a dairy maid, coming home with chapped hands and clothes reeking of soured milk, I scrolled through my phone. It was filled with images of women like Vivian, women with a purpose. I tell Vivian that I know she'll do the right thing for herself and her family, but of course, this line doesn't comfort her much.

The next morning, my name is on the card for that day's group date. Ten women are called, half of the remaining bunch, Winna and Jazmin included. This time, our ambiguous message is ***Love can save a life. Love, Dylan***, which means I'm certainly going to be sent to my death. The dress code is "athleisure, but pack a swimsuit." It's strange to think about how our group has already shrunk nearly a third in size since we began filming nine days ago: nine women down, twenty-one more still standing.

After an hour-long bus ride, we arrive at what I'm pretty sure is Venice Beach given the prevalence of beachside cafés and people roller-skating. No one uses the beach for lounging, as the temperature barely crests over seventy degrees, though an avid contingency of slackliners bob precariously nearby. Sand sifts into my sandals and chafes against my feet. I want to slide them off, but a production assistant tells us to walk toward the water. They always need shots like this to introduce the scene. A scream rings through the distance, not coming from the cement path with all the people but from the ocean. I turn my head, and far out in the water, a figure's head bobs. I look toward production, hoping they'll indicate who, in the event of a taped civilian death, will be in charge. A cameraperson across from us has its lens pointed at the lifeguard tower. Its door swings open and two extremely hot, tanned people run toward the sea, and I realize what's going on. I'm almost flattered that Dylan is willing to fake die in the ocean to shock us.

I elbow Winna, staring agape beside me. "It's Dylan," I say.

"What?" she asks me. I point to the cameras trained on the lifeguards, who paddle to him on their boards. They circle Dylan as he splashes; then he stops for a moment and begins an impressive forward crawl back toward shore. The lifeguards flank him like dolphins behind Poseidon. I wanted him to commit to the bit, but apparently being dragged back to land would be too emasculating. When he stands on shore, he shakes out water from his hair, a bit like a sweet dog, except he has lovely abs.

"Today," he says, "we're going through lifeguard training."

I shed my T-shirt and flouncy shorts down to my black one-piece with strategically placed sexy slits. I didn't bring any bikinis with me so that I wouldn't have to agonize over whether I'd wear one. Production has bath towels, which they allow us to wrap around ourselves for warmth before we start filming. The other women look beautiful, some waifish and others taut but curvy. When I was a child, women with brittle bones were considered desirable, tall and birdlike with white hairless skin and penciled brows. Models had wide doe eyes and looked a bit like aliens. I tried to shape my body after them and largely succeeded, but now it's clear I'm off-trend. Staying beautiful only gets harder as time passes. Leigh goes over to Dylan to ask if he will apply sunscreen to her back and the cameras eat up the scene. She has a tiny waist, wide hips, and strong legs tanned in places that never hit the sun. Winna does a front walkover in the sand, fanning her limbs in the air. A production assistant cheers us on saying, "*Baywatch*, babes!" CPR dummies are strewn across the sand where we stop. The male lifeguard asks for a volunteer, and we all raise our hands. I worry that Miranda will make my life harder after the interview yesterday, and I want to remind her that I'm game, that I want to stay here. I can be good at this if she'll let me.

"You. In the one-piece," the lifeguard says, and I wish I had worn a bikini. Whenever I raise my hand, I never expect to get called on. "Lie here," the lifeguard directs me. The lifeguard pumps the dummy's chest, then directs Dylan to do the same to mine. My hair fans out around me, and grains of sand dig into my scalp. My vision goes red from the pulsing sun behind my closed eyelids. Dylan's hands press against my sternum, fingertips spanning my rib cage. Two of his fingers slip into the cutout holes of my suit as he gives me fake compressions, damp across my skin, like Rob's at the club night. My breath matches his pace in tiny gasps. I still my whole body, playing dead. All the women are watching, and a fleeting sense of power rises in my throat. I arch my back into his touch, wanting to look seductive.

"She seems like she might need some mouth-to-mouth resuscitation," the female lifeguard says, and the male lifeguard laughs. When I open my eyes, Dylan's face hovers above mine, features in silhouette. His hands move to either side of my face and he bends down, placing a kiss on my lips. With my head wedged in the sand, I couldn't move away even if I wanted to, which I'm not sure I do. His long eyelashes nearly touch his cheekbones when his eyes are closed, and I snap my eyes shut to avoid being caught looking at him. I deepen the kiss, wrapping my arms around the back of his neck. He runs his tongue along my bottom lip in response. I want to show everyone that I'm a good kisser, and I open my mouth. We're making out, my brain keeps telling me. Look like you're enjoying it. Make him want more. When he pulls away, the rush of power is gone. I sit up so quickly I almost knock my forehead against his chin. My body flushes from neck to ears. His blue eyes watch me, waiting for something, though I'm not sure what.

"Thanks," I say to Dylan at the same time as the voice of the male lifeguard booms over me, directing the women to save the lives of their own dummies.

"For what?" he asks. He wipes stray grains of sand off my shoulder blades, his large hands cupping their contours. No one is near us for a second, though one camera eyes us from far away.

"Oh, I don't know. It was nice." He laughs, and I can't tell if it's at me. It's like the first night when I thanked the driver all over again, as though my main personality trait is being grateful. He'll get bored of me soon if I don't start showing him I have other charms. I guess the kiss has taken care of that, though, because now he's gotten a taste of me. Low waves quiver across the dark expanse of ocean. I want to get out of my body, out of my skin that's sticky in the sunlight, my too-fat cheeks burned red from the attention, my unvarnished fingernails bitten to the quick. I pick up a handful of sand and pour it through my cupped fingers. "Do you want to go swimming?" I ask him.

"I can't now." I follow his eyes back toward the women. One stares at us as she waits for her turn to use the dummy, hoping to catch him alone for a moment. I know now that I shouldn't monopolize his time for more than a few minutes in order to keep the peace, but when I'm with him, I feel like I'm where I'm supposed to be: not sidelined, not in a girl chat, not scrubbing my delicates in a bathtub because the laundry is broken again.

"Of course. It was a bad idea."

"It wasn't bad. I want to, but it wouldn't be right." He stands up and offers me a hand. It's a small gesture, but since I get so little of him, I chew on each tidbit until it's cud in my mouth and I'm the stupid cow. My whole body jitters like I underwent an exorcism as Miranda places me in front of the camera. She asks about what happened. I tell Miranda that yes, Dylan kissed me, yes, it was perfect, no, I don't care about what the other women thought about it, yes, I felt a spark, yes, I like Dylan, yes, I like him so much, yes, I like him more than I've liked any other man I've met, yes. I answer with whatever Miranda wants me to say, because the sooner the interview is over, the sooner I can be led by a production assistant to slip through a full restaurant to a bathroom, where girls will snap blurry photos on their phones as I go by, knowing I am part of *The One*, until finally, inside the stall, I can turn the faucet on and pat cold, wet paper towels to my face and armpits.

I came here because I decided that most of the problems in my life would be solved if I tried harder to be noticed. After the dairymaid debacle, I tried to do something fun on Instagram, a challenge where I would post a photo of the same tree every week over the course of a year to illustrate how everything changes, but the change is always beautiful. During that time, I got the same order of frozen yogurt for lunch every Monday to hype me up for my job: kid-size plain with dark chocolate chips and mochi. That was the level of inspired thinking I had access to. Twelve weeks into the project, the woman stopped me on the street and asked about *The One*. The tree didn't seem to be catching on. I wanted real attention. That's not so terrible, since even Jesus died with a bunch of adoring followers. After my moment came, the sun on my skin, and a hot man pressing his lips to mine, all I can imagine is the faces of the women watching me thrust my tongue down Dylan's throat. It was like the rush of a selfie, posted in the seductive whirlwind of golden hour lighting. In the bathroom, vulnerable after the scrutiny of everyone's gaze, I swish the warm tap water through my teeth, regretting that I parted my lips for him. I would have been better off with the changing leaves.

At the evening portion of the date, two men come from the kitchen of the restaurant, holding trays of pigs in a blanket and tiny crackers.

"These are my two best friends, Micah and Landry," Dylan says after his standard toast. "They're here to help me make some hard decisions this week."

Winna sweeps him away, and Micah and Landry place the food on high tops and start picking women off to grill them. No one seems surprised at their presence, but the idea that I'd let my boyfriend's friends break up with me on his behalf doesn't seem normal. When I ask Jazmin about it, she says it happens every season and that they're trying to root out a crazy. She unwraps the pastry dough and eats it, since it's the only vegan thing here tonight, and I eat all her remaining hot dogs until I start to feel sick. Brandi, the roommate I'm least close to, pulls me to a small sitting room in the corner of the restaurant. I await my due punishment for Dylan's kissing me in front of the other women and plan how to apologize.

"I have something that I need to talk to Dylan about, but I'm not sure how to do it. It's just—it's something from my past that's hard to talk about," she says, fiddling with the edge of her dress.

"I get that," I say, mind changing tack. I flip through the horrible things that can happen to women that she might feel like she needs to disclose to him.

"You seem like you've been doing so well here. I thought you could help me," she says, surprising me. We aren't that close in the mansion, but I'm glad that she thinks I could be an expert here. Brandi tells me she's afraid of his judgment. I don't know how to tell her in front of the cameras that it's not Dylan's judgment that she should be worried about. Once she says it, whatever it is, she can never take it back. Even if it's never aired, someone else knows, and that's a flinty piece of control you can never regain. Brandi begins to cry, and I wrap my arms around her. When I lean in close, I see a line of foundation under her jawline, dark and unblended.

"Let's go to the bathroom," I say. "We can get you cleaned up."

"The bathroom is occupied," the production assistant says. The moisture from Brandi's eyes has begun to blur the dark makeup around her waterline. She dabs her eye with the corner of a checked throw pillow.

"Can we get some tissues then?" I ask. The production assistant nods and sends a text. Brandi shakes her limbs out to brush off her bad feelings.

"Don't feel like you need to do anything before you're ready," I tell Brandi.

"But what if he sends me home before getting to know the true me and I lose my chance?" she asks. This triggers her tears again, though she presses her lips into a tight line to hold them back.

"Your chance at what?" I ask.

"To find love," she says.

"You'll have other chances," I say. A fat gray tear rolls straight down her right cheek, a type of crying so neutral and pretty I've only ever seen it in movies. It leaves a pale streak where her foundation thins. "The tissues?" I ask the production assistant. She clicks her phone screen on and shrugs. "I'll get some," I say.

Down a flight of stairs, I find an empty women's restroom so large that it has a small sitting area in a dark corner with a mirror for touch-ups. There are six stalls, one for over half of the women on the date. I crumple up a large wad of toilet paper and jog back upstairs. Brandi's producer, Andrea, crouches in front of her, telling her she did a great job and that conquering her vulnerabilities is the key to showing Dylan that she is here for the right reasons.

"I know," Brandi says with a nod, seeming cheered by those words. She grabs the wad of toilet paper I hand her. When I turn to leave again, the camera is still rolling.

When Micah and Landry come to speak with me, it's easier than talking to Miranda. They tell me that Dylan has said great things about me, and their hard-hitting questions involve things like the best Super Bowl party snack. My answer of buffalo chicken wings sends them into a frenzy of delight. They make a joke about us already having been to the Casita, and they're pleased to hear I had no idea what that was when I entered its hallowed halls. Micah shares a story, taking a serious tone. Dylan had been in a relationship before Suzanne with his high school girlfriend that lasted seven years. She was the most beautiful woman in their town, and Dylan was the star of the basketball team. They thought they were going to get married. As time passed, they struggled with infidelity, meaning that the fiancée kept cheating on Dylan, not one-night stands but sustained flings with coworkers or acquaintances.

No one could figure out why she had such a hold on Dylan, but he stuck by her. They went to counseling at their church, and Dylan never seemed to waver. Eventually, the ex-girlfriend tried to sleep with Landry, and that was the end of that.

"He's got a big soft heart," Landry says, shaking his head. "And he's got scars, scars that run deep in his soul." Micah asks if I knew that. No, I didn't, I assure them. I tell them that Dylan's a good guy, and I'll look out for him after they leave. I wonder how Suzanne reacted when he told her that story, back when he was a contestant itching to please the person with all the power.

The next day, Sam and Vivian go on a group date, so I ask if I can join Winna in her extensive stretching routine. She stands in the room I frequent the least in the house, the study where we receive our necklaces, and pulls at her limbs with a resistance band. Tight bike shorts grip her pointed hips and muscular thighs that look hewn from marble. Then I glimpse her gnarled toes, like twisted roots of a tree forced to grow around rocks. Swollen calloused bulbs top her knuckles, and even when flexed, her toes are skewed sideways as though perpetually pressed. Before I'm caught staring, I move my eyes to Guava, who sleeps nearby. He has started to follow Winna around the house all day, ever since she started sneaking him cheese from the produce drawer. She leads me in stretches, few of which I can do. Then we use two decorative waist-high urns as barres as we continue. She teaches me the positions and gives me small corrections. It's better to be aligned and unable to lift my leg higher than to be falsely bendy at the expense of form. Don't let my pointed feet collapse inward. Neck long, chin high, buttocks tucked. An hour or two passes. I'm blissed out by the order and the precision by the end of it, my body limber and my mind clear.

"Don't tell anyone," I say, "but Micah and Landry told me Dylan was once engaged to a woman who cheated on him relentlessly, and I don't get it. You put his face on a dating app and there has to be a feeding frenzy. Women are piranhas out there."

"Yeah, he told me about her," Winna says. It never occurred to me that Dylan would have told one of the other women about this since he didn't tell me. I try not to think about what that means.

"Why did he propose to someone like that?" I ask. If I had my phone, I would be able to find out. Why do people stay after cheating, why do people stay in relationships that aren't serving them, why does everyone get so stuck in their own lives?

"It could've been the classic devil you know versus the devil you don't," she says.

"Do you have one of those?" I ask.

"I think sometimes I'm so afraid of being undervalued that I don't put myself out there in the first place. That's part of why I'm happy to be here. I'm trying to be better."

I nod in recognition. There are times when I feel like my faults are so endless that anytime someone has a fear, I relate to it. I can identify with every bad emotion, but so rarely with the good. My own devils, the bad ones, float around my head like pixies, shooting my brain with their tiny arrows, but Winna is right that I keep them close. I'm not sure what I would do without them.

Sam and Vivian come back from their date to eat dinner and

change for the night portion. As we discuss who might go home this week, Sam eats a peanut butter sandwich so thick with crunchy peanut butter that the slices of whole wheat bread seem like an afterthought. She lifts her fingers, coral-painted nails trimmed short, in front of her mouth as she talks and chews, too excited to restrain herself. I slide my smoothie to her so she'll wink at me and kiss my cheek. She proceeds to drink the rest of it, and I'm happy to watch her buzzing. On the date, they had their tarot read to suss out their compatibility with Dylan, and she snuck in her first kiss. I can picture her in a crush of green velvet curtains in the mystic's room, his long fingers in her thick hair, the tranquilizing smell of incense in the air. That's what I would have wanted, to be somewhere alone and in the dark. She asks if I've kissed Dylan yet.

"Yeah, I have," I say. "On the beach yesterday."

"Oh, yeah, I heard about that, a major make-out. Did you think he was a good kisser?"

"It didn't feel like it was even me doing it," I say, sounding more defensive than I'd like to.

"Why'd you come here?" Sam asks. "You're not meant for this place."

"Oh, easy," I say. I shudder out of my strange mood. "Desperation. You?"

"So I can sling vitamins on Instagram, obviously."

"Do you really think you could do that afterwards?"

"Absolutely," she says. I tell her I've thought of it, too, in moments when I'm forced to imagine a livelihood outside my former desk job. For the first time, I tell someone I got fired.

Sam laughs at this. "Cowards," she says. "Afraid you'd shine too bright, I'm sure."

"What about you?" I ask her. "Why did you come here?" I know little about her life before, only that she was a manager at a coffee shop in Chapel Hill where college boys who drive $60,000 Jeeps flirted with her all day but barely tipped.

"I'll tell you later," she says, brushing me off. When she stands, I take in the full elegance of her outfit. Her hair is in a slicked chignon, held up only by a gold two-pronged pin. She wears a loose pink dress, almost as sheer as a slip. Big pearl earrings dangle toward her square jaw, and her makeup looks sparse but for her cayenne red lips. If I'm not meant for *The One*, she certainly is.

I limp downstairs the next morning dressed in my outfit for Necklace Night, sore from the ballet. We have to be ready by 9 a.m. so we can do pull-asides all day. Sam, Winna, Vivian, and Jazmin are sitting on one of the outdoor beds by the pool. Wyatt stands beside them with his eyebrows raised nearly to his hairline.

"Jazmin's going to pierce my nose," Sam tells me. She has a wild look in her eyes, half ready in a long lilac dress, but with her hair still in the bun from last night, the ends springing out in small coils.

"No, she's not. This isn't *The Parent Trap*. You're not at summer camp," Wyatt says.

"Exactly, we're baby Lindsay Lohans," Jazmin says, only more thrilled by the comparison.

"Where are you going to get a needle?" Wyatt asks. He widens his stance, which seems like an unconscious assertion of his masculinity. Unfortunately for him, no one cares.

"Winna brought a sewing kit," Jazmin says.

"Winna brought a sewing kit?"

"Of course," Winna says. "I'm like a Boy Scout. I'm always prepared."

Sam and Jazmin plan in Spanish while Wyatt listens, though he doesn't understand a word. Winna and I don't either, but I'm happy to watch them. Wyatt brings out his phone and shows us all an image search of infected nose piercings, asking Sam if this is what she wants to look like on national television. It doesn't have the desired effect. Jazmin watches a video of an infected piercing being lanced and says it reminds her of when we first popped my pimples. Sam barters with Wyatt, saying Jazmin won't pierce Sam's nose, but they want to do stick-and-poke tattoos instead. Jazmin sketches a lot, using it to unwind after her days of rescuing animals, and splays her fingers wide, showing inky doodles between her knuckles. She's done them before.

"With what?" Wyatt says.

"We'll do it with my liquid eyeliner," Sam says. "Unless you get us ink."

Wyatt says nothing. Sam and Jazmin wonder out loud what would happen if they stabbed themselves with a sewing needle covered in eyeliner, had an allergic reaction, had to get hospitalized, and then have Frank Dyer, the creator of the show, Wyatt's boss, find out that Wyatt had known about their plan all along.

"There'll be footage of you as our accomplice," I say, gesturing toward the sky. "Isn't this place rigged with cameras?"

Within a half hour, a production assistant brings the ink, and by the time it arrives, the other women have convinced me to get one as well. Jazmin does Winna's first: the outline of a crescent moon on her injured ankle in honor of her last name. Vivian gets her sons' initials between her fingers. Sam goes next, asking for a hibiscus flower on the crease where her hip meets her thigh. She tugs up the hem of her formal dress and Wyatt begrudgingly turns his phone to Jazmin with a picture to copy. Her leg is long, stretching across the daybed as she reclines like an ancient Byzantine princess, the kind fanned with palms and fed grapes. She laughs, so happy, radiant, and for a second, it feels like I want to slip into her skin.

By the time it's my turn, Wyatt has left, saying he has work to attend to as this is his actual job. I tell Jazmin I want the smallest eye she can manage on the side of my rib cage, a secret mark from my time here. The five of us lie on the bed, pressed close to each other. Above us, sunlight moves through the diaphanous linen canopy.

"You know," Sam says, "I used to hate it when I watched this show and would see the women cry after leaving a week in. They'd hug all the other women and say, 'Visit me,' or 'I love you.' But time is different here. I feel like I could have known you my whole life."

Hours later, after the kickoff toast at Necklace Night, our pod of roommates goes to a set of chairs by an outdoor fireplace to chat. Dylan is off with the first woman who grabbed him to play some kind of game of giant checkers that she arranged. Wyatt comes over to Jazmin and gives us an appraising look.

"You know," he says, "you'll have to stop complimenting each other's dresses and talk to Dylan at some point."

"Poor Wyatt. Are you jealous that we're not complimenting you?" Jazmin asks. Our group laughs. Jazmin complains about how, on her group date, Andrea assigned her to wear a leopard-print outfit. She says they're trying to make her look like Scary Spice, in case anyone forgets for a second that she's Black and hasn't gotten sent home yet. A few hours pass until Miranda gets me for my turn to talk to Dylan. She asks if I plan to kiss him again.

"He was the one who kissed me on the beach," I say, my voice cold. "And he had to be prompted."

"Are we in a fight?" Miranda asks. She gives me a puzzled look. "That kiss was hot." Before I have a chance to answer, she speaks again. "Don't do things because I say so. Do them because you want to stay here. I'm only telling you what I think your best strategy is."

"Strategy?" I ask her.

"If you want to marry someone, your best strategy is to let them kiss you sometimes. That's all I'm saying," she clarifies.

"Noted," I say. She tells me to wait for a second as she goes over to talk to Dylan and his producer, Terry. Luckily, this means she dismisses the woman he's talking to on my behalf.

"I planned something," Dylan says after we hug. "Don't worry. You'll like it. And if you don't, we don't have to do it."

Maybe the brazen kiss on the beach was a fluke. Maybe he's trying to make it up to me; maybe he, too, wanted a gentler moment for us, not in front of everyone with sand lodged in the creases of our knees and elbows. Dylan leads me down a set of stairs to the lowest terraced area of the backyard. We pass the Casita, and I'm grateful he doesn't take me there. A large metal livestock tank sits in a small dirt patch filled with steaming water. A few tea lights flicker behind paper lanterns on the rock wall, and a bottle of champagne rests on a high side table. There are even a set of small steps to use to get into it. "You said you wanted to go swimming," he says.

"I'm supposed to do things for you," I say. Hanging lights twinkle above us, making up for the lack of starlight.

"If you like someone, your best strategy is to do things for them sometimes," Dylan says. I look to Miranda off to the side, catching the camera in my glimpse, and she smiles at me, wide enough to show her teeth. A production assistant brings me to a blocked-off area where I change into a swimsuit, a bikini, not one I packed but in my size nevertheless. I put up half my hair into a small bun and wish for a mirror. I shave every day now that I'm here, to pass the time, but all of a sudden I'm worried I missed a spot. By the time I return, Dylan is waiting for me in the tub in his swim trunks. He stands to offer me a hand to get in, and steam radiates off his chest. I keep one arm wrapped around myself, covering the new tattoo because I'm worried he won't like it.

Until now, I never pictured the way I would fall in love for the first time. I wasn't sure what it would feel like or what I would enjoy about it. I was afraid I wouldn't know how to act, but it's getting easier and easier to imagine. Somewhere up the hill, in the mansion, eighteen other women wait to speak with Dylan, but he chose to be here with me in our own enchanted corner. It's as though all I wanted from a man was to be desired and after that I can act as a mirror. I feel surrounded by copies of myself, alternate versions of me all urging me to be closer to Dylan, and I let myself act on their desires: to start to fall in love.

When it's time to hand out the necklaces, Micah and Landry stand on either side of Dylan. They say the names instead, as they've decided who is right for Dylan, even though they've only met half of us. They call my name early, and I smile at them both widely to show my gratitude. Brandi, before the ceremony is even over, begins to cry. Jazmin rubs her arm in comfort, but that doesn't quiet her. No one seems to be stopping the proceedings.

"What's going on, B?" I ask.

"I slept with Landry before coming here," she confesses, and takes a step forward. She faces Dylan. "Landry and I slept together at the Wagon Wheel music festival last summer. The one you three went to together. Dylan, I thought you should know."

She wipes at her tears with the inside of her wrist. So this is the big news she alluded to earlier.

"I'm sorry, Dyl," Landry says, "It's true."

"It was a one-time thing," Brandi says. "But I know I can't stay. Landry, though I don't have feelings for you any longer, it wouldn't be right for me to stay here given our history."

"You will find a great guy," I tell her as she hugs us goodbye. Someone will see her on here, sweet and earnest, and fall in love with her before they even meet. She hugs all of us, even Micah, Landry, and Dylan, and goes home. It's hard to imagine that Landry would have punished Brandi for their one-night stand; he and Dylan would be raked over the coals for slut-shaming. Maybe she knew she would be going home soon and found it more dignified to leave of her own volition. I try to picture Wagon Wheel, an arid hotbed of former and future contestants of *The One* eating at taco trucks. Jazmin and Sam earlier had started to theorize about the world we were dipping our toes into by simply coming here, a world totally outside the scope of my imagination when I signed up. Being on *The One* can become a career if you know how to build your brand.

When I return to my room, Sam is in a large T-shirt with her back pressed against the wall of my bottom bunk, hunching so her bun doesn't get caught in the slats above. She uses her book light to read the Bible, but the room is otherwise dark. I have no idea where the rest of our roommates are.

"Sorry for being cagey earlier," she says.

"Don't worry about it. I felt bad for prying," I tell her, sitting on the floor to do some stretches. The right side of my neck has been sore for days, even before doing the ballet.

"It's not that," she says, folding the book shut over her index finger to hold her place. "I don't like talking about it."

"We don't have to. We can talk about anything you want."

"Don't tell anyone here," she says. "They'll make me into the sob story." She looks at the ceiling the entire time she speaks, and I hold my breath, afraid any sound or movement on my end could break whatever stroke of luck that precipitated this disclosure. Sam owes $88,477 in student loans, the payments each month more than her rent. She went to UNC out of state as a soccer recruit on a scholarship. Her mom died after her first year from a swift course of stage 4 triple-negative breast cancer. Sam took a semester of leave to be with her as she went on hospice care. They never tried radiation or chemo. Before she was homebound, she and Sam used the remaining portion of her savings on a three-week trip to Mexico. After, Sam tried to pump her with calorie-rich foods: buttery casseroles, McNuggets and fries, chocolate peanut butter pies, homemade Frappuccinos with extra whip. Still, she wasted away, in the ground seven months after the initial diagnosis. When Sam returned to school, she couldn't keep playing soccer, quit the team, lost her scholarship, took out loans for tuition. Her aunt, the only family she had left, moved to Chapel Hill to keep an eye on her, but still, she barely passed her classes. Her GPA tanked. She had planned on going through the recruitment process for a consulting company for a lucrative postgraduate job offer.

"I was going to get rich, but instead, I got depressed. So yeah, I'm effectively an orphan without a cent to my name, with negative cents to my name. I need money—and to fall in love and have a husband, but also I need money." She sucks in a long breath but doesn't cry. "Don't say you're sorry for me."

"I wasn't," I say. "I was going to offer to start a fight with you in case you wanted some extra screen time, you know, entertain the masses. I'll be the bad guy."

"We'd get mega ratings if we did it half naked, but let's save that as a last resort," she says. She finally looks at me, and I can breathe, too. I said the right thing. I didn't disappoint her. She picks the Bible back up and scoots over so I can join her on the bed. "So, when is this supposed to get good?"

"There's dragons at some point, magic fish, the plagues." She rests her head on my shoulder, and I take the book from her lap. "And, of course, we can't forget the entire section of erotic poetry."

She raises her eyebrows, and I flip to the Song of Solomon. She asks that I not read over her shoulder. I fidget and linger until the thought that I'm bothering her overwhelms me. I go to brush my teeth. The Jesuit school I went to for college gave me a merit scholarship worth three-quarters of my tuition, and my parents paid the difference. For spending money, I nannied in an expensive suburb for $22 an hour, and when I graduated with my $46,000-a-year admin job, the world opened up for me, whereas Sam's had closed tight. When I come back, Sam is looking toward the door like she has been waiting for me.

"Get this," she says. "'Tell me, you whom my soul loves, where you pasture your flock, where you make it lie down at noon; for why should I be like one who is veiled beside the flocks of your companions?' Pretty good, right?"

"Yeah," I say, "pretty good."

In Winna's mirror, I stretch my neck taut and run my knuckles across the muscles there. I tilt my head as I evaluate the color of my dark circles, the healing of my pimples, the texture of my pores, and the pain crescendos. That's what is going on, I realize. For days now, I've been moving my head so that my good side always faces the camera. It's like Winna's feet, the hyaluronic acid in Vivian's lips. It's like what my mother said the first time my eyes watered as I plucked my eyebrows: pain is beauty. It's like what the marines say when they exercise: pain is weakness leaving the body. It's like the tragic confessions we make to Dylan. I turn my face to my bad side. This is what Sam's life could be like after the show, changing outfits multiple times a day to get the selfies she needs for the week and hitting the same angles again and again. She didn't mention many specifics about the care she gave her mother in her last months of life, but I've seen enough movies and heard enough stories to get the gist: diapers, sores, pain medications, rolling beds and a growing laundry pile, the strange smell that overtakes the house, cracked lips and rattled breath, twitches, hallucinations, whatever other side beckoning the person forward, that endless siren song of peace. To picture Sam holding all that makes me want to dry heave, though I'd never let her know it. It's like what the Bible argues: the suffering of the present is worth the glory that will be revealed.

HUNT

A FEW DAYS later, Emily comes to Miranda in the basement, complaining that Anna Mae told Jazmin that she overheard a PA talking on the phone about how Miranda told the lifeguard before the date even started to pick Emily as the volunteer on the beach.

"What? Who said that?" Miranda asks. Emily explains again, her hands fluttering around her face in distress. It's a good mannerism, cute for television. Miranda wonders if they've got it on film yet.

"So is it true or not?" Emily says. She's much shorter than Miranda, wearing socks with holes on the big toes while Miranda wears her wooden clogs from a boutique that only sells shoes made of Italian calf leather. At the meeting before filming started where everyone weighed in on who should make the final casting cut, Emily's photo came on screen. "Wife-size," Miranda remarked, looking at her measurements and weight, and all the room nodded. "Brunette Polly Pocket," Andrea agreed. Wyatt said she looked easy to produce.

"I can't believe you think I'd do something like that," Miranda says instead of confirming that it is in fact true. She puts her hand on Emily's shoulder. "Next you're going to tell me you're a flat-earther or something."

"Not yet, but I feel like I could believe anything right now."

"I know," Miranda says, and really, she does. When Emily goes upstairs, presumably to continue fantasizing about Dylan, Miranda goes on the hunt. She calls the PAs to the production room and makes them stand in front of her cubicle. She holds up a finger for them and scrolls up and down her in-box so they have to wait. She slips her phone from her pocket and sends a text to her husband about getting sushi on her way home tonight. Then she starts grilling for the loose-lipped individual. She reminds them that every inch of the house is mic'd, and they'd better come forward now.

"Don't make me have to find out who did this," she warns. She kicks up her shoes on the desk so they stare at her expensive soles as they twitch. This is how you build character. After her first season as a production assistant on *The One*, Miranda worked so hard that her period stopped for six months. She dropped twenty-five pounds, only eating those sleeves of peanut butter cracker sandwiches and Hostess Donettes. She got berated and belittled by

Frank, realizing the more she seemed fazed by the interactions, the more they happened. She hasn't faltered since.

None of the assistants crack. "We have access to your phone records." This isn't strictly true, but they don't need to know that. They stare at the ground in silence, and she's surprised none of them rat each other out. "Go through the audio," she tells them. "First one to find out who peeped gets a bonus. The other person gets fired." They stand there, stock-still like open-mouthed guppies. "Go," she says. "I said it's a race."

WEEK THREE

ON MY WAY to the kitchen, Sam chats with Wyatt in a corner. Overnight, cool air drifted through the windows that had been left ajar, leaving a chill. I tug the sleeves of my sweater over my hands and clutch at the hems. Sam calls me over and points at the spare coffee she made on the mirrored credenza. She's clearly Wyatt's favorite, and Wyatt's other women have started to resent her a bit. I rub the walls of the ceramic tumbler. It's a light roast, tasting like acid and blueberries but forever burned by the faulty machine.

"You should start playing a reveille over the speaker system instead," Sam says. "Why waste time knocking?"

"What's a reveille?" I ask.

"You've never been bugled awake?" Wyatt says.

"Let me guess," Sam says. She looks Wyatt up and down. "Band camp?"

"Horse camp."

"No. Even better."

"I'm a man of many wonders."

"I know you are," Sam says. I take another large sip of the coffee. Seeing them flirt is almost worse than seeing Dylan with the other women.

"I'll start breakfast," I say, itching to leave.

"You ever been to sleepaway camp?" Wyatt asks me.

"Nope," I say. "This is my first time."

"I promise I'll make it good for you," he says. His laugh rings down the hallway as I walk to the kitchen, and I bristle. I make toast from the butt ends of a sourdough loaf. Only half of the girls in the house eat gluten, so there's usually some lingering pastry in the communal food pantry. The rising sun streams through the huge windows, and the rays warm my face. I can picture my eyelashes sparkling in the light, casting my features in a golden glow like a filter. I shake my hair out a bit, the ends of it dusting across my shoulders. My top lip is fuller than my bottom one naturally, a desirable trait these days. I arch my back against the counter, letting my nipples push against my thin sweater. If this was the morning after I slept with someone, the man would come downstairs and see me like this, young and lithe, bathed in light. I wouldn't notice him, caught up in my own moment, but I would look beautiful, so natural and unencumbered that he would have to fall in love with me.

The toast dings and I'm jolted from my daydreaming. When I go to grab the slice, it burns me and falls through my fingers, sliding under the gap between the dishwasher and the floor. I reach down on all fours to grab it and come across a spread of lost Cheerios, chopped pecans, and other shriveled food scraps. I'm surprised the house isn't infested with rats at this point. As I stand, I notice a camera pinned in the corner of the room, high on the wall by a hanging three-dimensional sculpture of sound waves. I stare at it for a moment too long, watching it watch me. This is what I have felt throughout my life, that someone could be watching me and that each moment is an opportunity for me to be desired. I could be walking to work in a crush of people in winter, all disguised in our scarves and hats, and feel a pair of eyes gaze down on me from above, telling me to be beautiful, telling me that if I only tried hard enough and was vigilant enough, someone could fall in love with me that moment. I decide I'll still eat the toast.

"Living room," Miranda says as she barges into the kitchen.

"Good morning!" I answer, trying to establish the kind of bond that Wyatt and Sam have but without the flirting. I butter my toast and hold it in my mouth, grabbing my journal with one hand and my drink in the other.

"Ditch the baggage."

"Miranda, it'll get cold. I haven't eaten since those tiny canapés before the cocktail party last night." As I whine, Miranda points to the toaster, a smaller separate appliance from the toaster oven, since the toaster oven doesn't work. "I've already buttered it," I say, mouth half-full as if the transition from whining to pouting will sway her stony mood. She takes the toast from me, sets it on the counter without a plate, and reaches around to unclip my hair. In the next room, she points me toward an open place on the couch next to Winna.

"Look happy."

I contemplate the remaining possibilities for the group date: paintballing with no protective gear, belaying down some vertiginous cliff, rubbing each other with canola oil and doing a slip-and-slide, eating slugs at a market but in a flirty way, talking to an elderly couple in a nursing home who have been married for seventy-five years and seeing how actual marriage applies to our reality show. Winna elbows me deep in the side. When I look at her, I see a camera behind her head trained on me. Leigh, date card in hand, stares at me expectantly. The woman on my right shakes my knee. I can never remember her name. Miranda warned me that I needed to look happy, so I do. I smile and put my hand on my clavicle.

"I can't believe it's my turn," I say. He'll be here in fifteen minutes. In large bubbly handwriting, the date card reads, ***Emily, let's see how large our love can grow. Love, Dylan.*** I can't imagine this is Dylan's handwriting; it looks distinctly feminine. I wonder which production assistant was pigeonholed into becoming the show's designated calligrapher.

"A greenhouse?" Jazmin says, looking over my shoulder.

Sam picks out my outfits from our now joint clothes collection. Winna helps me pack a go bag with my outfit for tonight, and Vivian does my makeup. Jazmin stuffs all my stray objects into my suitcases. Before each solo date, the woman has to leave her packed suitcases by the door in case Dylan decides the relationship isn't working. I leave my toiletries in the bathroom and tell the other women that if I die and never return, they can keep my deodorant. I want to pace as I wait for Dylan, stuck in LA traffic somewhere, but then I'll sweat on Sam's nice baby-pink top. I ask if I can go back inside and get my sad slice of toast abandoned on the counter. The production assistant says no, and Winna offers to get it on my behalf. Even she takes a long time to return, but by the time she's back, she's holding two slices with banana, peanut butter, and honey on top.

"One half-eaten slice of buttered toast isn't enough for breakfast," she admonishes me. "And you can't eat the date food."

"What?" I ask.

Sam nods vigorously. "No one eats the food at the dinner portion. You have to eat before," she says.

"Is it plastic? Is it poisoned or something?"

"It's real food," Winna says. "But it was cold by the time I got there on my date."

"And the mics can hear you eating," Sam says, "and you'll be trying to make Dylan fall in love with you. Chomp, chomp, chomp. It's not attractive."

I take a meek bite of the toast. "Okay, no eating."

Eventually, Dylan pulls up in an icy blue convertible. Leigh runs and wraps her legs around his waist as he spins her in a circle from the momentum. I look to Sam, who stares back at me with the same blank expression. We have begun to look toward each other whenever something happens in the house that we hate: the woman who calls herself a mixologist and makes foul-tasting drinks for Dylan throughout the week; the woman who calls Dylan her hubby; the idea that we should run to greet someone as opposed to doing the normal thing, approaching from far away and avoiding eye contact until we've reached an appropriate enough distance to say hi. It makes me feel like I can read her mind. The rest of the women line up to follow. When it's my turn, he walks me to the car with his hand pressed to the small of my back, urging me forward in case I have second thoughts. As we peel away, dust rises up in a cloud to coat the other women, leaving them covered in a film of dirt and resentment.

We follow a black SUV. They have rigged an enormous camera to the back of the car, which watches us as we breeze down the highway. Dylan takes my hand and tucks it under his, placing it back on the stick shift. I don't like it being there, imagining my anxiety will induce a spasm that causes us to stall out on the highway, crash, and die, all our last moments caught on film.

"Hi," he says, and smiles. He looks pretty today, more normal than at last night's ceremony with Micah and Landry. Though I know it's not true, it feels like I forget what he looks like in daylight. I've mostly seen his face paled in the studio lights around the mansion.

"Where are you taking me?" I ask, though, as expected, he tells me it's a surprise. I asked Miranda to give me a hint, and she said that *The One* is all about romantic gestures, that they're the perfect fodder for building a strong connection. She said that the things that happen on the show would never happen on the outside and that's what makes the couples so strong. She's right that each time he pays me a bit of special attention, the tendrils of my affection for him wrap tighter and tighter. We sit in a comfortable silence until we pull up to a sign for an airfield.

"Dylan," I say to him.

"Emily."

A helicopter waits like a grasshopper in a mown grass field. Even though I had never seen a full episode of *The One*, one thing I knew in advance is that you can never be shocked when a helicopter shows up, but that doesn't stop the awe I feel looking at its massive black frame, bigger up close than they seem flying overhead.

"You ever ridden in one?" he asks.

"No," I say. This should be obvious because I'm a regular person. "Have you?"

"Once," he says.

"Why?"

"Suzanne," he says, and I get the feeling talking about his ex is going to get cut from our love story. The red lights blink off from the cameras, and I move to leave the car, but Dylan steps out and walks around to my side. My door is open a crack, but I wait and let him open it the rest of the way for me.

"Now will you tell me where we're going?" I repeat. My usual next line of question would be "What's new?" but it has been approximately twelve hours since I last saw him. It feels like middle school when I got my first cell phone and texted my friends constantly but had nothing to say. I messaged everyone "what r u up 2?" though we were never up to anything but talking to each other.

"No," he says, and smiles. He puts the giant headset over my ears, and I worry the gesture has messed up my hair. On the first night, he surprised me with his ease. By ourselves, it's harder to think about what I like about him, what I know and what I want to know. I don't know what else to say to him. When I'm with the other women, their presence encourages me. Maybe I am too competitive: Dylan is like a luxury handbag, where the demand for the good increases as its price rises. The group dates are easier when I can model myself after the women, the way they cock their heads when Dylan enters the room and pitch their voices a bit higher.

In the air, a cameraperson sits so close to us that if I were to stretch out my legs, I could play footsie with him. Dylan and I press up against each other, unable to talk over the whir. Without the pressure to talk, I like him more. Though objectively a private helicopter ride is an exceptional life experience, our stillness lets me imagine a different life for us: sitting in the waiting room of a doctor's office reading old *Time* magazines, waiting for our kid's recital to begin in eager darkness, chatting on our couch as a soapy television episode starts. It's reassuring to feel like I'm not being spoiled by my life of luxury here, that there's a possibility at the end of this that I'd still want a normal life and that that life could be with Dylan. Out the window, patches of reddish dirt break into forests, heading northeast I can only presume, to the sequoias.

Miranda, Dylan's producer, Terry, and the rest of the crew meet us at the park after finishing their chartered flight. Wide trails snake through enormous trees, trees so large that I could live inside their girth comfortably, the square footage larger than my old apartment in Boston.

"I love him," I say, and touch my hand to the bark. It feels different than I expected, crispier and more fragile. Dylan puts his palm over the back of my hand and intertwines his fingers with mine. "This is the perfect date. I love being outside."

"Yeah?" Dylan asks me. I tell him about taking trips with the outdoors club in college up in the White Mountains, though I only did one per year, when we would dress up in costume for Halloween and drink beers at the summit. I lean my back against his body as he leans his back against a tree. A camera shoots what I can only imagine is B-roll, since this doesn't seem like compelling conversation for the masses. I feel like a Patagonia model. He tells me stories of hikes around Denver, his favorites, where he wants to take me: waterfalls in winter with icicles so large that they're opaque, aspens and their fluttering leaves turned yellow in the fall, ferns unfurling in the springtime. He speaks of them with such admiration and tenderness that I'm happy to hear him talk. The producers ask us to move around to various patches where sunlight breaks through the canopy so Dylan can reach down and kiss me artfully among the giant trees. It's better than the beach, our first kiss a sloppy show compared to this muted tenderness. It almost feels natural. On a bench at the base of one of the trunks, the Golden Necklace waits on a thinly sliced geode. We sit on either side of it. I cross my legs, then uncross them, and cross my ankles, wanting to look relaxed.

"Emily," he says, "you have such a genuine energy that I've never encountered before. When I'm with you, I can tell what a good heart you have. I see so many similarities between us. I wanted to offer you this necklace now so you know how I feel about you. I can't wait to continue this date tonight and to spend even more time with you next week."

"Thank you. I never imagined you would be so nice," I tell him, not being able to think of a good speech in return. Winna told me she got the Golden Necklace over dinner, so I wasn't expecting it now.

"Anything else?" Miranda says from behind the camera. It's the first time she has actively produced us during a conversation, but I can see why my response was insufficient. Even something as simple as "I feel the same way about you" would have been better.

This makes Dylan laugh. "Don't worry, Miranda," he says in my defense. "I like her the way she is."

I smirk at her, happy to have someone on my side, and kiss Dylan's cheek in thanks. "Oh, get a room," Miranda says.

"Okay," he says. "Take us back to the Casita." He says it as a joke, but ever since the first night, its presence has lingered in the back of my consciousness. Sometimes, at night, I try to imagine having sex with Dylan, his long frame draped over mine and the huff of his breath as he thrusts into me. The Casita is a few steps from the mansion, where the rest of his girlfriends live. I could only sleep with him there if I got drunk enough to not be in my head, but not so drunk that I make a fool of myself.

"Again," Miranda says, turning to Terry, who nods in agreement.

"Thank you," I say. "I can't wait to continue our time together."

"Dear God, put the necklace on her already," Miranda says. The camera approaches as he does. It's different from Necklace Night, when I stare at the women as he clicks the latch shut. Now he pulls close to me and reaches behind my head to do it by feel.

"When I imagined coming here," Dylan whispers in my ear before pulling away, "I wanted someone like you to be here, someone I could be myself around."

"Me, too," I say, and heat rises in my cheeks. The secret I keep from him, one that feels so perverse that I can barely acknowledge it myself, is that everything I've done here is tinged with falsehood. When I close my eyes when he kisses me, I don't see stars, but the twinkle of lights in the black camera lens. When I fall asleep each night in my bunk bed, I prepare sweet lines and fun facts to deploy in moments like these. I've been rehearsing my whole life to be the kind of woman that Dylan could fall in love with. This morning, as I waited for my toast, I practiced turning my face toward the sun to glow for him. Miranda offers to take a photo of us on her phone when we stand under a hollowed-out part of a tree trunk that arcs over the path where we walk. Dylan and I reach our fingertips up wide, still nowhere near to touching the wood. The artificial shutter clicks. Dylan kisses me and the shutter clicks again.

"You'll have to send me the photo when we're out of the bubble," he says, taking my hand back in his. He's been close to me this whole date, touching the dip between my shoulder blades, brushing hair away from my face, rubbing his thumb against the inside of my wrist. It makes me shiver.

"I don't have your number," I say, imagining entering the flood of his direct messages on social media after the show, trying to regain contact.

"You think by the end of this you won't have my number?" he says. I cock my head at him. Before I can answer, the producers tell us we're going to a second location for a short hike along the river. Dylan and I are separated into different SUVs for the car ride. They don't want us to talk about anything off camera. That's a privilege you can only earn if you go to the Casita together.

"Emily," Miranda says, turning her whole body toward me from her seat in the back with me, "I heard that line about exchanging phone numbers."

"Yeah, what did that mean?" I ask. I want to hear someone say it out loud, that I could win this whole thing, that he's going to pick me.

"Dylan is going to be your husband," she says, wanting me to repeat the line back to her, to feel the words form across my tongue.

"Dylan is going to be my husband."

"This is good for you," she says. "You look happy." The whole day has felt like it has gone too well. I'm getting sucked into a magic space where I believe Dylan likes me more than the other beautiful women at the house. We approach an eddy in the river only a few minutes into the hike. A wooden bridge spans the mouth of the opening, a perfect perch to look out at the view. Below the greenish water, I can see the clear sandy bottom.

"Do you want to go in?" I ask Dylan, sick of the shots of us leaning against each other on various large rocks and tree trunks. We could use a new backdrop for our picturesque memories.

"Are you serious?" he says. He looks toward Terry, who nods in approval. "Let me say this will not be as warm as the hot tub."

One cameraperson stays on the bridge, and the other follows us down to the smooth rocks that slope into the water. Miranda removes my mic pack for me. Her cold, nimble fingers work against my back, reaching into my shirt to the waistband of my flowy shorts. When I return to the pool's edge, I turn away from the camera and pull my shoulder through my shirt. It feels indecent to strip in front of its lens, down to the matching set of heather gray cotton underwear: a thin-strap bra and high-cut underwear, opaque enough to not worry me about the optics when wet. Dylan looks away from me as though to afford me privacy, which is sweet. I take a few bounding steps and squat down when the water is deep enough to submerge my whole body. My jaw clenches at the cold, but it's not as bad as I expected given the temperature of the air. I let out a tinny, shrieking laugh at its bite on my skin. Dylan steps his feet in and waits.

"Haven't you ever done something dumb before?" I ask him. "You have to do it all at once."

In the center pool, I dip my head below the surface. My hair floats suspended around me, obscuring my view of Dylan's approaching legs. The quiet hum of the current matches the whir of my mind, and I hold my breath there for a few moments. The icy water fills even my ear canals, runs between my toes, laps the back of my neck. Dylan is close to me now, up to his waist, and places his hands on my shoulders. I know I must be eye level with his penis, limp and shrunken from the cold, and it feels as though I'm confronting my fate. I rise in the practiced way of a young girl, face up toward the sun to not emerge looking like a wet mop. Without the mic packs and without a boom nearby, this may be the only moment I get with him away from listening ears.

"Can I ask you something?" I say. I wrap my legs around his hips, balancing back in his arms to get a good look at his face. His body shields mine from the camera. As he holds me up, his fingers skim across the scalloped edge of my underwear.

"Anything," he says. "Always."

"Do you know already? Who it's going to be at the end of this?"

He smiles at me, all dimples. "I have a hunch."

I kiss him now, the first time I initiate it. With my eyes closed, the water feels like it rushes all around me, though I'm sure the river is as steady as before. My skin sucks in all his body heat wherever we touch. He pulls me closer to him, and while I know that the cameras are watching me, that Miranda watches me, that a production assistant who works over eighty hours a week to make my life beautiful here watches me, I part my lips in return. Miranda told me to be brave. He can do whatever he wants with me. They can all do whatever they want with me. I twist my fingers into his hair, and when he makes a noise, I know no one can hear it but me.

"That was impressive," Miranda says as I change out of my wet bra and underwear behind a tree. She stands with her back facing me so she doesn't see me naked. In her outstretched hand, she holds Sam's shirt and my shorts, neatly folded for me to pull back on.

"Thanks," I say. "I'm dressed."

"You look fucked," she says, but she's smiling as though this is the highest compliment. My wet hair soaks my collar and my feet are covered in a layer of orange pine needles. Miranda flips a compact open from her pocket so I can wipe away flecks of mascara. Given Dylan's and my respective states, filming for the day portion of the date is over. We make our way back to the SUVs and toward a lodge where I will snack on appetizers and get ready for tonight.

If I were to time travel and tell myself at my desk job a month ago about this night, I doubt I would have believed it: the warm lodge with two large fireplaces and exposed wooden beams, electric tea lights in small red glasses hanging from twine along the edges of the room, the table with two chairs close together set with a tablecloth and an embroidered runner, a full set of glittering cutlery—four forks, three knives, two spoons, a bowl, two plates, three glasses—and on the other side of that sit two cameras on tripods, larger and more expensive than anything on my side of the room. The $257 gray metallic wrap dress of ethically sourced deadstock material that I borrowed from Winna makes me look beautiful. Food from the lodge's kitchen, chicken parmesan with a turnip salad garnished with flowers, is in front of us, but it's cold and stiff-looking. I pluck a violet off the top and eat it, feeling decadent. We drink from the glasses of red and white wines in front of us. Dylan makes a toast to a beautiful day with a beautiful woman.

I tell him how my parents met: organizing canned soup before their confirmation in the basement of Our Lady of Heavenly Virtue, the same church I've attended my whole life. My mother slipped on the laminate parquet floor in her ballet flats, and my father helped her up, gingerly catching her elbow. After three months, though they were only seventeen, they were engaged. They married a year later with their parents' permission. It was not altogether different from what I did by coming here, a romance doused in the accelerant of not being able to consummate their physical desires, theirs for religious reasons and ours for logistical ones. My parents love that story and won't mind me broadcasting it to the world. Miranda knew it was gold as well, telling me to wait to share it until the right moment. I deploy it with ease. I tell him that is how I believe my journey on this show can work, that it's in my blood to fall in love fast, and the powerful force of desire can make people behave beyond the pale of their own imaginations. He brightens when hearing hints of my Catholic upbringing, thinking that God, among other things, connects us. Dylan shares the story of his parents' meeting, also engaged and married within a year. These whirlwinds are our history, spinning us toward each other.

"I guess when you know, you know," Dylan says to me.

"I've always believed that," I say. Nothing I say about myself here needs to be true; it only needs to sound true. I thumb the Golden Necklace, and he hooks his finger in it, pulling me forward for a kiss.

The next day, after two hours of sleep, Miranda comes to get me in the room. My shoulder aches from its twisted position on the charter plane ride back from the national park, and I stretch from side to side, hearing my tight muscles crackle around my bones. Everyone else must already be awake. Production didn't make anyone stay up for my return last night, given we got back at 5 a.m. Even the fine lines at the corners of Miranda's mouth and eyes seem more papery today. She tosses a barely thawed Eggo waffle on my bed and tells me to eat it while I dress.

"You're needed for a girl chat," Miranda says. Next she drops the Golden Necklace at the foot of my bed, and the comforter sucks it into its folds. "Wear that," she says.

I clip my hair back with blue barrettes by my ears and tuck my oversize T-shirt into denim cutoffs. My roommates sit next to each other in silence in the large circle of wicker chairs and a plush couch by the pool, a cameraperson hovering in the background. Laura sits in the circle as well, having returned from her grandmother's funeral last night, but she's quiet among her own set of roommates. She doesn't look like she's grieving or recently landed from a twelve-hour journey from Fairbanks, Alaska, back to LA. In fact, she looks healthful and well rested, so much so that I'm envious. It must be the sweet serum of social media flowing through her veins, the pulse of the world rejuvenating her outlook, or the wildness of her small arctic town as the northern lights tremble across the sky each night.

"I knew you'd get it," Vivian says, catching my eyes first. The women cheer a bit as I come over, which is equal parts sweet and embarrassing. I nestle in between Vivian and Sam on the couch and recount the date in loose detail. As friends, they all want to hear about how it went, but since they're also women dating Dylan, some of whom have spent significantly less time with him, it feels mean to tell them of all the strange, affirmative moments of the date. Winna especially has stopped talking about Dylan around the house, excusing herself for a glass of water whenever the gossip gets too detailed. All I want to do is ask Laura what she read about the season while she was back in the real world. Sam told me that people start researching contestants as soon as they're cast, writing blog posts with old headshots and making early guesses for the winner. Laura has that knowledge tucked away in her silent blond head. On the internet, people could find out about my cross-country times from high school meets, the award I won in college for my senior thesis in psychology, the post I wrote to fundraise for my spring break Habitat for Humanity trips. If someone was persistent, they could find my old Pinterest account from middle school when I wanted to redecorate my room in pale green and eggplant purple, though my parents never let me get beyond color chips for it. I'm sure there are more remnants of my life out there, strewn around in strange places like bones picked clean. Though I have only been away for two weeks, the world outside the mansion feels blurred. For Laura, it must still be vivid.

A card comes in not only with the information for the date today, but also that the eliminations this week will be made from the results of an exam.

"What's the exam based on?" Anna Mae asks.

"I don't know," Ashley, the girl who read the card, says. "It just says, 'Each of your connections will be tested.'"

"Except yours," Sam says, totally unhelpfully, and elbows me in the ribs.

After half the house leaves on a group date, I fall asleep by the pool. When I wake from my plastic wicker chaise lounge, Sam is journaling beside me. She's left-handed, the edge of her hand inky black from running over her messy scrawl. She touches the side of my face, feeling the ridges from the chair indented on my skin.

"You're stamped," she says.

"You are, too," I say, and point to her hand.

"I'm glad you got the necklace last night," she says.

"Why?" I ask.

"I'm going to get sent home soon." Panic flares across my limbs and I sit up in the chair. She must know something that I don't know. Something must have happened while I was away yesterday.

"What, why? Is this about the exam?"

"Maybe. Don't tell, but I asked Wyatt. Since you're staying here anyways, it doesn't matter if you know. He said it's trivia about

Dylan and stuff. He's going to evaluate our answers for compatibility and rank us. The lowest three scores will have to leave. It's not that, though. He doesn't care about me. He has known who his top girls are since Night One. The rest is theater, and I'm waiting here until they thin me out, which would be a real bummer, since I haven't wooed the American public half as much as I'd like to yet."

"No, you're not leaving," I say. Wyatt wouldn't let it happen, though I'm not sure how much control he has over that kind of thing. I also won't let it happen, though I have less control over it than anyone.

"What do you mean, no?"

"We can talk about it later."

"You'll be fine without me," she says, her voice soft.

"You're not leaving." Someone splashes in the pool close to us and it ends the conversation. As it gets dark, I take off my swimsuit and change into my pajama shirt. I pull on a pair of underwear from the bottom of my bag, needing to do laundry soon. There's been a backup since the repairman came, each girl fighting to get in a wash cycle after days of not being able to use it. When the fabric of my underwear touches my labia, a burning sensation runs across my skin. I try to scratch it, but it only causes me more pain, not relief. I take the underwear back off and hop onto the countertop in the bathroom, the surface so chilled it causes goose bumps across my butt and legs. In the mirror, I try to figure out if anything looks amiss: cottage cheese discharge or whatever other unappealing symptoms I've heard can come with having a vagina. As far as I can tell it looks fine enough, wrinkly and alien, only more red than usual, but I had been itching it rather aggressively. In the room, I ask Sam if she has ever had a yeast infection before. She has, in college when she didn't bring enough underwear to an away soccer tournament.

"I hate to do this," I say.

"You want me to look at your vagina," she says.

"Yes." She follows me to the bathroom, where I spread my legs for her. She stays a far distance away, but asks me to move into the light more. In middle school, I taught three girls how to put in a tampon like this, having learned from an American Girl book that my mom slid over to me one day without a word in place of a puberty talk. We squatted in a circle in the gym locker room. Once, I even pulled one out of a girl. She had gotten it stuck there after inserting it dry, not on her period, trying to prove that she, too, had started to menstruate. A few weeks later, I told my mom to buy me a razor when she was out shopping next, so I knew I had truly become a woman. Another girl taught me how to shave the curves of my ankles and the tendons behind my knees without nicking myself. Here, I've returned to the cyclical economy of girlhood.

"Yeah, you need Monistat ASAP. It's probably from sitting around in a wet swimsuit all day. Want me to tell one of the handlers?"

I nod, and she goes downstairs. Back on my bunk, I burrow

under my comforter, naked from the waist down, and wait for Sam's return. I want to feel ashamed for being unhygienic, but Sam's nonchalance is a potent antidote. I hope that Dylan never finds out, lest I sully his fantasies of our future time in the Casita together. Nearly an hour later, Sam knocks on the door, waving around a box with a set of seven syringes and a thick tube of cream. She's also carrying a plastic bag full of candy bars.

"Look what they got us," she says. "Let's party." She chucks a Snickers at me. I say I want a better candy bar, and she tells me I'll take what she gives me. Then she throws a Butterfinger on my bed. Her skin is luminous, a high flush across her cheeks as though she's been needing a sharp dose of excitement. I never thought I would be excited about a yeast infection, but it shows the depths of the situation I'm in. We skitter down the hallway with me still half naked, clutching my last pair of clean underwear and the box to my chest.

"I can do it for you if you want," she says as I unfold the directions with tiny print and squint at the various languages. She unwraps a kid-size Almond Joy and pops the whole thing into her mouth at once, smacking as she chews.

"I don't need you to do it for me," I say. "I just need a demonstration."

Sam places one of the syringes onto the opening of the ointment container and extracts a bit. She mimes like a flight attendant in the safety demonstration. "Put it in your vagina and shoot it up there like a tampon."

"This is gross," I tell her, and take the syringe from her hand. I place one of my feet high on the counter to spread my legs and squirt the goo, thick like hair conditioner, inside me.

"Don't sneeze for a bit afterwards or it'll all come out on your pants."

"You're making it worse," I say. She snaps a Twix bar in half and takes a bite. "So, about you going home."

"Emily, I'm flattered that you went out of your way to get a yeast infection to corner me like this, but we don't need to continue the conversation."

"Turn the faucet on," I say. The sound of the water should drown out our voices in case anyone comes by. "You're not going to get sent home."

"And what can you do about it? Give me your necklace?" she asks. Her voice is still resigned, but she sits on the toilet seat, at least willing to listen to me.

"No, I'm going to help you."

I tell Sam about everything I know of Dylan, what he told me on the date and what I noticed about him over the past weeks. The insides of his forearms are a bit ticklish, but he likes when you rake your fingernails there anyways. It makes his thick hairs stand up from their follicles. He likes basketball, so bring up that you went to UNC, he'll like that. Go Blue Tar Heels, or something, right? He has a younger sister who is obsessed with K-pop. She's fourteen. Do you know anything about K-pop? No? BTS has seven members; Jimin is your favorite. He scars easily, can't get tattoos because of it, but likes them on women. You can show him the new hibiscus flower. He wants four kids, no more, no less. He hates Disneyland—no, Disney World. Tell him you hate both or, depending on how it's going, say you like them, the gigantic turkey legs, just to fight with him a bit. Tell him you'll go there with him one day and show him the good stuff, how to enjoy the happiest place on earth. The happiest place besides here, of course, you can say. He'll like that joke. He'll think you're being real.

Two days later, at the necklace ceremony, I stand off to the side. Dylan quizzes the women on food he likes, his past relationship history, the names and ages of his siblings, all the cities he's lived in, his hobbies, his star sign, his love language, whether a man should pay on the first date, what the best holiday is, and what charitable causes he supports. The women hold up whiteboards with their answers, and a production assistant keeps track on a secret scorecard. Sam gets second place. I bite the inside of my lip to prevent myself from smiling so hard I draw blood, and the taste of iron fills my mouth as she walks up to him. As she turns to face us, she catches my eye. She really is so pretty. He'd be an idiot to send her home. Dylan plucks the necklaces off the silver branches of the jewelry stand until there is one left. Laura, one of the Laurens, and two other women all wait with pained expressions. Dylan picks up the necklace, twists it around his finger, and pulls it close to his chest, acting agonized. Laura will stay, though the ordering makes it seem like she's in jeopardy. How cruel it would be to send her home after the death of her grandmother just because she missed a week of learning more about him. He's not that much of a prize.

"Laura," he says into the silence, and the exhale of her relief moves through the room. The host tells the other disgraced women to pack their bags and leave the mansion.

"The rest of you also need to pack your bags . . ." Dylan pauses. Sam smiles when I look to her for reassurance. "Say your goodbyes . . . to the mansion. Tomorrow, we're going to Iceland!"

PREPARATION

"WHAT DID DYLAN'S ranking earlier say?" Miranda asks Terry. He reads her the sheet of paper: Emily, Winna, Laura, Sam, Anna Mae. Her two girls are holding the top spots, and all her plans are starting to reap their rewards. Sam's the only strong contender Wyatt has left, but his face remains cool. They're in the production room, surrounded by large screens rolling through the footage of the week. It's 3 a.m. The fifteen women and dozens of staff fly to Iceland the next night. Her teeth feel mossy after eating twelve mini 3 Musketeers bars from the bowl that craft services sets aside for her.

"Jazmin dropped off?" Andrea clarifies.

"Yes," Terry says. "She hasn't been on there since last Tuesday, so that's been"—he pauses to count it out, days blurred in everyone's minds during the frantic preparation to begin their travels—"five days."

The last season with a male lead, he eliminated all the Black women by the fifth episode, and people on Twitter took notice. The last lead story producer got fired over it to appease the masses. They replaced the white man host with a white woman host, one who's even approaching middle age. Frank had made a comment that Miranda should like that, seeing a woman like herself on-screen and in power. Miranda scheduled a new six-week Botox filler appointment right after that meeting. At parties in the off-season, Miranda talks about all the initiatives the show is doing for diversity. They hired a full-time DEI consultant to run affinity groups for the staff. Wyatt, Filipino, replaced the old producer. They post their internship opportunities on HBCU job boards. Her friends tell her how admirable it is that the show is trying to represent real people's lives. They'll have to get Jazmin back up on his list. Winna, who's Korean, was an early bet for the winner, or maybe even the next lead, and Sam, she's half Mexican. People will like that.

"Who does he want on the solo date this week?" Wyatt asks.

"Laura, but we can't give him that yet. See if he'll go with Vivian. Tell him that they can ski down a glacier. We've got to keep him separate from Emily for next week. Did you hear what he said about the phone numbers?" Terry says.

Miranda smiles, happy that someone else brought up how her girl is in the lead. Emily keeps getting better and better. She knows, though, that there's a fine balance when they create the arc of the season. For the most part, the relationships need to inch along at the same pace. Terry works with Dylan on picking the dark horse, someone lurking on the side of the pack who is ready to become a front-runner. Miranda looks at the stream from the camera in the corner of the kitchen. She always misses it once they start to travel. She likes to watch the women cook together, the way they hold out wooden spoons for each other to taste pasta sauces. Earlier that week, as she drafted the date card for the solo date, Emily came into the kitchen. That girl's gonna win, she thought. Look at how she shines, awash in all that sunlight.

A few hours later, Miranda returns to her small two-bedroom house in Santa Monica. Her husband sleeps in the middle of the bed on top of all the blankets with a pillow over his face. He rouses easily when she enters, complaining that she hasn't been home in three nights, and that she's about to leave for more. He doesn't usually mean it. He loves when she's away and he can eat microwaved tortilla chips with shredded cheese on top and call them nachos.

"Why're you still giving them your everything after all these years? What have you gotten?" She doesn't mention her bonuses made the down payment on this house, one they never could have afforded on only his salary. "I'm serious. You're obsessed with your job. It's like an addiction. I can see your brain scheming even when you're home sometimes. You think I can't tell, but I can. It's creepy."

"I don't want to fight," she says. "I want something else."

She crawls onto the bed and moves her hand into his boxers. He kneels to give her more access and undresses her. It happens like this, each night before travel, since they started dating fifteen years ago, when she was still a production assistant. That's why she came home. She pulls her lace bralette over her head and gets on top of him because she knows it's the way he finishes the fastest. It's also the most work for her, but maybe that's why he likes it the best. She can sleep on the red-eye. The sex isn't about her at this point. It's part of getting ready to leave, like packing. No, she thinks, that's mean. She would never want her husband to know she had that thought even in passing. As she moves against him, their limbs stick together slightly, his tacky and damp from sleep. She thinks about the show's allusions to sex, the slow backing away of the camera as the interior lights flick off. Her husband is right that she can't get enough, that the show flashes through her mind even as she rides him. The sex in her life would be better if she could use her producer's sense of pacing, her taste for anticipation. Early in their relationship, she got a flickering thrill from acting out her desire for her husband. She seemed like she wanted him so badly, and the pretense made her want him more in practice. Her husband groans beneath her, shuddering to a climax. Even if you start by faking your feelings, the show sweeps you up in the wave regardless until everyone comes crashing down at once.

WEEK FOUR

I'VE NEVER LOVED an airport more. Feeling like a child again, I walk with Sam and Jazmin into the snack and magazine shop. If asked why all these beautiful women are traveling together, we've been told to say that we're higher-ups in an essential oils pyramid scheme going to a conference. Now that we're out in public, it's obvious how fake the club night was. We're not even allowed to go to the airport bathroom within sight of our gate without a production assistant. Sam picks out the largest, value-size bag of Swedish fish and three celebrity gossip magazines that I don't recognize.

"I have to know what's happening with Meghan Markle. I'm

always so worried about her," Sam says. Jazmin grabs a bag of Bugles, which I didn't know people still ate, three bags of Sour Patch watermelons, and a box of Milk Duds. "We're going on a plane, not the movies," Sam says as Jazmin unfurls her selection into Sam's basket.

"I haven't seen a movie in almost a full month, and we'll be in the air for fourteen hours. That's at least a quadruple feature," Jazmin says. She adds in a large bag of Flamin' Hot Cheetos. "For Winna. I hate those things. She asked for Takis, but they only have these. I hope she won't be disappointed."

I find a paperback of the latest Irish murder mystery novel and nearly collapse. It's 528 pages. I pull it off the shelf and clutch it to my chest, buoyed by the idea that for a few hours of my life I could escape the inanity of my own thoughts. Though our first flight is a red-eye to Boston where everyone is encouraged to sleep, I contemplate spending the whole time reading. I slap it against Sam's arm.

"Do you think they'll let me get this?" I ask. Sam takes it from my hand and peruses the back.

"Watch and learn," she says, and stuffs it below all the snacks. She pivots toward Wyatt. "Dad, will you buy these for us?" she asks, putting on a puppy face.

"Put those magazines away, but I'll get you the rest," he says. Sam gives him a look, but she acquiesces as Jazmin tells the cashier about Guava, who has been sent to her parents' house in San Diego now that she's traveling. Jazmin's always doing that, even making friends with the peripheral staff for the show, the lighting people and the location scouts. It's a superpower, her charm. She urges Wyatt to show the woman a photo of Jazmin and the dog at the mansion, and he obliges, flipping through his camera roll with one hand and sliding the snacks one by one toward the till with the other. I stand behind him, staring at the sliver of the book's spine that peeks out beneath the other items. He pulls it out and stares at Sam, holding it toward her with his eyebrows raised.

"It's Emily's, and hasn't she been so good?" Sam puts her arms around my shoulders and rests her chin against my neck. I offer him a high-watt smile.

"I'll read it on the plane and give it back to you by the time we land, I promise," I say. "I'll do whatever Miranda wants. I'll be so good in Iceland, I promise. I'll start a fight. I'll tell Dylan something outrageous about myself."

"Fine," he says, and pushes it through to be scanned. Sam kisses his cheek and stuffs some of the candy into her bag.

"Don't you think Wyatt is more handsome than Dylan?" Sam asks no one in particular, bouncing on her toes. Wyatt rolls his eyes. "Will you buy us lattes next?" she says.

"How the hell did she get Wyatt so wrapped around her finger?" Jazmin asks when they're out of earshot. "I wish Andrea was like that."

At the Starbucks, Sam decides we all should buy three drinks: one hot, one cold, one for hydration, something I have never done in my life.

"You've never had a Fizzlé before?" Jazmin says, shocked when I tell them I've never tried the latest fad brand of seltzer.

"I've heard of it, but I've never had one. I'd never buy that kind of thing for myself."

My parents never let me drink sodas as a child, so I never caught onto the appeal of carbonated drinks. It always seemed like a frivolous expense when I was grocery shopping, despite seeing entire pallets of the drinks lining the bottoms of other families' shopping carts, so I knew they must have been good. Wyatt opens a can before we pay and passes it to me. "Here," he says. Jazmin and Sam wrap their arms around me as I take a sip. The flavor is subtle and crisp, and I take a larger drink. In my subconscious, I knew that if I let myself give in to the temptation of luxury, I'd never be able to stop myself afterwards. Wyatt snaps a photo on his phone. "Baby's first Fizzlé," he says, patting my head patronizingly as he shows us the photo. "I couldn't be a prouder father."

Our layover in Boston gets delayed, and the producers gather us in the international terminal in Logan, a place I've never been to before. Growing up, we never traveled out of the country. My father said he didn't like the inconvenience of passports, while my mother said that he was simply afraid of flying but too ashamed to say it. I'm happy to be close to home and watch the sun rise over the horizon, where a few miles in the other direction, my old life used to putter along uneventfully. I try to get everyone excited about eating Dunkin' Donuts bagels, insisting that they're extremely reliable and the perfect traveling snack, but only another contestant from Rhode Island agrees with me. Wyatt walks over with me to the Dunkin' kiosk, needing to grab another coffee himself.

"Thanks for the book and for the food," I tell him after he pays. I mean it more than I can convey.

"Don't worry about it. We all have to have our little pleasures here," he says. I wonder what his pleasure is as he bought nothing for himself at the airport stores but a giant bottle of expensive Smartwater and a black coffee. As I watch a small screen playing the news without sound by another gate, a red box flashes up saying there's a breaking story. There's been a shooting with ten people confirmed dead, more wounded. It happened overnight in Chapel Hill. I look at Sam across the terminal, reading the prologue of my novel to the women crowded around her on the floor like a teacher with a picture book.

"Close your eyes," Wyatt says when he sees what I'm watching.

"What?" I ask, glued to the news. It was at a bar. The shooter died of a self-inflicted gunshot wound. He grabs my shoulders, pulls me away from the screen, and starts cursing under his breath. I crane my neck to watch more clips of the throngs of people illuminated by strobing ambulance lights, and he yells my name so loudly that people at the airport turn and stare. He tells me I need to stop looking at that, that I'm going to sit down, be a good girl, and eat my bagel in silence.

"Don't say a word to anyone." He, Miranda, and Andrea will be back in a few minutes. Sam tries to do an Irish accent as she reads the dialogue. The red banner on the screen flashes through my mind again and again, but for some reason, I do exactly what he tells me.

Miranda speaks first upon the producers' return, the most senior of the group. "We wanted to let you all know about something that happened while we were in the air. You might see it on the news while we're waiting here. We don't know a lot yet." She describes a shooting: a man, twenty-one, at a bar in Chapel Hill. Miranda glances at Sam, but Sam remains expressionless. Twenty-three people dead already, not sure how many wounded, mostly college kids. A balcony overlooking an open patio space in the back, fish in a barrel. The shooter killed himself before the police got to him. A manifesto sent to the local news, posted online, sent to a therapist. Warning signs, but no one put them together. One of the women starts crying first, making muffled unobtrusive sounds. Soon I start crying, too, as do the women around me. Even Miranda tears up as she tells us. It seems contagious, the sadness of the outside world.

"He was one of those incels," Miranda says, and I can picture what happened now. Anxiety sets over me, my throat tightening further. Though I know the show hasn't aired yet, I envision the shooter watching me, watching us all vie for Dylan's affection. I can picture how he looks: a pale shadow, dark-rimmed eyes from lack of sleep, his square-set jaw, but a tremble in his hands with rage or with fear. I'm the kind of woman that man wanted to shoot, and what's worse is I understand why. The man doesn't need to be alive for me to be unable to shake my fear. There are so many waiting in the wings to fill his place. Wyatt pulls Sam aside, handing her his phone so that she can make calls to her aunt and a few friends in Chapel Hill. Andrea leads us to an empty gate with a television screen, and we huddle around it. Someone requests that we get on Twitter, the news is always better there, faster.

"No," Andrea says. "No social media."

Sometimes, the news flashes excerpts from the shooter's two-hundred-page essay, called "The Doctrine for a Just Society," on the screen.

> *Since elementary school, before I even knew what sex was, I have been denied by women. It is the tragedy of my life to never experience what even evil, shallow men have, men uglier than me, poorer than me: the pleasure of sex, the desire of females, to love and be loved in return. Females hold the power to dictate which men will rise and which will be humiliated, though they pretend to be subjugated by us. This is part of their strategy, their great deception, the straw man, quite literally that they erect as their oppressor. None of them are innocent in this. This is the basis of the War of the Sexes. I was at the bottom of the ranking, not even worthy of their revulsion. To be ignored was worse than being scorned. After the first Battle, I am sure they will know my name, even if they only utter it in disgust. Real men, the ones who have been Awakened to the cause, will utter it in power.*
>
> *All I want in the world is sex, but I have been cursed by females not to be able to access it.*
>
> *If women were cordoned off away from men, we could exist in a free world, a world without sex.*

I will shoot the most beautiful females first, the ones whose denials of me hurt the worst.

The plane rolls into place in front of the gate, and Andrea shuttles us away from the screen. Sam reenters with Wyatt as we board, and I hold back from the line to wait for her.

"All good," she says. She even gives me a thumbs-up. As soon as we get settled next to each other on the plane, she slides an eye mask over her face and falls asleep. We arrive in Reykjavík in the afternoon. Our hotel is one floor of a tall, mirrored building that rises above the entire city. A production assistant swipes us into our rooms, as we aren't allowed to control the keys. We're upgraded from the bunk beds at the mansion to each sharing a king-size with another woman in suites nicer than anywhere I've ever stayed before. Production makes us redo our room tours twice because we don't seem enthusiastic enough. There is a telescope in a corner and an art easel in another as decoration. The theme is vaguely nautical. Everything is shiny, like we're inside a disco ball.

"It's 4 a.m. in LA right now," Anna Mae reminds the camerapeople.

"The more convincing your faces, the faster you can get your beauty sleep," Wyatt says, and I realize again how much I dislike him. Regret burns in my throat that I let him tell me what to do when I saw the news about the shooting, that I let him grab me and tell me to keep my mouth shut. The shooter thinks that I'm the one in control, after all, and maybe I could be if only I had a bit more backbone.

All the women have stopped talking about the shooting because what else is there to say. Across the ocean, in a hospital in North Carolina, the people will die or be saved. Some remain in the in-between, but I won't know about any of their fates until my time here is over, stuck in my own kind of in-between, this fever dream of a television show, spellbound from trying to fall in love. When we watched the news, they interviewed a girl a few years younger than me, standing in front of what looked like a dorm building. She said she heard the loud crack and her body started to tremble. She immediately knew what was happening. She had seen enough news stories to know how these types of things go. I couldn't listen to her whole interview. In truth, we flew away from all that; even the events that shake the news with their tragedy can't alter our trajectory. I'm a raw nerve to the real world now, too sensitive for its seismic shifts. I change clothes, don't bother to shower, and lie atop the plush comforter in the room I share with Sam, Winna, and Vivian. I try not to fall asleep and fail.

"There's only so much sunlight here in a day," Miranda says when I complain about her waking me up for a filmed walking tour of the city. When we go outside on the cobbled streets, the sun is already setting. The red roofs of the houses are thin lines between their stucco exteriors and the long pink dusk. Arm in arm, we go downhill toward the center of the city. We pass a bright turquoise house, then a marigold yellow one. I breathe in great gulps of the cold, fresh air. The sensation of the chill in my lungs refreshes me after our weeks in California, after the stale dry air of the plane. My skin feels scrubbed clean, my tiredness washed away.

Iceland seems not like a foreign country but a foreign planet: no trees, the dark craggy rocks peeking from low green moss, the tower of Reykjavík's eminent cathedral pocked like honeycomb, the babies bundled in blobs of down. A camera moves behind us, capturing our wool trench coats and scarves in silhouette as we stare at the view. It was nice to bring out a new corner of my wardrobe for the trip, having gone through most of my warm-weather clothes. Those are the topics I have the bandwidth to focus on now: which plaid scarf to wear, the navy or the red. Two production assistants come down balancing fifteen hot chocolates across four trays for the remaining contestants. I take a sip of mine, and Miranda tells us to look happier.

"I wonder if he ever came to the café," Sam says. Her voice is soft, and we look out at the smooth sheet of the ocean stretching out before us, gray and shimmering. On the other side of the bay, wide low mountains topped with snow are bathed in lilac light.

"Don't think about that," Jazmin says.

"I don't even want to imagine you there," I tell her. She takes another sip of her hot chocolate. We don't talk about it again for the rest of the night. A line from the shooter's manifesto keeps running through my head on a loop: about how all he wanted was "to love and be loved in return." If I said that here and believed it with all my heart, any lead would keep me for weeks to come.

The next morning, our group date card reads, ***Let's knattleikr. Love, Dylan.***

"It's got to be some Viking blood sport," Sam says as we get ready. She brushes clear mascara through her brows. "Do you think it's bad not to believe in God, even though he gave me such good eyebrows?"

"You're in a good mood this morning."

"Of course I am. My life has never been easier. What do I have to be sad about? Have you seen our bathroom? It's literally the nicest thing I've ever stepped foot in. The bathtub here is bigger than my entire bathroom at home. I can't wait to soak all night long."

I don't say anything back, but I'm worried about her. I've been trying to imagine what it would be like for the shooting to happen somewhere close to my friends or family. One night before this all happened, Sam told me about what she loved about North Carolina. Some weekends, she would take her car and drive west toward the mountains. She'd put a quilt and pillow in the backseat and sleep in her car, stopping at every honey stand and stone fruit orchard on the way. In the summer, she would go to the top of the grassy, bald-faced mountain before the tourists descended, eating her breakfast of wild blackberries as she hiked to the top. She said she'd sit there all morning, turning in a circle so she could take in the view from every angle until the noise of the crowd started to bother her. As a kid, she moved around a lot with her mom, and she said that this was her way of reminding herself that she was her own home.

We arrive at an open, neatly trimmed field where Dylan stands between two large ginger men in brown tunics. They all hold wooden staffs in their hands, with Dylan holding a tennis-sized leather-stitched ball in the other. Knattleikr, as Sam guessed, is an ancient Viking blood sport.

"A mix of lacrosse, field hockey, and tackle football," Dylan says. With some combination of throwing, whacking, and sprinting, we are supposed to hurl the ball across the field and score points. The team with the most points will spend the rest of the evening with Dylan, and the others will return to the hotel to wallow in their defeat. The producers send us to a changing room to dress in our new team colors: Winna, Leigh, Ashley, four other women, and me in black woolen tunics and leggings, with Sam, Jazmin, Laura, Anna Mae, and the rest in white tunics.

"What about Sister Wives as our team name?" I overhear Sam saying to the other group. They start to laugh.

"Put a harness on your prize pony, Wy," Miranda says.

"Sam," Wyatt says, slicing a finger across his neck for her to cut it out. She blows him a kiss.

The game begins slowly, each woman afraid to commit in earnest to sloshing around in the mud. The Viking descendants at the edge of the field yell encouragement at us, like "Pummel her!" or "Hit her with your stick!" Winna whispers to me that it seems like they have been promised a cash reward for stoking our competitive instincts. I start to run so hard that the cold air makes my mouth taste like copper. After Leigh scores two points, Laura elbows her in the face and her nose gushes blood.

"I'm sorry," Laura screams. She looks toward the sidelines for the medical team. She takes off her tunic and offers it to Leigh to stop the bleeding. Her sports bra is neon pink, and she hovers behind Leigh, fretting, as her skin goose pimples from the cold.

"Get away from me," Leigh says as Laura's shirt soaks up her blood. "You've done enough. And put a shirt on, for God's sake." The gaps between her teeth shine red as she speaks, the blood from her nose pooling in her mouth. A girl down the field vomits. Laura apologizes to anyone who will listen to her, insisting it was an accident. I don't want to see Dylan badly enough tonight where I'd strike another woman, but the Viking energy in addition to the regular cognitive distortion we experience every day could've finally sent her over the edge. We pause play as Dylan helps Leigh to the medical tent, where a defibrillator rests casually on the table as though amateur knattleikr could be fatal. With half the camera crew focused on the Leigh spectacle now, Wyatt calls the game off early. Our team wins 2–1.

That night, our team goes to a hot spring resort an hour drive away and sits around a long wooden bar. It's a modern building, made of smooth gray cement and oily wood on the outside. Inside, it's all brushed-bronze lighting and mid-century modern leather chairs. Most of the walls are exposed dark rock, as though we're in a cave, but above the rock, racks of wine bottles have been inlaid. The necks of the bottles have been organized by color: blood red to gold sweeping across the wall like a pointillism painting. Dylan gives a toast, and Leigh takes him away soon thereafter. Two dark circles have spread beneath her under-eyes, and she stuck a dainty Band-Aid over her nose in case anyone forgot she's injured. An assistant producer asks if we feel like we've gotten enough time with Dylan today given what happened on the field. The temperature of the room rises as the eight of us discuss how Leigh has been capitalizing on a glorified nosebleed. I don't care much, having had a solo date last week. When Leigh returns, we stop talking abruptly.

"So, how are you ladies tonight?" she asks.

"We want to be honest with you about how we're feeling," Ashley begins in a measured tone. The first person plural is intended to be diplomatic, but only makes Ashley sound pretentious. "We feel like it's a bit rude for you to take Dylan away first after you spent so much of this afternoon with him. Some of us haven't talked to him at all today, you know. It seems a bit disrespectful to us."

"I talked to him so much in the day because Laura tried to break my nose. I could always do that for you if you're so desperate," Leigh says. Winna stares at me from across the other couch, eyes so wide that I can see the entire circle of her iris.

"Excuse me?" Ashley says.

"We wouldn't be here tonight spending time with him at all if I hadn't scored both the points for our team," Leigh points out.

"It was a team sport," Ashley says. "Look at Melanie over there, she assisted you for one of the goals, but she's not bragging about it like you are. It feels like you think that you're better than every other girl here. Why do you think you can take my time, Melanie's time, Emily's time?"

"Oh, I don't mind," I pipe in, trying to swerve as far away from this wreck as possible.

"I'm not surprised that you don't understand what I'm saying. You're so obtuse when it comes to other people's feelings," Ashley says.

"'Obtuse?'" Leigh says. "We get it. You're better than us. You're emotionally intelligent. You went to Columbia. We've heard it all before since you've told us so many times."

"That's not even what I'm talking about," Ashley screams back.

"No, but it's always what you imply," Leigh says. Dylan walks in and asks what's going on, that he heard shouting. Ashley and Leigh go silent, and Miranda, thank God for her, airlifts me out of the situation. After what feels like the longest pull-aside interview of my life, where I discuss the Leigh-Ashley feud in detail, Miranda brings me to Dylan. She tells me to change out of my cocktail dress and into a swimsuit, another bikini I never packed. Dylan waits down in the hot spring for me, a boom mic hanging over him. I step into the milky blue water, surrounded by steam that obscures the windows to the room where the other women are. He takes my hand in his and flips it over, running his index finger over my palm. A wooden bridge with thin metal railings rises over a portion of the lagoon, encased in mist.

"Remind you of anything?" he says, gesturing to the pool.

"So pruny," I say, smiling and tugging on the tip of his finger. He must have been in the water for a long time as he talked to the last woman. He leans back onto the black volcanic rock. It suits him here, the dark rocks matching his hair, his blue eyes matching the water.

"You and I are always swimming together," Dylan says. "There must be some kind of poetic reason for that."

"There are worse ways to pass the time," I say. I do a breaststroke around the pool a bit, letting the warmth envelop me after the chill I caught from being in a cocktail dress in Iceland in the middle of March. The sound person swings the boom over me. It picks up my splashes. I must look like I belong in a luxurious place like this. Miranda tilts her head, indicating I should move back toward him. This, after all, isn't time for my leisure. "Bad night?" I ask him.

He laughs. "You tell me. You were in there."

"You could always take it as a compliment when women fight over you."

"Do you take it as a compliment when men fight over you?"

"I wouldn't know," I say, but he doesn't believe me. He pulls me to sit beside him on a flat stone slab in the water. In college, I slept with four men, and since, I've slept with one. At no time have they fought over me, or even fought to continue to have sex with me. Sex with them was something that happened at night when I was tired and felt that the time had come in the natural progression of our relationship where no longer having sex would be strange. It was never particularly good or bad, just something I did.

"Sometimes, I feel like you're keeping secrets from me, Emily," he says. This time, I laugh at him.

"If only I were that interesting."

He tells me that he finds me very interesting and he kisses me. Later in the evening, he gives Leigh the Golden Necklace.

In the night, I wake up to two beeps coming from the hallway. The overhead lights in our room switch on. Winna screams. There must be an emergency somewhere. Vivian gets out of bed quicker than a firefighter, maternal instincts flaring. In a worse turn of events than an actual fire coming to burn me and all my nicest clothes, two camerapeople and Dylan enter. The beeping sound was merely them unlocking our hotel room door. I put my head under the pillow to hide my face from whatever horrible footage they're seeking to gather here. Vivian's solo date apparently begins predawn.

"Fuck," Sam says. Something clicks. "The one night I wear my mouth guard." She slips her hand under my pillow, and something wet trails against my cheek. I yell Sam's name, ripping the pillow off and seeing the opaque mold of her teeth right where my face was. I rub at the damp spot on my face. She mouths an apology to me.

"Do you ever sleep?" I ask Dylan as we hug hello. Last night's date ended a mere six hours ago. He kisses my cheek, where Sam's saliva has already dried.

"Too much to do," he says; then, in a whisper, "You look pretty." I roll my eyes at him. He turns away from me to address Vivian, who has nonchalantly attempted to wrap the comforter around her body in an effort of modesty, having slept in a crop top and truly tiny boxer shorts. "Vivian, put on your best snow bunny suit, because we are going skiing."

She packs a bunch of printed-out pictures of her sons into a tote bag and slings her formal outfit over her arm. You'll do great, we tell her, bleary-eyed. She makes sure the blackout curtains are pulled together and tells us to go back to sleep, that she'll spill all the details tonight.

At the more reasonable hour of 8:30 a.m., Winna, Sam, and I go to the common area for our catered breakfast. Ever since I was a child, I have been obsessed with buffets. I love the blue Sterno flames licking the base of the broad stainless steel trays. I love weddings and hotel breakfasts and all-you-can-eat restaurants where you pay by the pound. In the common area, piles of fruit cut into geometric shapes take up an entire table, surrounded by a ring of full glasses of orange juice. The hot-bar section has fluffy scrambled eggs and a wide array of unfamiliar meats. A white tablecloth, speckled with batter, covers a round table with irons to press out crispy waffles. I grab something from each station, as I pride myself on being an equal opportunity eater. Sam picks up three miniature cartons of drinkable yogurt and brings them to our table. She splits open the packaging and downs them one after the other.

"That's disgusting," Winna says.

"Come on. Those things are tiny," she says. Cars, half the size of those in the United States, circle around a roundabout below us and go their separate ways. Farther out, the bay opens up toward the mountains we saw yesterday, now pale yellow in the morning light. "You want to hear something?" Sam says, and Winna nods.

"I didn't know anyone from the shooting, who was there or who got hurt or anything. I don't think I even knew anyone who knew anyone. Which is good, you know, that I don't know anyone that died. It was mostly college kids. I should be happy about it. But I keep feeling like I wish I did because the whole thing happened and it was huge. I wasn't a part of it at all."

"Oh, Sam," Winna says. I can't think of anything to add, and my only strong instinct is to get up and get her another carton of yogurt.

"It feels like my world is so small that I'm the only one in it."

"We're in it," I say. "Or, at least, you're in mine."

Sam plucks a cube of melon off my plate and pops it into her mouth. She takes a long time to chew, and we sit there in silence, watching her process. "It's twisted, isn't it?"

"Which part?" I ask, thinking she's talking about the shooter.

"I'm not so different from the producers," she says. "When the tragedy hits, I want to be right up next to it."

That night, two assistant producers organize us for a girl chat as we wait for Vivian to return from her date. They've become mandatory in the recent weeks as there are fewer women to lob questions at. Do the stakes feel higher now that we've left the mansion? Do we feel like our relationships are progressing quickly enough? What is the tenor of the group these days? What about Dylan meeting our families? What about us meeting his? What about overnight dates, when all the remaining women get a night in the travel Casita, unfilmed in bed together? Are we ready? Are we falling in love? Deep into the night, another producer comes in. She walks over to Vivian's two packed suitcases in the corner and rolls them out the door.

"I guess Dylan has started to make hard decisions. If he can't picture you as his wife, then there is no reason for you to stay around," Anna Mae says, breaking the hush that fell over the room. I can feel the eyes of the other women on our rooming group, but I can't look away from the blank wall where her suitcases were.

"At least she can go back to her kids now," Jazmin says, and we all nod in agreement. Jazmin moves into our room that night, taking Vivian's space in Winna's bed.

The morning of the necklace ceremony, I go to my interview with Miranda in a cordoned-off hallway of the hotel, lined with decorative wire sculptures.

"Things seem to be going well with Dylan this week," Miranda says as I get my mic pack rigged up, and I tell her I agree. "He told me, and keep this between you and me of course, that he really likes you."

"Wow," I say.

"There's one piece missing, one barrier still in your way." I would say that there are eleven barriers in my way, those being the other women. "He needs to know more about you, your soul, you know."

"My soul?" I ask, wondering if I'm going to have to do some serious religious talk with him. I could muster up something good and convincing, that my faith is so important to me. I start to dredge up Bible stories that I remember from high school and their moral takeaways.

"Like, what does being a woman mean to you?"

"Miranda, what are you talking about?"

"With everything going on in the world right now, this would be a good conversation to have with him. It would mean a lot."

"Mean a lot to whom?"

"You shouldn't talk about the shooting specifically, per se, but it could be powerful. Dylan even said so himself, that he wants a wife who can change the world with him. Are you a feminist?"

"Yeah," I say, "I guess."

"Full sentence."

I stare at the camera lens and back at her. "I'm a feminist."

"Do you want to raise your daughters to be strong women?" I don't say anything back. "Come on, Emily. We need to have this conversation. This isn't only a show about falling in love. It's an opportunity to be real, to effect real change, and do real talk."

"You think this could matter to people?"

"We want you to be the mouthpiece for this. You're great at this kind of stuff. Everyone agreed. We'll give you two hours tonight at the cocktail party to talk with Dylan and no interviews tomorrow."

"Okay. Okay," I say, and start talking. Young girls watching could hear something that resonates with them, even if it only affects a few of them. There are times in my life that I felt like being a woman was hard. I've been catcalled; I've had to buy a decade's worth of overpriced women's razors and deodorants. A drunk guy grabbed my ass at a college party. I've never had an orgasm during sex or even come close. At the club night, Rob, a stranger, slipped his fingers into my dress a bit, which the show heartily facilitated, but I don't mention that part. Everything has been standard, but I guess that's what they want me to talk about, that those experiences could be worthwhile to draw attention to. Miranda tells me that she hears me.

"Don't ever let people make you feel like trying to find love isn't a valid pursuit. All our lives as women we're told that it's the most important thing that will happen in our lifetime, but when you come on a show about finding love, finally doing what they told you to do all along, you're mocked. That's why I do this job, because this shit doesn't get any more real."

"All I want is to love someone and be loved in return," I say.

"What?" Miranda says.

"That's what the guy said, the shooter." He and I are like two fishes staring at each other across the sea, the same polluted water pumping through our gills. Except he's dead, and I've never killed anyone.

Back in the room, Sam already has a necklace slung around her neck. Wyatt let her call in sick to the necklace ceremony after she threatened to tell Dr. C she was having trauma-induced burnout, so Dylan came up to give it to her early, filmed of course, with Sam in bed clad in a terry cloth bathrobe. Wyatt told her to look like she had a cold, and she gingerly coughed twice for effect.

"In reality, I couldn't figure out what to wear," she says. I can never tell how serious she is being. Conversations with her are like being surrounded by fun house mirrors, all deflections and feints, running into walls, then stumbling across a sudden moment of clarity. She offers to touch up my makeup. I don't want to tell her about the plan for my talk with Dylan tonight, since part of me feels like she should be the one to do it. Then again, I didn't even mention the shooting in the interview.

"I don't know what I'm doing here," I tell her as I sit on the toilet seat. She stands above me, riffling through the makeup brushes in my bag.

"You got fired, so you didn't have anything better to do," Sam says. She pulls out a flat-topped brush and pours luminescent drops of liquid highlighter on the back of her hand.

"I'm serious." She dapples it across my cheekbones so lightly I barely feel the bristles. "How are you okay right now? Aren't you supposed to be the one bugging out, not me?"

She shrugs. That's how it always is: everyone else is fine, and I'm thrown off-kilter from the tiniest thing that has nothing to do with me. Maybe I'm one of those empaths. With the residue of the highlighter, Sam taps her fingers from the inner corner of my eye to the outside edge. My breath becomes shallow and a panic rises within me and I clench my teeth to suppress it. When I kiss Dylan, I always try to squeeze my eyes so that no light gets through. I like to be immersed in darkness, and if I time it right, a cool wash of peace comes over me like a burial shroud. I close my eyes now, relishing the sensation of Sam skimming blush across the bridge of my nose.

"It's good you have short hair. It always looks cute. You don't have to style it much."

"Sam, what if I don't even like Dylan? What if I've just made myself like Dylan? What if being here has made me like Dylan against my will?"

"You like Dylan," she says. "And Dylan likes you. You don't have to overthink it. You deserve to be happy."

I know I deserve to be happy, but I don't know how. If I knew for certain that Dylan could be the person who brings me happiness, the kind that could last for decades, I wouldn't have any of the problems I have now. Someone knocks at the door to the hotel room. I'm five minutes late to get on the bus.

"She's shitting!" Sam yells back.

"Three minutes. You better be ready," Miranda says, her voice far away in the hallway.

Sam grips my face with her fingertips, her other hand slanting an eyeliner pencil toward me. She wants to do my lower waterline. "Look up," she keeps saying. "Look up, look up." Every time she gets too close, I flinch. She pinches my chin in scolding. "Stop that."

Sam's eyes watch me, focused but not seeing. A small wrinkle forms between her eyebrows as she concentrates. I close my eyes, push up off my hands, and kiss her. Her lips are smooth and full. A small breath huffs from her nostrils in surprise, but then she kisses me back. The spiderweb of nerves inside my body and across my skin flares up, like a power surge the second before an outage, the kind that blows out lightbulbs. As she pulls away, she laughs a bit. She smiles at me and says my name in a soft voice.

"Emily."

"I should go," I say, and sprint out the door. The sound of my name from her mouth rings in my head. Emily, Emily, Emily. When you do something dumb, you have to do it all at once.

EDGE

MIRANDA HAS STRATEGIES that make her the best producer, and in the tinny blue light of her hotel's bedside lamp, she starts to use them. Dylan shifted the rankings every night this week up until Necklace Night, Sam rising and falling, Emily pushed off the top spot, Leigh for a moment soaring high. Back in LA, the air-conditioning at her house broke and her husband won't stop calling her about who to get to fix it, even though she's halfway across the world in a country where A/C is the last thing on her mind. It all started with that shooting, a bad omen, but Miranda can use it to her advantage.

Earlier this week, after they landed in Reykjavík, Dr. C met with the remaining women for an hour session each to check in on their states of mind. Though the meetings are confidential, Miranda has electronic access to the broad-spectrum notes. Some of the women are sad; some talk about gun control in various political diatribes; some worry about their families at home, as though they had forgotten about them until they were able to glimpse the news again.

Her other small tricks are as follows: wake up earlier than everyone else to lift weights so that her mind stays sharp and her body stays tight, maintain a keto diet in fits and starts to counteract her candy habit, get Botox every six weeks so that she looks young enough for the contestants to relate to. The real secret, though, is that she watches the other producers' pull-asides. She's gotten insights into the lead this way before, ideas for who to press on the next week, questions to ask her own girls. She can't imagine Andrea or Wyatt doing it. She wouldn't have the time to if she ever got a normal night's sleep. She watches one from Wyatt and Sam after the shooting. Sam is drunk, clearly, with her hair tossed up in a loose bun.

"How's your relationship with Dylan these days?"

"Good. What do you want me to say? He's one tall drink of water. I'd like him all to myself, but unfortunately he has fourteen other girlfriends right now."

"Say that you're hoping for a solo date soon and I might give you one."

"I'm hoping for a solo date soon. We have so much that we could build our connection on. Being with him in that capacity would solidify my strong feelings at a critical part of our journey."

"Nice. Off the record, how're you doing with the shooting? How was calling your aunt?"

"White men are unhinged, collectively, as a group. You and I already knew that."

"Your current boyfriend is a white man."

"We all have our vices, embarrassing as they may be."

"What do you think the hardest part about being here is?"

"Have you ever waited on a charter bus for an hour for a date with fourteen other women to start? I've never wasted so much time in my life."

"Serious answer."

"I take it we're back on the record."

"Yes."

"The hardest part of this journey is all the learning I've had to do about myself."

"Like what?"

"How much free food I can eat at the breakfast buffet. Kidding. No. Sorry, I'll be serious. I know you want to get to bed. Sorry, what was the question? Oh, I'm trying to learn what 'be yourself' means. People say that all the time here. Be yourself, be yourself, but like, isn't everything I do being myself given that I'm the one doing it?"

The girl is so magnetic on screen that for a second, Miranda wonders if she's going to win. Sam did rise to the top spot on Wednesday, so there's a chance. *The One* isn't a popularity contest with future viewers, though. Dylan would have to fall in love with her, and despite Wyatt's best efforts, she doubts it's going to happen.

There's nothing good in the interview. Miranda works so hard when there's no end in sight, no measurable goal to achieve beyond her own satisfaction. She'll never be the showrunner. She's at the highest rung of the ladder. It's like sharpening the edge of an ornamental blade. If it ever got the chance, it could glide through a sheet of paper with one bite of steel. People look at it hung on a wall and admire the fine craftsmanship, but no one ever appreciates all the damage it could do if only it was allowed a little more power.

WEEK FIVE

WINNA, JAZMIN, AND I don't flick on the lights as we come back to the hotel from Necklace Night. We pace around the room, scraping off our makeup and stuffing our bags for the next destination tomorrow as Sam sleeps. Even at the whoosh of the flushing toilet, she doesn't stir. I check on her and check on her again, dreading the moment when I will have to lift the comforter and slide into the bed next to her. I didn't think about the fact that I'm literally sleeping with Sam when I kissed her. I wasn't thinking much of anything, in fact, except that I wanted to. Dylan never even flitted through my mind.

The next morning, she rolls out of bed before me as usual, though the expensive mattress barely trembles. Without her, the temperature beneath the blankets drops, and I huddle into myself to stay warm. In movies when couples are forced to share one bed, they wake up intertwined, their love for each other such a strong force that their bodies can't help but gravitate toward one another. My subconscious is too disciplined for that. At breakfast, Sam waits at a small round table for Winna, Jazmin, and me, the first time the four of us have been able to debrief since Vivian was sent home. Three empty cartons of drinkable yogurt surround her bowl of fruit. I dawdle around the buffet until Winna and Jazmin have already sat down. Their heads lean close together over their coffees, talking in soft voices.

"I had a pull-aside with Wyatt this morning," Sam says, looking at me only to fill me in, then continuing to recount the story. She doesn't seem to be paying me any mind. Her nonchalance makes me reel, as though I'm the only one obsessed with the kiss, the feeling of it. It's all I can think about, like a leech on my brain stem. Maybe it wasn't a big deal to her. She kissed me back. I know she did. When I close my eyes, I can still feel the chill of the toilet seat and the sweep of her tongue across my bottom lip. I choke on my orange juice. The three of them stare at me and Jazmin slides me her water glass.

"Wrong pipe," I say.

"He said that Vivian got sent home even though the date went well. Dylan said their relationship wasn't progressing as fast as the other ones here and that he didn't want to keep her away from her family any longer. Wyatt said she had told Dylan that she was falling in love with him."

"Jesus Christ," Jazmin says.

"I know basically all of us are going home at some point. I just never imagined it would happen to one of the five of us. I know that's stupid," Winna says. "Has anyone ever heard of where we're going today?"

"Madeira, I think. Isn't that a kind of wine?" Sam says.

"Not a clue," Jazmin says.

I take another sip from Jazmin's water in silence. In order to get through this, I need to cleanse myself. As a child, when my hands were covered in the film of Elmer's glue, I would peel off large swathes of it from my fingers and fantasize that it was my own skin. Each cell in my body is constantly working, reproducing and replacing itself, so every seven years, I'm made new. I need my cells to work faster than seven years. I need a twenty-four-hour sprint.

As we board our flight, I find out that Madeira is an island way off the coast of Morocco, but technically part of Portugal. I use the time in the air to make a plan. My main problem is I kissed my roommate, and my secondary problem is that, while I like Dylan when he's in front of my face, whenever I separate from him, our relationship seems like a dream. Not in the way of something I imagined for myself and finally achieved, but more that it doesn't seem like it's actually happening to me. With him, I exist in an altered state of consciousness, a personality I molded from whatever bits I thought could be useful on a reality show.

In my conversation with him last night about gender, I told him that I was followed once late at night after I left a friend's sorority formal. I was in a tight dress and high heels, tipsy and tottering around with my phone wedged in my bra strap and my ID card, debit card, lipstick, and dorm key slung across my body in a tiny chain-link purse. I felt someone's gaze first, a kind of intuition, and turned around. There was a large white man behind me dressed in a brown hoodie and shorts. I turned this way and that to make sure it wasn't a coincidental destination match. I walked faster, swerving under streetlights, and still he was behind me. Finally, I saw a group of five college boys leave a dorm in sweatpants. I walked right into the center of them, and they all looked at me strangely. When I turned around, the man was gone. One of the boys offered to buy me a slice of pizza and said that I looked like I needed to relax, that he could help me relax. They all laughed. I told Dylan I was shielded by their masculinity until they remembered their masculinity could be a threat, too, because it made me sound smart. When I planned the line, I pictured Dylan nodding along, whispering "women's rights" to himself. I almost made myself cry from recounting, though I wasn't sad at all.

"That's the thing. Stuff like that happens all the time," I said. After, Dylan squeezed my hand. I shivered each time he called me strong and lovely, as he assured me none of it was my fault.

It was only half true, though. It happened once, and I didn't think much of it. Last night, though, I felt vulnerable and paranoid. I wondered if I would be dead if that group of boys hadn't happened to leave the building at that exact moment. I shouldn't have tried to walk home alone, though it wasn't more than a mile, and I should have brought a bigger coat to disguise my outfit. I fell asleep imagining how many miles away the closest woman was locked in a basement. I want everything that comes with being pretty: choices, money, goodness, respect. Try as I may, I can never get the calculus right in my head. Some days, I would choose being beautiful over anything else in the world.

In the late afternoon, we arrive at a pink hotel in the largest city on the island, with a sloping terra-cotta roof, perched atop an ocean cliffside. Its grounds, dotted with neon blue swimming pools, snake down to the roiling ocean. The producers choose our rooms based on the pairs from last week, but now it's two of us to a room, and I try not to think about sharing a bed with Sam again tonight. We go straight out on a deck overlooking the ocean, with checkerboard floors and wide white archways. Below us, two camerapeople film us as we scream, "We love you, Dylan!" We do another take screaming, "Olá, Portugal!" Then another, "Hello, Madeira!"

A date card for the week's only group date comes: ***Let's slide into love. Love, Dylan.*** It's addressed to Winna, Sam, and me, along with seven others. The two not listed, Jazmin and another woman, will have solo dates later in the week. An assistant producer lobs questions into our semicircle.

"Jazmin, you got the season's first Golden Necklace and now you're getting your first solo date. How do you feel knowing that your connection with Dylan is about to get stronger?"

"I'm excited to have a day alone with Dylan. Sometimes, when we're apart for days at a time, I start to miss him."

"There has been some discussion about the maturity of the remaining girls here. Anna Mae, what do you think about that?"

"Who discussed that?" Winna asks with an even tone.

"I'm not at liberty to say," the production assistant says. "Anna Mae?"

"There are definitely a few girls on the younger side here," Anna Mae says. She stares at Sam, twenty-six; Jazmin, also twenty-six; Winna, twenty-three; and me, twenty-four—the youngest girls still here. We linger in the silence, Sam peeling large chunks of sunny-yellow polish off her nails and littering the ground with the scraps.

"You're all so young," Ashley says. "It's a fact."

"You're only a year older than me, Ashley," Sam snaps back. The cameras eat this up.

"But when you say it like that, you're insinuating something about our maturity," Jazmin says. "Something beyond our literal age."

"We've noticed some behaviors in the house that make us question the remaining women here," Ashley says. "I wouldn't want to call anyone out. I don't believe in that."

"You're calling us out right now. What do you think you're doing?" Jazmin says.

"I'm starting a conversation."

"She's calling you in," Anna Mae says, as though that means something different.

"I'm feeling attacked right now," Ashley says. "The energy I'm getting is a little aggressive, given that it was vulnerable of me to bring this up."

"She brought it up," Winna says, pointing to the production assistant. This somehow brings us all back to earth.

At dinner in the hotel restaurant, Laura comes over to our table. She doesn't sit with us, just stands on her way to the bathroom. She's always pretty, but now she's especially so in the dim flickering candlelight. Her blond hair, dyed pale and highlighted even whiter, is tied in a bun on the nape of her neck. Her teeth are similarly luminescent, almost turquoise. They must be so sensitive from the whitening treatments that her whole face buzzes when she chews on an ice cube. Chewing on ice cubes seems too unladylike for her, though.

"Don't worry about them," she says, casting a glance over to Anna Mae and Ashley. "They're mad because basically your whole rooming group is here and you're all young and beautiful."

"Everyone here is young and beautiful, including you," Jazmin says.

"Any one of you seems like you could be with Dylan," Laura says, dismissing Jazmin's compliment. "And you all always hang out with each other. They're intimidated."

"And you're not?" I ask. Laura shakes her head. I hadn't realized it could bother the other women, how our room always stuck together, that we're the youngest here, that so many of us have stayed until Week Five.

"I'm too old for cliques. I like you guys," she says. "I'm not here to get into fights."

"We like you, too," Winna says.

"Good," she says. Laura, in springy steps, leaves us. I ask how old she is, and Winna tells me she's thirty-one.

"I'm losing my mind," Jazmin says. "I thought it would be better outside the mansion, but still all I do is get drunk and hear people complain."

"Emily," Sam says, and my name from her lips starts ringing between my ears like last night all over again. I look up, and her face is so glowy and perfect, I know it can't be real and that I'm merely spiraling every time she pays attention to me. "They said you spent like an hour and half with Dylan last night."

"Yeah, what'd you talk about?" Jazmin asks.

"Oh, Miranda said she thought it could be good for me to talk about what feminism means to me."

"Did you bring a tri-fold poster board or something? Were you workshopping your Common App essay?" Sam asks. I can't tell if she's trying to be mean or not.

"It was pretty weird," I say, and turn to Winna. "Did Miranda say anything to you about it? She said she's making women's issues a focus of the season."

"Definitely not," Winna says.

"What do you mean?"

"It makes sense that she asked you," Winna says.

"Why? I actually don't know a lot about it."

"Every season they get some white girl to talk about girl power or her parents' divorce. Jazmin, Winna, and I just get to talk about deadbeat dads and drug use," Sam answers.

"Then we get sent home right before we meet his family," Jazmin says. "Heaven forbid he have to introduce his parents to a Black girl."

"Hey, on my one-on-one date, Miranda asked me to talk about if I ever had an eating disorder, so don't be so stereotypical," Winna says. "I'm surprised she didn't ask me if my parents were hard on me or to shed tears over an old report card."

The three of them laugh. I hadn't thought about their positions, so focused on my own failures and successes. For the first time since coming on the show, I realize Sam's distinct advantage: the knowledge of the earlier seasons ingrained in her mind. If I were her, I could shuffle through past contestants and see the grand algorithm of the season illuminated above me overhead, like those night-lights that project constellations on a child's ceiling. Sam goes back to talking to Jazmin and Winna now. She always talks so quickly, like her brain moves faster than everyone else's.

"If people want to watch romance or drama," Sam says, "and we give them a dose of entertainment, then that's all well and good. What we know we're selling, they know they're buying, a free market exchange. If I'm out here saying, 'I was poor and raised by a single mom,' and the viewers are proud because they feel like the show challenges the system, it's not true. The studio is the system, and if anything worked against their interests, they wouldn't air it."

"Exactly, the incentives for us are completely warped. We're damned if we tell Dylan our life stories and damned if we don't," Jazmin says.

"Miranda and I keep talking about how showing different kinds of love stories allows everyone to see that their beauty can be transformative," Winna says. "But sometimes it all seems made up. I agree that people need to widen their perspectives, but I've been feeling like it's no longer about me, but a marketing campaign."

"We should unionize," Jazmin says, and they start laughing again. Candlelight flickers across Sam's lip gloss. I know I shouldn't have kissed her, but that doesn't stop me from wanting to do it again.

The next morning, the bus ride to the date lasts five gloriously short minutes. We pass the cruise port to our right, with ships bigger than whales, housing hundreds. That seems the closest thing to my experience now, trapped aboard a vessel moving far beyond your control. At first it seems like paradise, with unlimited food and fluffy towels folded each morning into a new kind of creature, until you realize that you've paid a great cost to be there and can't get off. To the left, the white stucco homes rise up on the surging hills that surround the coastal city. We meet Dylan at a gondola station by the ocean. His collarbone peeks out of a deep, unbuttoned Henley. Around him, frothy-leaved trees rustle in the wind. A gondola car soars above us, rocking as it moves over the city toward a nearby hilltop. We tilt our heads back and track it a bit, small and black against the clear blue sky.

"Today, I want to explore this beautiful island with you," he says. We cheer.

Leigh wrangles Dylan into her cable car. I enter a gondola with Winna, Sam, Ashley, two other women, and a cameraperson. I press myself in the farthest corner from the entrance, awaiting the first jolting swing off the platform.

"You've been weird recently," Sam says in the clatter of the gondola doors closing. Over the intercom, a man speaks in Portuguese, then English, describing all the things we shouldn't do during the ride: jump around, extend our limbs, be too volatile.

"I have not," I say back. We're both mic'd. I grip the bars on the edge of the gondola. The cameraperson films the other four women overlooking the view of the city. We rise over deep ravines, the houses getting larger but also more dilapidated as we ascend. Stray dogs run about the streets and chickens scratch around their hutches.

"Jesus, Emily, why are you freaking out so bad?"

"I need to focus on Dylan today," I say. "Intensely and without distraction."

"Am I distracting you?" Sam says. She presses her arm against mine. The scent of her bodywash comes over me, the same as when she leaves the shower, hair and body wrapped in damp towels. I do find her distracting and think I have for a while, but it was such a pleasant distraction that I didn't notice.

"No," I say. I turn to look out the back window. The ocean is a flat plane, reaching out so far beyond us I feel like I can see the curvature of the earth, arcing downwards. The rest of the crew arrives at the top of the mountain, and we pose for a picture on Andrea's iPhone, leaning over the railing looking over the city. Someday, months from now, it will show up on our Instagrams. We will all be following each other, or not following each other, and that choice will mean something. Strangers will notice who among the group I seem close to and post about it in forums, cheering us on. We're shepherded down the hill where we chat and watch taxis go by as we wait for Dylan to return to us from an interview. I've never waited this much for anything in my life. After a half hour, the camerapeople lift their lenses, one facing up the hill and the other on our faces. We hear cheering and a rumbling noise. Turning the corner, Dylan comes sitting in a wicker sled, steered by two men with flat-brimmed straw hats and orange boots with thick rubber soles. They skid into a stop in front of us. An empty fleet of sleds follows behind them.

There was a course of my life that never would have led me to this island in the middle of the Atlantic, skidding down the streets in effectively a wicker tourist trap, but I didn't take that track, so I get in a basket with Winna beside me. The sled drifts wildly from side to side, the wind whipping my hair across my face. The guides steer us through active intersections. Cars breeze by at cross streets as we tilt like race car drivers. I consider telling her what I did with Sam, screaming it out into the wind. I think of her words about the marketing campaign. I'm here for the average viewer to root for, the Middle American, the flyover, the suburb, my mom's neighbor as she watches her guilty pleasure show between baking a pound cake and caring for her 2.3 children. If the image of Sam and me kissing reached their screens, I can half imagine it being palatable. Two attractive women in love is like a bonbon for the masses, the sweetest type of blasphemy to stomach. Despite what I've done, I could still be the kind of woman that men want. That's how I ended up on the show, after all. My conventional beauty, my feminine packaging, gets me all kinds of free passes. When Winna and I get out of the sled, she turns to me and says, "I didn't know anything like this existed."

"Me neither," I say. I didn't know about a lot of things before coming here.

That night, we go to a tavern with barrels of aging Madeira wine lining the walls. It has a medieval look compared to the rest of the Mediterranean island, hulking gray stones making up the walls, a cast-iron bell looming from the ceiling as décor. I drink a glass, so sweet I almost can't tolerate it, and then another. I haven't eaten, haven't slept, and my stomach sloshes with alcohol. The pattern of the wood grain of the barrels starts to swirl in my vision, and I laugh at everything the other women are saying.

After class in middle school one day, we all had to go to confession, where we entered the tiny box with you on one side and the priest on the other. In the dark, you speak all your darkest secrets and then the priest forgives you on the Lord's behalf. One of my friends in school confessed to Father Sheldon that she thought that abortion should be very, very legal. I had never even considered that people could think that, let alone express the idea to others. I was starting to have thoughts of my own. I told Father Sheldon that I was questioning my faith. He asked me what parts, and I mentioned the beliefs of the Church, and again, he asked me to clarify. I didn't want to say abortion, because I didn't want to seem like I was copying my friend, so instead, I said, "Gay people." He hummed a bit and didn't seem to care at all. He prescribed prayer and I was dismissed. When I got home from school, my parents asked what the priest and I discussed. I didn't even consider lying; in fact, I was almost proud of my rebellion.

"I said I thought that gay people should have rights."

My parents were aghast.

"You let Father Sheldon know you support those people?" my father asked, incredulous. He couldn't even say the word *gay*.

"The whole church will find out," my mother said. I started to get nervous.

"Father Sheldon didn't make it seem like a big deal."

"I'll have to call him," my mother said. "I'll call him and tell him you're sorry or he'll never accept a dinner invitation again. What if he won't do cousin Bella's baptism now?"

My parents went back and forth and I stopped talking, ashamed. Eventually, they remembered that the nature of confession is private. It's as though the priest isn't even there, and you're in direct communication with God. That assuaged them, though I know they still worried, because a few months later, when the *Catholic Inquirer* published an article about loving the sinner and hating the sin, one of my parents cut it out and left it on my bed for me to read. I never discovered which of them did it or if they did it together, and we never talked about it again. Since that time, the community has softened a bit. I heard my father once say, in a loving way, "Everyone has a gay nephew these days," to comfort one of his friends over the phone, and I guess that could be considered progress.

When Miranda gets me to talk to Dylan, she can tell I'm drunk.

She grabs my shoulders with both her hands and squeezes them before we walk into the cellar together. I'm brittle under her touch, ready to shatter.

"You've had a hard week," she says. "You were vulnerable with him. You're exhausted, but you're in control. We've got this."

"I've had a hard week," I say, nodding along. "Honesty. I love being honest."

"You can't crack now." She hands me an Altoid. I pop it into my mouth and begin to suck on it, but she watches me intently, so I press it between my molars, wait for it to break, and chew it to dust. "He'll love that you're struggling. Men think they want an easy girl to fall in love with who will turn into an easy wife. But all they do is fall in love with a difficult girl, try to fix her, and end up with a difficult wife."

"Is that what your husband says?" I ask her. She doesn't answer and walks down the stairs to the cellar, which is seemingly hewn from the bedrock of the earth. It smells musty and humid, but we're surrounded by bigger wine casks now, all the more cinematic.

"You're my girl," she says, and Dylan stands there, kissing Sam. Miranda recedes to the shadows so fast that it takes me a moment to realize the cameras are on me. I clear my throat. They step away from each other, and Dylan rearranges his hair. Sam leans back against one of the barrels, glancing at the camera, then leveling a blank gaze at me.

"I didn't realize anyone was down here," I say, though this makes no sense. I never would've found this stairwell without Miranda's leading me there. I stare at Sam's lips, Dylan's hands. For a second, I worry that Miranda is trying to hurt me by making me watch Sam kiss another person. But there's no way she knows. She wants me to see another girl kissing Dylan.

"Is it okay if I talk to Emily now?" Dylan asks Sam.

"Of course," she says. Her wineglass, half full, is rimmed with a print of her nude lipstick. She leaves her drink there, not looking at me as she goes back upstairs. I'm still staring at the glass, my eyes all wide from the overly sweet wine coursing through my veins, when Dylan puts his hand around my waist. Someone from the art department comes in, clears their old glasses and brings new ones. Dylan must get a new glass for each girl he sees; gone are the lingering greasy fingerprints from where he grabbed our slick, moisturized skin.

"I'm having a bad week," I say.

"I know." He takes both hands of mine in his. A draft passes through the cellar, chilling me.

"You do?"

"I can read you, Emily," he says. "I see you." It's a nice thing to say, and if it were true, he would have broken up with me this morning.

"I felt like I should be honest with you about how I've been," I say. "Real talk." I can feel my head nodding slowly as I repeat Miranda's words, but it's beyond my control. He nods back at me, and I can't tell if he's mirroring me or if I'm mirroring him.

"I love that you can be honest with me. I know it's hard that we haven't had much time alone recently."

"Yes," I say. "That's it. I miss you."

"Nothing to miss now," he says. He leans across the table, his neck reaching toward me like a Slinky. I marvel at it, the way it seems to give him at least another foot of height, and I feel his lips against mine. His mouth tastes like the sweet wine, the same flavor on my breath; the same must have been on Sam's as well. Some people believe in divine hallucination, messages from God coming into your brain and giving you access to another world. That's what happened to Moses and Joan of Arc, if I remember right. I try to make myself have one and picture Dylan's and Sam's faces flashing in front of me as we kiss, their lips shifting back and forth underneath mine. His tongue darts into my mouth, and I open mine to receive it. I picture their features like shards in a kaleidoscope, swirling over their faces. I want to see which one the hallucination lands on, so that God can tell me what to do, but all I see and feel is Dylan, and all I've got is this world, no matter how much I want it to be otherwise.

When we get back from the date past midnight, Sam and I move toward the thin aisles on either side of the bed. Each piece of her jewelry hits the dresser with a plink. Her feet pad away from me, freed from her heels, as she goes to the bathroom. I run a makeup wipe over my face, staining it beige and black, and then use another. When I get into bed, my skin is sticky and tight. The sheets, in their astronomical thread count, breeze over my shaved legs. I lie on my side and loosen my limbs to feign sleep. Usually when I've tried to fall asleep the past three weeks, I've matched my breaths to Sam's small snores. The bedcovers rustle and the mattress dips. A loud motorcycle rips down the curved mountain road at the far side of the hotel.

"You want to forget it ever happened? I can do that. I'll do whatever you want so that you stop ignoring me," she says. There's a note of desperation in her voice, something I've never heard before, not even when she was worried about going home, not even after the shooting.

"I can't talk about this right now," I say, but what I want to say is, "I can't believe I had to see you kiss him." I grit my teeth and pull the blanket up over my shoulders.

"Of course you can't."

Since being here, I haven't thought much about the after, about going back home to Boston, where I'll have to get another job and clear my stuff out of my apartment so my roommate's boyfriend can take over my lease. Maybe I'll work at Trader Joe's, because they have health insurance. Sam would think that's funny, me in the tropical-print shirt like the ones she wears for fashion. Everything would change if my feelings for Sam were aired. I don't want to be a love-is-love spokesperson. People say that coming out means you can live authentically, but if that's the case, living authentically sounds horrible. The focal point of my life would become something I never wanted other people to be a part of. My brand deals would happen in June for Pride Month, when companies would want me to start selling multivitamins targeted for gay women in rainbow packaging. I'd sell a personal essay to a women's magazine called "I'm *The One* Who Came Out." I can still change course, though. I just need to be unimpeachably good. Sam exhales humming breaths as she sleeps. I lie awake for an hour and then another before I fall asleep.

To avoid her in the late hours of the next two nights, I go to the hotel gym, supervised by a production assistant. Winna joins, using a barre that lines the wall of mirrors on one side, and does ballet for two and a half hours straight. She can kick her leg so high that it's like when I was a child and would twist my Barbie's legs into contortionist circles. We talk about how she always thought she wanted to be an architect like her parents, but they knew that she was some kind of artist. Her childhood watercolors are so charming that they still hang up in the house. We talk about how being at ballet school and an all-girls Catholic school are like being on *The One*. I run on the treadmill until I feel like I could vomit. Then I wipe a large square with a bleach wipe on the springy matting of the gym and lie there until I catch my breath. Sometimes I run so hard, my teeth start to hurt. I think of becoming skinnier, of disappearing. If I threw a weight through this ground-floor window of the hotel, I could probably escape. Except I have no money and no identification. Even if I managed to find my way to a police station, production would find me, not to mention that I'd also be breaking my contract and subject to significant fines. The production assistant stares at me as I lie on the floor, but never asks if I'm okay. She mostly watches television on her iPad. The second night, she lets me watch a few scenes with her—a gritty drama, all shot in dark green and black, men with bruised faces—but I lose interest after a few moments and go back to lying on the ground. I thought I would relish seeing a screen again, but it's almost like I've lost the taste for them.

The cocktail party before the necklace ceremony takes place in the hotel itself. Miranda brings me to Dylan by an alcove in the hotel surrounded by tall white fluted columns. On a side table by a couch, there is a telephone with the receiver faceup on the table.

He presses a button and the phone emits a crackle. "Mrs. Boylan, are you there? I'm Dylan," he says.

"Mom?" I screech out. Miranda smiles at me. Terry looks close to giving me a thumbs-up.

"Honey!" she says back. I bend over the phone, and Dylan wraps his arm around my shoulder from behind me. He presses his large body into mine, enveloping me. "How are you doing? We miss you so much at home."

"I'm good, Mom," I say. Though we don't talk much usually, being here has made me think of them more. "I'm good."

"You raised a wonderful woman," Dylan says. My mom laughs, a high-pitched giggle. She's always been so pliant around men; she even preens for clerks at the grocery store. It must be a heritable trait. We chatter about where we are, how it has been, what we've seen. My mom is thrilled by the idea of Iceland, the way the sun shines all day in summer. After a few minutes, Miranda intercedes. With a swish of her hand, the camerapeople stop filming. She puts the receiver in my hand and turns it off speaker.

"It's just me, now," I tell my mom.

"Are you falling in love there, honey?"

"Yeah, Mom," I say. "I think I am." I picture Sam, her hands on my elbow at the club, her voice chatting as Vivian popped my pimples, the sound of her flipping thin pages of the Bible in the bunk bed above me, the press of her fingers as she passed me the mystery novel at the airport, the kiss in the bathroom. My eyes tear up as Dylan watches me. It looks good to seem like I love my mother so much. I let the tear roll down my cheek. The cameras switch back on. "I have to go, Mom," I say, choking out the words. "Thanks for talking. I miss you and Dad."

"She's so amazing," Dylan says as I come to sit over next to him. He seems genuine, despite not having any evidence for this. He puts his arms over my shoulders and pulls me in for a hug. "I know you miss your parents. I miss mine, too."

"It sounds like she liked you," I say. I have to be good right now. Miranda has done me a favor and I have to pay her back.

"Parents love me. What can I say? It's a God-given talent. Maybe I'll get to meet her soon," he says with a sly smile. Three weeks from now, the international travel will stop and the four remaining women will split up across the United States as Dylan visits our hometowns. He will meet our families, eat at our dining room tables, and ask our fathers for their blessings. I could be back in Ohio within twenty days.

"Wouldn't that be nice?" I say. To obscure my messy makeup, I kiss him. My mom sounded like she is no longer ashamed that I've gone on the show, but excited about all the opportunities it offers. There's a glimmer of hope that with enough time and distance, she and my dad could come around to the decisions I make for myself. It's as though I've become terrified to remember what their disapproval feels like, the fear of it worse than its ultimate sting. Our relationship could change if I tried hard enough to defend my decisions and to let them know that the outcome makes me happy. I think of Sam, and of confession. Believing that my parents, Sam, and I could look like a happy family in a Pride-themed paper towel commercial would be more delusional than believing any one of the many lies of this show. Besides, I haven't even talked to Sam since we kissed. It's like the timeline of the show has become an objective truth that I can't shake—kiss, meet the families, marriage—neglecting the vast possibilities of the in-between.

As we line up for Necklace Night, the smallness of our group dawns on me. Jazmin watches from the side, the Golden Necklace dipping toward her matching golden dress. We stand in two rows, five in front and six behind. We'll lose another three tonight. I get a necklace, second to be called behind Anna Mae. Winna and Sam get called after me. I take a deep breath. The three women who go home don't matter to me.

As we chat after, Dr. C pulls me aside for a talk in the hotel bar. She's wearing a long cream-colored sweater that reaches her knees. Her fine graying hair is wrapped in a loose chignon and secured with a thin silver clip.

"A quick chat," she keeps repeating, until she gets me alone and says, "Miranda tells me you've been struggling this week." Cropped chinos expose her crossed ankles, covered in thin navy socks.

"That's interesting," I say.

"In what way?" she asks. I feel like she should have a notebook in front of her, scribbling about my inane remarks. I've never been to a real psychologist before.

"I didn't mean anything by it. Just something to say." Dr. C flags down a waiter and orders a cappuccino, though it's past midnight, indicating this will not be a passing conversation. I ask for nothing but a glass of ice water. We sit in silence, me inspecting my fingernails. I pinch the skin on the back of my hand, and it stands up stiff, clearly dehydrated, before settling back down. The ocean is more volatile tonight, large crashes audible even from up here. "You don't tell anyone what I say here, right?"

"Everything stays between us," she assures me.

"I'm a stupid person."

"Say more." I'm surprised when she doesn't scold me for negative self-talk. I thought that wasn't allowed in therapy. In the past, there were girls I liked as much as I like Sam now. Theresa in elementary school before she moved to Illinois, Ella in middle school before she transferred to a coed public school, and Connie in high school before I headed to a Jesuit university and she went to OSU. They were my best friends and we spent all our time together.

"Why do I never know what I want?" I ask Dr. C. I thought I wanted to be those girls, to have their full eyebrows, purplish fingers, mauve lips, freckles on their collarbones, wide hips, fuzzy arms, square teeth. I envied their bodies and mannerisms, their quirks and their senses of humor, but I thought I wanted them for myself, to mold myself into their image. Over time, no matter how different we looked, we always started behaving like sisters, twins even: swapping clothes in the mornings, hair elastics in the hallway, socks in gym class, toothbrushes at sleepovers, secrets in the dark. I was never the kind of girl at sleepovers to try out things with other girls as "practice" for boys. Those were the ones who turned out gay, but I never did that. I had one gay friend in college, but he was a man and came out to his parents at ten years old.

"Do you want a lot of things and have trouble choosing?" Dr. C asks, in her sympathetic voice. No, I want one thing and never, deep in the recesses of my mind, thought I would be able to have it. "Women are often told they can't have it all, but that's a lie sold to us by men so that we don't even try. You can have all the things that men have, if only you expand your mind."

I don't want the things that men have. I increasingly want nothing to do with men. I've seen this type of conversation before, where another woman pinpoints the nebulous patriarchy as the source of all her problems. Dr. C says that the first step toward a solution is to do a guided feminist meditation, as though I could think my way away from *The One*, away from my upbringing, away from my own wants. She offers to let me borrow her phone at some point tomorrow to use a subscription-based app. She says I need to become more empowered in my body. I don't even ask what that means. I think of all the lies told to me in my life: by Father Sheldon, the nuns, my parents, basically every movie I've ever watched, *The One*'s existence on the earth. Women and men alike have sold me on ideas of romance, goodness, and happiness that roiled into a toxic sludge in my brain, where sickly flowers grew as my warped dreams. Dr. C can misread me as much as she wants. Months from now, viewers will leap to conclusions about my actions and behavior far beyond any of my original intent. The least I can do is try to read my own desire. I excuse myself before Dr. C's cappuccino arrives, and knock on the door to my room. Sam lets me in without speaking to me and moves through the filmy curtains, yellow in the moonlight, back out to the porch. Her body is in silhouette, leaning on the railing with her elbows. Her hair is in a long braid without an elastic. Cellulite marks the tops of her thighs.

"Sam," I say, breathless from the stairs that I took in twos up four flights. My gasping voice makes it sound like I'm about to cry. I stand beside her, and she turns to face me. I don't know what to do with my hands. "I'm sorry."

"You don't have to apologize. You have nothing to apologize for."

I know this isn't true. I don't say anything for a moment, looking at her awash in moonlight. Below us, the waves ripple across the surface of the water, sloshing against the rocks, though I can't hear them up here anymore. With the big moon is a big tide, reaching higher toward the hotel, toward us.

"I've never kissed a woman before," I say. She nods as though she had guessed this already. "Just you."

"I have," she says, though I, too, had guessed this.

"I won't do it again," I assure her. "I don't want it to be complicated."

"I'd kiss you back," she says, "if you did."

"That's good to hear." I stare at her, feeling confused and almost desperate, and then, after a moment, ask, "Should I go home?" I know why Sam wants, needs, to stay here: the more time onscreen, the more followers; the more followers, the more impressions; the more impressions, the more money in her bank account. Those tethers aren't keeping me.

"We're leaving for Italy tomorrow. Do you want to go home?"

"Maybe you'd go farther if I left," I say.

"Maybe I'd leave quicker without your insights," she counters. "What if we have another exam?"

"I'd be lying to everyone if I stayed."

"Weren't you already?" This stings a bit. She's seen me so clearly for so long. I put my elbows on the iron railing next to hers. "Dylan has seven other women here besides us. What difference would it make to him that we kissed once? He's kissed all of us as much as he wants."

Once, she says. Though I was the one to say we shouldn't do it again, I don't like it. I agree to stay. All else being equal, there's an 11.1 percent chance Dylan picks me. If I leave tomorrow, there is a 0 percent chance that I'll be on an all-expenses-paid trip to Italy next week. I'll take those odds. Sam and I don't move, don't breathe. The fronds of the fat palm trees shift in a passing breeze. Our eyes are open, shimmering back the water's reflection, mirrors for the sea.

That night, when we get under the blankets, we meet in the middle of the plush bed. In half sleep, I wrap our legs together like a cross-stitch. I could be satisfied with only this kind of closeness for the rest of my life, inching toward something but never getting there. In high school math, we learned about asymptotes, lines that creep infinitesimally toward a number but never touching it. Tomorrow we go to Rome.

MEETING

IN ROME, MIRANDA opens the door to the hotel room.

"Hi, Frank," she says. Frank reclines back on the enormous bed while Wyatt and Andrea sit on a couch in front of him. Terry is off with Dylan, congratulating him on another successful week of dating beautiful women. She perches on the arm of the couch, a bit unstable, and wishes she hadn't been last to get here. Frank, as always, is wearing denim shorts and a Lakers jersey. Newspaper articles always call him an eccentric, the mastermind showrunner, but everyone who works there mostly just calls him a dick.

"Okay, Wyatt, you start. What are the sitches with the bitches?" Frank says. Miranda clenches her jaw and reminds herself that she can stomach anything he says. He has used that line in every senior production meeting since she got promoted five years ago. Unfazed, Wyatt gives his update: the remaining three women he has left, lingering biographical details to reveal, psychological weak points to stomp harder on.

"Who's your top girl?"

"Sam," he says.

"You think she'll get you the bonus?"

"I'm hoping," Wyatt says. Andrea talks about her girls: Laura, Leigh, Jazmin. Miranda gives her update: Emily, Winna, and her long shot, Paige. She doesn't mention the cracks in Emily's facade that erupted this week, the frantic look in her eyes in interviews and the increased alcohol consumption. She had to send Dr. C in as backup, but the notes after the meeting were unhelpful, yabbering on about the heightened pressures of womanhood on the show, cultural barriers to success, and self-care. Dr. C prescribed a guided meditation for Emily today. When Miranda followed up with Dr. C in person about Emily's frame of mind, Dr. C suggested she should try one, too.

There are two ways for the women to break down here: manic or depressive. She wants the lower-tiered women who won't go as far to spiral out of control and the top girls to get sad and cry alluring tears. Chaos is only welcome as long as it's coming from the right sources, as long as it's within her control.

"I've got meetings in Positano all week," Frank says. They all know that by "meetings," he means doing cocaine on a yacht. "But I'll be back next week for Florence before we head back to the States. Oh, and before I forget, I'm disappointed there haven't been any ambulance rides yet."

"Noted," Miranda says. Miranda is good at creeps. She's good at difficult people and people on a precipice. There are stories from when she was a child and would go up to strangers at restaurants to ask about their lives. They were always so charmed by her, they'd tell her more information than any small girl needed to know. She seemed composed, like she could handle whatever they threw her way. At her mother's weekly women's card game nights, she would listen to them talk about love, their husbands, and their kids. They would curse and discuss their menopausal dry vaginas, and Miranda was so good at fading into the pleasant background that they never censored themselves in her presence. Her mother would even talk about Miranda in front of her, but the main focus was the problems her mother had in her marriage: Miranda's father's alcohol use and tempers. The next morning, remembering the drunken secrets she spilled, her mother told her she should be a police detective because the murderers would just let it slip that they did it in a casual conversation.

Frank stops her on the way out, after Andrea and Wyatt have already left. Sometimes, it depresses her that this is the man she works to please.

"You know you're my top girl, Miranda. Make something good happen this week. Who can you push?"

WEEK SIX

THE PRODUCTION ASSISTANTS keep trying to get us to say we're in the city of love as we shoot B-roll, but I'm pretty sure Paris is supposed to be the city of love. The light fades into violet around all the pastel buildings. Winna's heeled boots get stuck in the cobbled streets, so I link arms with her as she walks. A rush of pigeons flies overhead and Sam lets out a scream like she's witnessed a murder. We pass a gelateria with a long line snaking out its door. Though it's early spring, the Roman people and other tourists seem indifferent to the cool air. Our group unites against the producers, a rare show of strength in numbers: please, get us gelato, when in Rome, please. Sam insists that Wyatt search each flavor for her on Google Translate on his phone. Jazmin, Winna, and I huddle by them, trying to coordinate an ordering strategy.

"'Bacio'?" Sam asks.

"It says 'kiss,'" Wyatt says.

"What's a kiss?" she asks.

Wyatt leans down and presses a peck to her cheek. "That."

Sam's laugh drifts through the group, and a few women turn toward her. If another man kisses Sam, I might faint. I kissed her over a week ago now, though each time she's near me, it's as though it's etched on the backs of my eyelids. Want rushes through me, and I shake out my shoulders to rid myself of the energy.

"I've got this," Jazmin says. She slides through the crammed shop, making her way to the counter without people protesting. Wyatt watches her leave production's grasp, but doesn't make an effort to stop her. Through the window, she makes a man in a paper hat and bow tie laugh. He goes out of view for a moment and returns with a fistful of tiny spoons. She splays her fingers for him, and he places them between them one by one, so she can balance them all for us. She moves more carefully back out toward us, careful not to spill her prize.

"God," I say, "how do you do that?" Inside, the man in the paper hat watches from behind the cash register.

"It's called flirting, Emily. You should try it sometime," Jazmin says. I roll my eyes as she passes me the sample. "It's a chocolate-and-hazelnut flavor. It's based on a candy called a kiss, like how we have Hershey's Kisses. And Claudio says we should order everything con crema. Bacio is fine, he said, but we should try the pistacchio. Except for me, because he told me I should get the sorbetto di limone."

"Mamma mia, did you also figure out the building's monthly rent? Or their recipe for the gelato base?" Sam asks.

"What about a discount for us?" Winna says.

"An invitation to his nonna's Sunday dinner where he'll spoon-feed you tortellini?" I say.

Jazmin looks at Wyatt for a second with a frown. "I almost feel bad for you, Wyatt. We're not very nice, though usually it's directed at you."

"At least I get paid to be bullied by you," Wyatt says with a shrug. She hands him a sample, though I hadn't expected her to get him one. I wouldn't have. I suck on the plastic tasting spoon, gripping it between my teeth. I order the pesche con crema. When the assistant brings out my gelato, shuttled out to each of us in rapid succession, the sun has set too much to film anymore. I stand against the wall, looking into the bustling gelateria, where towers of cones rise above glass cases that seemingly hold hundreds of flavors. A child, poised on her mother's hip, licks off drips of ice cream as her mother pays. It's nice to be on this side of the glass for a night.

The hotel where we stay seems more like a rented house than anything, a single staff person organizing us at the base of a large staircase. Though the outside is plain, all the inside walls are painted with scenes from ancient myths, lyres and grape leaves in each corner, while all the furniture itself is slick and new. Since we started traveling, I've gotten a new barometer of wealth and refinement. I can tell what's expensive by looking at it. The wide-sliced log, covered in resin, acting as a glossy, terminally unused side table, must have cost thousands of dollars.

"Who are the two short women here?" the hotel manager asks in a thick accent, looking us up and down.

"Sorry, what do you mean?" Andrea asks, standing in front of us, our Mother Goose for the evening.

"The top room, it's for short people," he says, waving his hand a few inches above his pepper-gray hair.

Sam grabs my wrist, raises it with hers into the air. "We'll take it." The man gives a production assistant directions to our room. The print of her hand is still hot on my skin. We haven't touched each other since the last night in Madeira, though I've started to dream about it. Hot, flashy images of our bodies intertwined leave me damp and unfulfilled in the mornings, while she sleeps on next to me, unaware of my mind's swirl.

"What are you doing?" I whisper to her as the group starts to disperse.

"Top of the world in the city of love," she says. "What more could two roommates want?"

The assistant goes ahead and unlocks the door for us as we trek up the stairs with our luggage, first a wide flat marble set, then to a foyer where the stairs split into two separate staircases like a ram's horns, twisting up the core of the house. The room itself is sparsely furnished with low ceilings, a worn Persian rug by each bed, and a modern, bendy lamp. Between inlaid fluted columns, the walls have been frescoed in expansive pastel scenes: naked women, round and blossoming, twisting in sheer silks, chubby angels by their sides; naked women painted as marble statues; a woman in a golden chariot towed by a dozen cherubs, naked but for a breastplate. We go to our respective beds, Sam on the left and me on the right, mirroring the pattern we've been sleeping in since we graduated from bunk beds. The beds are so narrow and short they can't be standard-size twins, so low to the ground they might as well be mattresses on the floor.

"Do you like Wyatt?" I ask Sam, staring up at wooden beams above us instead of looking at her.

"Yeah, I like Wyatt," she says. She barely listens to me as she braids her hair, her fingers moving like a sailor's on knots.

"That's not what I mean," I say. I don't want to explain myself further, embarrassed enough as it is.

"Oh my God, Emily, do I *like* like Wyatt? Is that what you're trying to ask me?" Sam says, turning to face me.

"You're making me sound stupid when you say it like that," I say. I also know I'm being stupid, but I also can't stop myself.

"It's not like that," she says. She raises her eyebrows. "Are you jealous?" I shake my head no and she laughs. "I can't believe you're jealous of Wyatt and not Dylan."

"You don't like Dylan," I say.

"Everyone likes Dylan," she says. "That's the point of him. And if anyone has cause to be jealous, it's me. You're his favorite and you seem to like him."

"I'm not his favorite," I say, though I'm not sure it's true. It could be Winna. It could be Anna Mae. Though I picture Dylan surrounded by the sequoias, telling me he knows who it could be at the end of this, Dylan wanting to meet my parents, Miranda saying if I played my cards right it could be me. I picture us in the Casita on the first night, and I imagine him bringing me there again.

"But do you *like* like him?"

"No," I say. I want to circle back to Sam and Wyatt, not this track of conversation. Figuring out my feelings for Dylan is like finding a giant, ancient dust bunny under your bed and trying to figure out what it possibly could be made of. "Dylan's nice."

"And?"

"I'm supposed to like Dylan and I'm a good girl, so I do what I'm told."

"You're not that good," she says. She's giving me a look.

"Stop flirting with me," I say.

"Tried, failed," she says. "Sorry."

"You're too powerful. You need to use your powers for good, not evil."

"I'd rather use my powers on you."

"I'm going to dinner now," I say. "We have enough problems."

"Whatever you say, Emily," she says, brushing past me. Her toes are light on the spiral stairs back down to rejoin our group, as though she doesn't have a care in the world. Hot pans of pasta are in the center of the table, bread in baskets down the table, tiny bowls of olive oil so green it looks like it was pressed today. I love Italy.

The next morning, a date card comes that reads, ***Can you open up for love? Love, Dylan.*** Everyone but Winna, who has another solo date, is shuttled to a bar on the first floor of a hotel in the center of the city. All the lights are turned down low, though it's the middle of the day. Dylan and the host greet us, grinning wildly.

"Physical connections and openness are such important parts of relationships," the host says. "Today Dylan is asking you to write a personal story from your dating life to perform at this comedy club tonight in front of a live audience."

"What a shame," Sam says. "Guess it's not a gynecological exam, after all. I'm due for a Pap."

I've never done anything in front of a live audience and was hoping to go my whole life without doing so. Even as a child, when friends and I would talk about getting married, I could only stomach the image of a small ceremony. It's also clear they mean sex stories, of which I have none. In the back room, there are a bunch of props and costumes. A sexy schoolgirl costume is labeled with my name, and I look around for Miranda to complain. She says that it can be liberating for women to talk about their sexual experiences. I tell her, not really.

"Dylan wants someone who he can connect with on this level," she says.

"Tell him he can make me one of the final three and connect with me on an overnight date, then," I say. "He's not going to find out anything from me being onstage."

"He wants a wife who is fun," she says. The worst thing you

can do on a group date is be shy and not commit. If you laugh and try, then you look cool even if you look bad. Jazmin taught me that.

"I'm fun," I say.

She shoos me away. "Then go be fun."

Soon Dylan hands me a notepad and says, "Excited to see what you come up with."

"Hah," I say. "You and me both."

"Do you want help?"

"How would you help? Are we going to do something that you want me to tell a story about tonight?" I ask.

He laughs shyly. "I meant brainstorming or, you know, emotional support. A shoulder to cry on."

"Brainstorming out loud would do more harm than good," I say, but he sits with me anyways. Instead of working on my sex story, we sketch terrible pictures of each other. I can't get anything three-dimensional flattened onto a page. A camera films us doodling in a dark corner of the bar, and I know we look cute and natural. That's what people want to see when they watch us fall in love, that it comes together easily. We can hear a woman crying in a pull-aside interview, and the sound person asks us to move. Apparently, someone left here is still a virgin, and this event is giving her literal hives. A production assistant comes in with a bottle of antihistamines for her. An ambulance is called. A few minutes later, a medic hurries past us, filmed, with a red-plastic first-aid box marked with a white cross, in case we didn't realize there was an alleged medical emergency on set. Dylan tells me to follow him and takes me to an elevator. That's when I know he's serious about me, that he stays with me instead of comforting whoever is sick. He pushes his hand in front of the parted doors to hold them open for me, and the cameraperson films them shutting, saying they'll meet us upstairs.

"Where're we going?" I ask, alone with him for the first time ever. It will only last the ride up to the tenth floor.

"This is the hotel some of the crew and I are staying at. There's a Casita here," he says. "A place with some privacy."

"Okay," I say, though it's the middle of the day and sex is supposed to happen at night. I start to imagine how my breath smells. I had yogurt for breakfast and didn't brush my teeth again afterwards, so not especially appealing.

"They'll take off our mics if I ask," he says. "No pressure."

The elevator beeps and the doors open. He waits for me to get out, but I don't know the room number, so I stand in the alcove for him to lead me. He pulls out an electronic card from the back pocket of his jeans. Apparently, he gets his own keys. The suite we enter is completely standard with no belongings in sight. It doesn't even have the semblance of romance like the Casita did. At first, I thought he was taking me to his personal room, where I would be able to comment on his toiletries and the various states of his unpacking, but all I have in front of me is a blank slate. A cameraperson, Terry, and Miranda come in. Terry asks if we're good to go in here and Dylan says yes. Miranda repeats the question, a recent consent safety protocol of independent double checks, and he says yes again before I answer. The cameraperson asks for a shot of us kissing against the hotel door before they unmic us, which we both agree to, though I'm not sure I act convincingly passionate. He lifts my legs up around his waist and pins me to the door, so most of my face is obscured from the camera anyways. In ye-olde-days-style fantasy shows, after a grand medieval wedding, there's always a scene when the wedding guests escort the bride and groom to the bedroom so that she can be deflowered in a scant white frock. Now I'm still pushed into a strange public performance, but this time allegedly it leads to my empowerment. The women who fought to make sure other women didn't feel ashamed to have sex and enjoy it couldn't have possibly wanted this for the daughters of their revolution.

I'm not sure how I agreed to this by getting in the elevator with him, but by the time I got up here, it seemed out of my hands. The hum of the central heating kicks on. Alone again, Dylan kisses me standing up, then lifts me onto the bed. His long fingers slip beneath the hem of my shirt, running a line below my navel as he opens his mouth against mine. He palms my right breast gingerly, as though to be respectful.

"You taste good," he says, and flips us onto our sides. I can see the erection tenting his jeans, and he takes my hand in his and runs it up his thigh. I can't believe that he wants to have sex with me in the middle of a date with seven other women, but I stroke him through his pants a couple of times because it feels mean to pull my hand away as if his dick were a hot stove. I let it go on a bit, flipping on top and seeming eager to take off his shirt to deflect the attention off me. When he flexes, I run my fingers along the rivulets of his muscles; then I trace the trail of hairs to his waistband, so plush and thick. He starts to pant and twists his hands into my hair. He seems to be into it.

"I've wanted you for so long," he says, and I have to stop myself from thanking him. I stick my hand in his pants so that he won't say anything else. His jeans are so tight that I don't have a lot of room to move around, but I don't want to seem like I'm fumbling lest he try to get any more naked. I act more vigorous, even taking off my own shirt to pass the time. He pinches my nipples through my bra, and they refuse to harden at his touch, a disappointment. A bead of moisture from the tip of his penis gets on my palm as I continue to touch him.

"We should go back down," I say. "The women . . ." Even in the hotel room, they've taken the alarm clock, so I have nothing to gesture to.

"No, I know, you're right." He pecks my lips between each word, as though he can't get enough of me.

"I'll meet you down there," I say, gesturing vaguely to the bathroom as though I need girl time. When Dylan leaves, I wipe off my damp hand on the bed. I think about funny things that happened the times I've had sex, but nothing comes up. Being in the Casita with him now is probably the best story I have to tell. My first time was a one-night stand after a college party at the beginning of the school year. It was so humid in the dorm room that the windows fogged up, and he and I made patterns in the glass from other people's breath and sweat. He was going bald, though he was only a sophomore, and I liked the way that he didn't seem to mind. As we left the party together, people would shout "Hey, man," or "How's it going, bud?" at him, and each time he stopped, he would introduce me to them as though I mattered. It delayed the trip by at least fifteen minutes, but I was glad to know he was popular. It made me feel less vulnerable. Back in his room, he offered to go down on me and I politely declined. To his credit, when we slipped into the polyester sheets of his twin extra-long bed, none of it ended up hurting, even though I had been told it would. There were no spots of blood, so it didn't feel like a special event. I had heard that it would be quick, too, that boys can't last for that long, which I was hoping for, but that didn't happen either. It must have lasted at least ten minutes, because a late-summer thunderstorm rolled in as he thrust into me. I was on my back, staring up at the spinning ceiling fan. I imagined the roof springing a leak and rain showering me with cool water. Sweat beaded across his skin, and I kept worrying that's what would drip on me instead. Thunder shook the building and I clung to him tighter, which made him finish. I think it lasted so long because I wasn't showing much enthusiasm.

That night, before getting onstage for my performance, I take three shots. The stage lights start to make me flush, but the audience is smaller than I expected, only fifty or so, and half of that is *The One*'s staff. I wonder where they got the rest of the random Italian people from.

"I want to share something from my past that informed everything I know about how to have a strong physical bond," I say, and run offstage to put on a cheap polyester habit some poor handler had to fetch at the last minute so that I could do a sex education class as a sexy nun. Blood rushes to my head. All this acting has done me good; I finally feel believable. I whack Dylan around with a ruler a bit to seem fun. Jazmin talks about when a man fell asleep while having sex with her and does a spotless reenactment on the floor. Soon, Sam comes out dressed in the schoolgirl outfit. I can't listen to any of the words she says, and instead, I watch the way her body moves. She's been with women and she's been with men. Whatever I'm figuring out now, she figured out long ago. The audience starts laughing, and I focus on her. For once, I feel like the smartest person in the room. Everyone else gets Dylan, while I have Sam. Jazmin wins a special trophy for being funny, and Dylan kisses her in front of us. I don't even blink.

Back at the hotel, a production assistant waits for us to enter. "Girl chat."

Thankfully, Anna Mae complains before I do. "Can we do it after we shower?"

"Fine," the production assistant says. "Emily, how about you?"

"I'd like to shower, too."

"Winna's had a hard day alone here," the production assistant says, and starts walking into the atrium, expecting me to follow. She calls Winna's name, and Winna looks up from her hands folded in her lap. A cameraperson is already in there, rolling. Winna asks me what I did on the date.

"Public humiliation," I say, gesturing toward the part of the habit I'm still wearing.

"Again," the assistant says. "It's late."

"We shared stories from our personal lives onstage. We even got costumes."

"And Emily got some special time with Dylan today. He took her to the Casita while they were on the date," the production assistant says.

"It wasn't a big thing," I say. Winna presses her lips together in a thin white line. "We didn't do anything."

"Did you have a good time with him?" Winna asks me.

"Yeah, it was fine," I say.

"Fine," she repeats. "Was it off mic?"

"Yes."

"Winna," the production assistant says, "what have you been thinking about here when you had some time for yourself?"

"I'm in love with him." Winna's voice is splitting into a hundred pieces. "And he's in love with you. He might be in love with me, but he's also falling in love with you."

"Winna, I'm so sorry. It was five minutes alone. It was nothing."

"It's never nothing. Every second is something. I know how he feels about you." She starts to sob, the sound almost animal. I look around for something to give her, for something to do. Another camera is in the corner of the room, and I put my arm in front of Winna to shield her face from its lens.

"Hey," I say. "It's okay. It's okay." I try to sound calming, but I'm as panicked as Winna is sad. I've never seen her cry like this. I couldn't even have imagined her crying like this. She has always seemed so composed. It's not like we've talked about the fact she is in love with him these past few weeks. After a bit, she seemed like she didn't want to talk about Dylan at all anymore. Sam told me it's always that way. When the women start to catch real feelings, chatting about our mutual boyfriend gets precipitously less fun. Miranda sweeps in the room all of a sudden. She touches Winna under her chin, lifting it. She cocks her head toward the door. "Let's go for a walk."

"Miranda," Winna says. Her face shines with a great surge of relief, and she follows her out of the room.

"You're good to go," the production assistant says, already bored by me and looking at her phone. After my shower, I stare up at the ceiling. Though I don't want to be engaged to Dylan, there is still a part of me that wants Dylan to want to be engaged to me. I can picture him proposing, surrounded by flowers, floating on a giant raft down a slow river. I'd be tall above him in a flowing dress, and I'd get something I have tried for all my life, the moment from the storybook, the pretty man on his knees begging me to be with him. I always heard that in dating, men have all the power; then they lower themselves to propose and can never quite get back up.

Sam is still tipsy from the date. I can tell from the way she trots into the room. Her hair, still in a ponytail, is loosened, hanging lower than usual. When she's sober, she always splits the ponytail in two to pull it tight against her scalp. She immediately strips off her dress.

"Welcome," I say, moving to sit at the edge of my twin bed and face her.

"Rumor has it you went to the Casita with Dylan," she says.

"Wyatt?"

She nods. "So what'd you two randy teens get up to?"

"I touched his dick a bit," I say.

"I'm so proud of you." She pats the top of my head and pivots in front of the wall, a painted woman naked in silks behind her. She lifts her arm just so and tilts her fingers to match the pose.

"Wait, wait. What do you think?" She rips the sheet off the bed and drapes it around her waist, trailing a piece up her arm. I watched a video once where someone dropped a marble in a well and it whistled all the way down, so far down that you never heard it hit the water. That's what this is like, but I'm not sure if I'm the marble or the person waiting. I trace my toes along the lines of the warped wooden floor planks. "Come on, Emily. Give a girl a compliment."

"You don't need me to compliment you."

"And why is that?"

"You know what I think about you."

"Do I?" she asks.

"You know Winna is in love with Dylan, right? She loves him. She told me that today, while she was crying because a PA told her about Dylan and me in the Casita."

"Well, it's a good thing we don't. That could get awkward real quick. All us women in love with the same person, recipe for disaster. Someone could make a television show out of that." She's no longer in front of the wall, but riffling through her suitcase for the shirt she likes to wear at night.

"I should leave," I say. She slips the big blue T-shirt over her head: "Chapel Hill Fun Run Turkey Trot." The font is all broken up, hairline fractures along the capital letters from wear. She walks over to me, still on her toes, still like everything in the world is going exactly as she wants it to.

"And what, sleep in Miranda's room? What if I don't want you to leave?" she asks. She knocks her knee against mine. It would have been playful, but she lingers there.

"Sam," I say.

"Emily," she says. I look at her eyes and she looks at my lips. It's happening. It's like Dylan, except I want it so bad. She kisses me and my body does all sorts of things outside of my active control. Her mouth tastes like peaches and champagne. My eyes shut and the tip of her nose brushes against my face and I lean into her more, but she moves me back onto the bed. I'm on my elbows and she pushes my shoulders down until I'm flat on my back. She straddles me, her mouth moving up my jaw toward my ear. My pulse thrums so fast it's like a hummingbird in my throat, like I'm choking on my heart. She runs her hand up my shirt and touches my chest. Her tongue licks my neck for only half a second, and I make a noise without meaning to. I clap my hand over my mouth. She laughs at me, sitting up. Some number of old people must die every year from this, hearts going out during elderly sex. It has to happen somewhere. It's happening to me right now from making out, and I'm only twenty-four.

"That's fun," Sam says, shaking out her hair. The elastic must be somewhere in the sheets now. The insides of her thighs are still pressing against my hips. My face is so hot. It's like Australian pavement in the summer, the kind you can cook an egg on. It's embarrassing, but Sam doesn't seem to notice.

"Mm-hmm," I say. "Fun."

"Jesus, you look wrecked," she says. "You are wound up so freaking tight. Seems like Dylan didn't help you out with that." She taps her fingers against my belly down the line to my underwear. I shift my hips, and she swings her legs off me, giving me some space.

"He assuredly did not."

"So are we doing this?" she asks me.

"Doing what?" My heart hasn't slowed down a beat.

"Whatever we want."

"Okay," I say.

"So what do you want to do?" she asks me, but I don't have an answer yet, though I can feel one forming, circling around my head like an asteroid caught up in a new planet's gravity.

I say nothing, and next to me, in the lingering silence, she falls asleep. I check my pulse every ten minutes to see if my heart rate will ever slow down. Her body is like a furnace, so hot to the touch it makes me sweat. Someone could come in here to wake us up in the morning so that we see Winna off for her date. My heart rate rises again at the thought of being found out, so I move to the other bed. Later, the world lightens through the skylight above us. Sam's hair fans out around her on the pillow, and the pink rise of the sun washes over her skin. She could be one of the women in the painting on the wall. That's what I like about her. She could be anything she wants to be.

Two days later, Sam and I go to Jazmin and Winna's room to dress for the cocktail party. Jazmin clips the Golden Necklace around Winna's neck. It's strange to see anyone other than Dylan do it. Week after week, it's always his hands hovering by our throats, snapping the clasp shut.

We go to a bar overlooking the craggy edge of the Colosseum. It's nice. Everything here is always so nice. And that's partially why I stayed, isn't it? To enjoy myself a bit on the most expensive vacation of my life. When you leave, you not only have to abandon your hopes of marrying your Prince Charming, but you're also plunged back into regular life: no free Bellinis, no organic produce; doing dishes so you have enough pans to cook with, cooking, then needing to clean the pans again. Dylan tries to give a more rousing speech this time. Perhaps he can sense that morale is down since three women are going home tonight. It's the same number that always goes home every week, but now that there are only nine of us, it feels more intense.

"*Roma* backwards is *amor*, the Italian word for 'love,' and this week, I definitely started to see myself falling in love with the women in this room."

You love someone, you're in love with someone, you're falling in love with someone, you're falling for someone, you can see yourself falling for someone, you're starting to see yourself falling for someone, you can imagine starting to see yourself fall in love with someone. It seems like this is supposed to make us feel better, but all I can think about is how I can make myself fall in love with anyone. They don't even need to be there; they don't even need to exist. All I need in my own corrupted brain and my closed eyes before I fall asleep at night, twisting fantasies from the gossamer of my imagination. Laura grabs him first, drawing him away from our semicircle.

"So, a few of you haven't gotten much chance to solidify your connections this week. Anna Mae, Leigh, and Emily, right?" a production assistant says. "Emily, are you worried at all about not seeing Dylan a lot this week? Besides your time in the Casita, of course."

"There's always time in the night before the ceremony to check in with where we're at," I say, not taking the bait about the Casita.

"God, you're stupid," Leigh says to me. I lift my head, startled. There was a ticking bomb in the room, but I wasn't listening to the countdown. "There's women here who have to try and try to get Dylan's attention. I ask Andrea every date, every cocktail party, multiple times, when I can talk to Dylan. You're led there, towed like a horse on a halter. You don't even know what the rest of us have to do. You're in your own bubble. You're in the Casita with the blackout shades down."

"I didn't know," I say. I also don't know how I didn't know that's what the rest of the women had to do. Is this what it is like for Sam, Winna, and Jazmin? They must hate me, too, then. No wonder Winna started crying this week. I look at them, but all their eyes are on Leigh.

"Is this what your whole life has been like? Getting everything and not noticing? Is that why you're so fucking dumb all the time?"

"Hey, that's enough." I hear Sam's voice. "You can't talk to people like that."

"Don't try and tell me what to do," Leigh says.

"It's not her fault that Dylan doesn't like you," Sam says. "It's yours. So why don't you sit with your own inadequacy instead of yelling at her?"

Sam spirits me to a hallway. It seems like the kind where restaurant staff should be bustling, but since we're the only patrons, it's empty. A cameraperson follows, and I move far away from her so as not to arouse suspicion.

"She's right," I say. It's like the conversation in Madeira, where Sam, Jazmin, and Winna talked about how the world works, and I sat there, dumbfounded, consumed by my own self-centeredness.

"She's not," Sam says. "They had you pegged since before you answered the surveys, since some casting person saw your screen test and thought, 'America will love her.' It has nothing to do with you."

"It feels like it has everything to do with me. It's my fault."

"We're going to need something else," the production assistant says. Sam looks at me, a question in her eyes. She wants to drag me away again, but I won't let her. I don't need to be towed everywhere.

"Leigh's mad that she's going to be sent home," I say. "I know that's it, but still, words hurt. It's like Dylan said. People are tense because they're starting to fall in love. It's sad that hers won't be reciprocated."

"Love is a powerful force. It can change people," Sam says, parroting back the clichés of the show.

"*Roma* backwards is *amor*," I say.

"Not helpful," the production assistant says.

"Tell me what to say and I'll say it," I say.

"Can you call her a bitch?"

"No," Sam says.

"A comment about her having roid rage? An impersonation? I don't know, something juicy."

"You're right about Leigh getting sent home. Dylan doesn't want to marry a girl like that," I say, emphasizing the last words as though they mean something in particular.

"That'll do," the production assistant says, and leaves us in the hallway, but Miranda, as always, comes to get me. As she walks me over to the corner of the restaurant where Dylan is with another woman, I ask her about why she brings me over to Dylan.

"He asks to see you in particular," Miranda says. "Especially tonight. He wanted more from you this week after the Casita. You got him riled like a stallion."

For a second, a spark of anxiety shoots through my body. They're going to bring me to interrupt Leigh and then we'll have to fight again. But when Miranda opens the door to the side room, it's only Anna Mae, who leaves Dylan without a huff. I do all the things I usually do with Dylan: we kiss, talk about our futures in abstract language, make meaningful eye contact, laugh. I tease him. He stares at me. We kiss again. It's all going exactly to plan.

His blue eyes are so pretty when I look into them. If he knew what I'm doing with Sam at night, I wonder what he'd do to me.

At the ceremony, Dylan calls up Anna Mae, Sam, Laura, and then me. Fourth on the roster is later than I've ever been, but in some ways, it would be a blessing to meet a producer in an SUV at the end of the night, my packed suitcases already in the trunk, and be shuttled back home. At least I'm not waiting for the last necklace, like Jazmin, Leigh, and two other women are now. He picks it up from the tree stand slowly and lets the pendant swing in the air a bit. Those other two women are goners. One is smiling like she hasn't realized that yet, but it's going to come down to Leigh, who starts fights, versus Jazmin, the only woman in the group to get two Golden Necklaces during her time here. He pauses. The sound of our bated breath gets picked up on our mics.

"Leigh," he says.

Jazmin's face is so still it almost seems like she isn't breathing. The host says her usual lines, releasing us from our lineup, and Winna, Sam, and I rush over to her. Sam wraps her arms around her first, but Jazmin doesn't cry. Her jaw is tight and square.

"One of you needs to get engaged," she says. She kisses each of us on the cheek before pivoting on her heels and walking up the purple carpet toward Dylan. After they hug, they whisper in hushed voices, but they're both smiling. I itch the tattoo she drew across my chest, another eye to help me figure out the world with. Winna and Sam tear up. I start to cry from looking at them, and somehow I end up being the most distraught. Whatever happens, the season will be over in fourteen days. I'll see her again soon enough, but it will never be like this. All of us, young and pretty and together. It was almost like being a girl again, and I can't get that time back.

At the hotel room, I rip off Sam's false eyelashes. She unlaces the back of my corseted skintight dress.

"Did I ever tell you Spanish is my first language?" Sam asks me. I shake my head. "I didn't learn English until I was in grade school. When I was little, it was just me and my mom in a whole other language. I told Dylan that tonight. That's why he called me up so early."

"We haven't talked about your family that much," I say.

"We haven't talked about yours either. Wyatt thinks I should tell Dylan next week about my mom. He says I'll make it to hometowns if I disclose my story, but that's the whole fucking thing. We go to Chapel Hill together, no parents, no grandparents. It'll be me and my aunt in either my tiny apartment or hers. I'd seem pathetic."

"So don't tell him," I say.

"Final four, though," she says. "I could be the next One. Wyatt says that's what he's pictured me as this whole time, America's next darling to torture."

"Would you say yes if they asked you?" I can picture her on the other side of the limousines that first night, the mansion looking like her gaudy castle. The men would go crazy for her, coming in salsa dancing and saying, "I'm loco for Sam." They would find a man whose single mom has died, too, so they can bond over it.

"Even with Wyatt's powers, I shouldn't think about it. You're the kind of girl they'd ask."

"I don't want that. You know that I don't want anything else."

"You always say, 'You know, you know,'" Sam says. "But I don't. You never tell me things."

"I still think about the shooting. Do you?" I ask her.

"Yeah," she says. "Sometimes I wonder if coming here saved my life. I've been to that bar before. Maybe the universe is trying to keep me alive, while I always thought it was trying to kill me."

"All I keep thinking about is how"—I pause, the words stuck in my body—"not wanting to be with men can be punishable by death. Being here with you, I feel like, one wrong turn and I'm about to die."

BITE

MIRANDA HOVERS OVER Kenji's shoulder at his desk, where he sits all day and will sit long into the night. It's not her job to do this, but everything becomes Miranda's job toward the season's end. She makes the drama, everyone makes the arc, and Kenji makes you believe it. He searches through the pull-aside transcriptions, looking for the perfect utterances for the words Miranda needs from Emily. He has linked together half a sentence so far: "Dylan is / my / dream man / but / . . ."

Screen Emily, though Real Emily does not know this yet, has started to fall in love with Dylan after their time in the Casita. Neither can resist the raw passion that's exploded between them. Real Emily has been quiet about it, worried about the other women still there, but Kenji can make Screen Emily ripen before their eyes. Miranda was able to manage her better this week, get her into the Casita and get Winna to cry beautifully about it. The rankings are in her favor now.

"Dylan is / my / dream man / but / I'm not sure / he / loves me / yet. / By the end of this, / I think / he could. / I think he will."

Whenever she feels bad about twisting her fingers into the precise strings of Kenji's job, she reminds herself that she got him this job. She sensed potential in him when he was a lowly transcriber, one of the dozen who type up the most banal audio of the season to tag it for this purpose. It's her gift, after all, to find people in the rough and polish them to their Platonic ideal. Now he plucks out words and strings them together like Christmas lights. He searches through the log for love.

Miranda reminds herself of the contract the women signed. She always rereads it at the start of every season, a soothing balm, before passing it along to her girls. It gets her in the right frame of mind. After she places the stack of legal documents on their tiny nightstand at the hotel in LA, she grips the shoulders of the woman in front of her. Read this, she says. This is your life and you need to know what you're doing with it. It says you can be filmed twenty-four hours, seven days a week, through hidden and open cameras. Once it's filmed, the Studio can disseminate the footage and audio as they see fit. It says "throughout the Universe in perpetuity," as though aliens in a million years will watch it. The audio can be cut into embarrassing or derogatory slices at the Studio's discretion. They can concoct phrases you never said. Here, there is no such thing as a false light. After floating around space for a million years, when the aliens finally get a chance to watch the tapes, it will both be entirely unbelievable and a pristine snapshot of our cultural moment, of our lives. You could learn everything you need to know about people from watching it. Miranda believes that, truly.

She shuts her eyes as Kenji plays clip after clip for her so she can tune into the emotion rather than the phrases themselves. When the producers keep the women in pull-asides for too long, the audio takes on a different cadence. The women's voices drop into a scratchy drawl, and their thoughts become looser. Those are the best moments, when the woman says something so honest it makes Miranda's teeth ache. It's like peeling an orange in one clean spiral.

"Dylan is / my dream man / but / I'm not sure / he / loves me / yet. / By the end of this, / I think / he could. / I think he will. / All I want is to love and be loved in return."

WEEK SEVEN

OUR VILLA IN Florence has the perfect Mediterranean style that the sprawling mansion in LA tried to emulate, the kind of place that has not only a garden but grounds as well. Miranda tells me that since there are only six of us left, we each finally get our own room.

"The numbers get easier from here," she says. "Only two women leave this week. You don't have to be with the other women all the time. You can reclaim a bit of yourself now."

Though this was supposed to make me feel better, it doesn't. I had expected to be with Sam for the rest of my time here. I've grown used to her presence, the way she sleeps and rises, the way she gets dressed sock-shoe sock-shoe every morning. I go to Sam's room across the hall, leaving my door propped open with my suitcase. Her windows face the driveway, lined by spindly cypress trees, and mine face the vast olive grove on the other side. As she unpacks, she pulls a pastel yellow silicone vibrator from her suitcase. It's about the size of her hand, with a flat top coming to a rounded edge, like a large lipstick bullet. Without visible buttons, it's so nondescript it could almost be a modern desk sculpture.

"This is the reason I've done so well here," she says.

"I didn't know you had that."

"Well, yeah," she says. "I wasn't going to masturbate in front of you earlier. That would have been, like, sexual harassment or something."

"I thought I was the reason you did so well here."

"All these women are so sexed up from making out with Dylan, having horny dreams about him every night and thinking horny thoughts about him every day. They can't stay clear-eyed. Not me," she says, shaking the vibrator a bit as though it's a trophy. "It's even waterproof."

"Can you stop wagging that in my face, please?"

She zips it back up in her suitcase. "Given everything now, I thought you should know." She flops back on the plush bed. There are flashes here and there when it's just us two, and I forget what I'm doing here. When she's happy like this, it's almost as though there aren't a million cameras ready to be switched on outside our door.

"Thanks," I say. "You're such a thoughtful person."

We get mic'd in the hallway for B-roll. I'm greasy from the flight and my hair is stiff with the cornstarch I use as dry shampoo. I try to pin it back in an effort to disguise how bad I look, but this is what they get for making us film as soon as we arrive. We have all stopped complaining about the routine for the most part: land, unpack, shoot no matter how tired we are. We go out around the gardens, lined with busts and vases. There's a fountain, water glinting in the evening light. A cramped chapel is tucked at the edge of the villa's property, marked by a tiny, nondescript cross at the top of the door. A statue of Mary with open arms is outside the entryway. Church shots are kept to a minimum, so the cameras don't follow us. After all, it would be terrible if the show were marketed as the Christian dating show it really is, given that the lead and more than 80 percent of the contestants are devout. The rest of the women peek in and then head back to the garden and the sunlight, but I follow Sam all the way inside. The door knocks shut behind me, blocking out most of the light but for a small stained-glass window at the front. A car rattles by on the other side of the wooden door at the far side of the church.

She goes over to the door and presses her hand against the warped frame. "Should we make a run for it?"

"It's a nice chapel," I say instead of answering her question. I haven't allowed myself to think about the after with Sam. "I'm sure tons of people get married here."

"Can you picture it?" she asks. She steps away from the door and back toward the main altar. "Do you, Emily . . ." Her hands are pressed in front of her heart—I think she's trying to imitate a priest, but she's clearly never been to church. "Wait, I don't know your last name," she says.

"What?" I say, though I heard her just fine.

"Do you know mine?"

It feels like I do, or that I should, like it's something she must have told me long ago, the first night at the mansion, but I've forgotten. I know Winna's last name—Moon, for her tattoo—and Jazmin's because it was on Guava's dog bed. I knew the Laurens' initials: K and N. "I guess I don't," I say.

"Espinoza," she says. "My mom's. You?"

"Boylan," I say.

"Boylan," she says, stretching her lips wide to accommodate the new word. "Emily Boylan. Huh."

"You don't like it?" I ask.

"No. That's not it," she says. Another car roars by, filling the chapel with its sound. Her face is splintered in jewel-toned fragments of light. "Emily Boylan, do you take Dylan Walter to be your lawfully wedded husband?"

"Don't be like that." The chapel door flings open again, filling the room with sunlight.

"We need you by the rose bushes," the production assistant says, and we go back to the gardens, where we walk through prim hedges, arm in arm. Over the olive grove toward the city, the basilica suns itself above the surrounding roofs like a turtle on a log. After dinner, Sam convinces Wyatt to let us go for a run around the grounds even though it's dark. She keeps saying we're jet-lagged and that our sleep schedule is off, even though we've been in the same time zone for nearly a week. Miranda is in a pull-aside interview with Winna somewhere. They've been grilling her ever since she cried to me last week, and each time she leaves the interview room, I can't tell if she feels better or worse. We haven't talked one-on-one since our filmed chat. The only time I feel bad about what I'm doing here is when I think of her.

Sam and I run up and down a grassy path between cypresses until my shirt sticks to my skin with sweat and my stomach churns. Sam, taller than me, bounds ahead in long strides that I push myself to meet. I break first, sitting down on the grass at the top of the hill. I pant, and Sam sits next to me, knees up by her chest and arms hugging them in close. When I catch my breath, we walk back up toward the house. In the shadows of the villa, I reach out to hold her hand. It's the first time I've done it. Somehow, her hands are smaller than mine. I wouldn't have guessed that by looking at them, but her fingers are stubby and her palms are round. As we're about to go back to the light of the house, she pulls me toward her, closer to the shadowy patio wall. She doesn't say anything, just looks at me for a moment with her face close to mine. She squeezes my hand and then leans in, kisses me. It's quick, a peck, but I go back for more. There are stars out here, no more Los Angeles smog, no more exhaust particulates filling my lungs, no more wildfire smoke casting down from the mountains. Her breath is humid by my face, mixing with this fresh air. I breathe it in. She pushes me back against the wall into the full shadow of the staircase. The short hedge-maze garden is lit behind us, but we're all in the dark.

"I'm gross," I tell her. She goes to kiss my neck, running her tongue where she can taste the dried salt of my sweat.

"Like I care," she says, and kisses up my jaw back toward my lips.

"We should stop." The skin of my back where my shirt has ridden up rubs against the stucco of the wall.

"Why? We're on a run, okay?"

"We should go through the church door, like you said."

Sam raises her eyebrows. "I can't," she says. "I promised Wyatt I'd try to be the next One."

"I don't care about Wyatt," I say. "I don't want to have to be so worried."

She takes a step toward me, puts her lips on the hollow of my ear. "So stop worrying," she says. She parts my legs with her knee.

"I'm not going to have sex with you in a bush," I tell her.

"Fine," she says. "Somewhere else then. Let's go inside."

I drop her hand, and she follows me back toward the house. She pulls an ivy leaf from my hair and waves it in front of my face, smiling like she did with the vibrator earlier today. I pluck it from her fingertips.

As soon as I step through the door, Miranda comes up to us. "Where were you two? Was Laura with you?" she asks. I slip the leaf into my shorts pocket, careful not to crush it and careful for no one to see. I'm becoming sentimental. Before we can answer, she pulls us to the living room where the rest of the women are waiting.

"Here she is," Andrea says, and pushes Laura toward the edge of one of the couches.

"Date card. Sam, sit. Emily, read."

I pick up the folded note from the table. "'Anna Mae, Emily, Laura, Leigh, Winna. Love is like a priceless work of art. Love, Dylan.'"

Winna shakes Sam's leg. "Your first solo date!" she says.

"I'm happy," Sam says, preempting the question from Wyatt on the sidelines. "I can't believe I haven't had one yet. It's such an important time, so much to talk about with meeting families next week."

Wyatt pulls Sam aside for an interview. Upstairs, the women peel off to their rooms until it's just the PA, Laura, and me left walking down our wing. The PA unlocks Laura's door, but can't find my card and has to run back downstairs for a second.

"I wouldn't have sex in a bush either," Laura says as she waits with me.

"What?" I ask. She doesn't answer. "How much did you see?"

"Enough. Don't look so freaked, though. I'm not going to say anything."

"Why?"

"I've got bigger fish to fry," she says, and before I can ask what precisely those fish are, she goes into her room and latches the door behind her. In bed, I run over and over again what I'll say to Laura tomorrow. Maybe I won't bring it up at all. She doesn't have any proof, just her word against the two of ours. Maybe I could call her a homophobe and then I would automatically win the argument because she would seem bigoted. But her being a homophobe would mean that Sam and I were, in fact, kissing in the garden. I need to talk to Sam, but her footsteps don't come. Wyatt must be on her case about the date, pushing her to talk about her dead mom. I fall asleep hoping she's okay.

The next morning, it's raining so hard that they don't mic us at the hotel. I scarf down some untoasted bread and butter, a mini yogurt, and a hard-boiled egg with salt and pepper. I keep looking around for Sam, but I guess they no longer care about getting the group date's parting shot now that there's only one girl to wait on the sidelines. Our van follows the twisty roads down from the villa's hill through the city to a piazza filled with statues. Winna rubs my neck with her strong fingers.

"You seem tired," she says.

"I'm okay," I answer, leaning into her touch a bit. "And besides, I should be worrying about you."

"I'm okay, too. It's just been a lot these days."

I miss Jazmin and Vivian. I miss the bus chock-full of women, hot from all our bodies pressing against each other and eager to hear whatever music is on the radio. By the time we get to the city center, the sun has started to peek through the clouds.

"Dylan's running late," a production assistant says as we hop out, surprising no one. "Look at the statues. I'm taking espresso orders."

Instead of lining up to put in my coffee order, I part from the group. I'm so sleep-deprived that the light hurts my eyes, so I go to a shady corner of the square by the clock tower. I'm pretty sure the statue I choose to stand in front of is Michelangelo's *David*.

"In physics, one of the basic theories is that the mere observation of something changes its behavior," Laura says next to me, so close that I'd only have to sway in the wind a bit for my shoulder to brush against hers. "Even an atom, things that don't think. It's probably happening to poor David right now."

"What are you," I ask, "a closet physicist?" I don't mean to sound like such a bitch, but she could be holding a knife to my throat and I just haven't felt the edge of the blade yet.

"I'm a middle school science teacher," Laura says. She doesn't seem mad at me or my comment, though being a middle school teacher could be the reason she has been able to stay on the show for so long. She's steeled against all outrage, verbal lashings, and hysterics.

"I knew that," I say.

"That's what happened to you here," she says. I don't answer for a moment because it's what happened to everyone here. "I needed to get out of Juneau. I need a different life," she tells me. I also came here needing a different life. "He might love you now, but once this is over and five years have passed, he'll still love me."

"I'm not going to leave here with him," I tell her. "You don't have to worry about me."

"Winna?"

"I don't think it's her, not quite, but it might be. Anna Mae?" I say, casting a glance back toward the rest of the girls.

Laura shakes her head.

"Then my money is on you. Get engaged."

"I'm trying," she says. We stare up at the statue together. The straight slope of his nose almost reminds me of Dylan a bit, the way he looks like any other hot man. "I won't tell anyone."

"Thanks," I say.

"You know," she says, "he's not even the real one."

"Dylan?"

"No. The real *David*'s in a museum. Acid rain and all that, can't keep him out here. Imagine that, we come all the way to Florence and aren't allowed to see the actual art. Funny how that works, huh?"

"I guess," I say. She pinches my arm, lightly, lovingly almost, and goes back to the production assistant. It's weird how she drifts in and out like that. I wonder, for a second, if she might be my guardian angel, but then I realize I just haven't slept at all the last few days. David's penis is small for his giant body. When Michelangelo was making statues, there must have been a time when he chiseled too deep, and a chunk of David or whoever cracked off and scattered across the room. I feel a bit like that, like I whittled myself down too thin and all the meaty shards of myself are now spread on the floor. When Dylan comes, we sculpt self-portraits out of clay. This is sold to us as mission-critical to baring our souls to each other and falling in love. Mine looks like a piece of sludge with Bambi eyes, panicked at the newfound realization that it has started to exist.

That night, I get drunk quickly due to my lack of sleep, lack of food, lack of water, and lack of general health and well-being. My face looks swollen as though I've suffered from a mild allergic reaction, and I kiss Dylan extra enthusiastically, slipping my tongue into his mouth and my hands under his shirt. It's not like kissing Sam; his jaw scrapes against my face, his lips moisturized only with petroleum jelly and not fruity gloss. I'm sure he's never used a sugar scrub on them. We somehow end up horizontal on a chaise lounge. I hold his face between my hands as he covers his body with mine. He becomes hard against me, but I don't do anything about it this time. Men and their penises are no longer my problem.

When all of the other women have gone back to their bedrooms after the date, I slip a coffee filter between my door latch and the jamb to keep it propped open and knock on Sam's door, still buzzed. She opens it a crack, as though someone bad could be there, but when she realizes it's me, she opens it wide.

"I think we should have sex," I say.

"What makes you say that?"

"Because I want to."

"You know, I've been thinking that for a long time." She sits back on the bed in that long T-shirt she's always wearing, and I want so badly to see her body underneath it. I've seen her naked before as roommates for weeks, but it's all so different now. I'm still in my dress from the date, petal pink and short. I kept it on because I know I look good and I am trying to seduce her. "You're drunk," she tells me.

"I know." I go over to the bed and straddle her lap. She laughs at me a bit and I kiss her to swallow the sound of it. "Isn't it fun?"

"Mm-hmm," Sam murmurs as she kisses across my collarbone. I get off her, wrap my arms around my back to grab my zipper, struggle, and then turn my back toward her so she'll do it. She pulls it down slowly, careful not to pinch my skin or catch my hair. Her knuckles run down the ridges of my spine, and the dress falls to the floor in a pile at my feet. I shimmy my underwear off. She takes her shirt off the way boys do in movies, crossing her arms by the hem and pulling it over her head in one fell swoop. I get back on top of her and my chest presses against hers. I kiss her, then pull away to tell her I love kissing her.

"Thanks," she says, laughing again. She flutters her legs a bit to help me tug off her underwear. I press my lips against hers harder now, and she lies back on the bed. When I open my eyes for a second, I feel like I can see through the skin of her eyelids into the churn of her brain. I want to be underneath her. It's like she can read my mind because within a second she hovers above me, her hips grinding into mine.

"Where is it?" I ask. Her pupils are blown wide like black saucers.

"What?" she asks.

"The vibrator," I say in a half whisper. She leans over and pulls it from under the bed. When her body is away from mine, a wash of cold air prickles against my skin. She places it on the bed between us, and I stare at it and don't move.

"Have you ever used one like this before?"

I shake my head. "Haven't used any before. Just my fingers," I say. She puts it in my hand and I push my index finger against the flexible tip.

"Try it," she says. "See what you like."

I listen to her because Sam always has good ideas. She turns it to the lowest setting and I press it against myself. Sam kisses me and I start to make noises. I say her name appreciatively. She covers my mouth with her hand and, for a second, looks toward the door. I kiss the inside of her palm. She smiles and kisses my cheek. Soon my legs start to shake. Her mouth is on my throat, the hollow point where the necklace's pendant sits each week. I stop thinking about the necklace. She grabs the rise of my hip bone with one of her hands.

"You're so good," she says. "That's it."

My eyes flutter closed, and a moan vibrates past my lips. She tells me that I'm good again, that I can relax, that I feel good underneath her, that I should let myself come.

"Yes," I say, and keep saying, until my limbs feel like pixie sticks with all the sugar drained out of them. I kiss Sam, hands on her breasts, as she uses the vibrator on herself. It must take less than a minute or longer than an hour.

The next morning, Sam wakes me up, shaking my shoulder hard. I grumble at her; then her nails dig into me so hard that I open my eyes to slap her away.

"Are you kidding me, Sam?" a man's voice says from the corner of the room. I pull the sheets up to my shoulders, even though my naked bottom half is already covered and I'm wearing Sam's T-shirt. The vibrator comes loose from the comforter, thumping to the floor. Wyatt looks at it. "We had plans," he says through gritted teeth. He gestures at me as though I'm not here. "Crew is coming up here within ten minutes. What am I supposed to do, have them film this?"

"No," I say, shuffling up.

"You." He points to me. "Quiet." Sam gets out of the bed, stark naked in front of him and seemingly unperturbed. Wyatt's eyes don't flinch from her nudity. She throws me a pair of shorts before grabbing any of her own clothes, and I pull them on under the covers.

"It's fine," Sam says, finally putting a T-shirt from her suitcase over her head.

"It's not fine," Wyatt says. "It's anything but fine."

"It doesn't change anything," Sam says.

"You're my last girl here and you're sleeping with the Wife?" Wyatt says. "You've got to be kidding me, Sam."

I grab my underwear from the floor. My dress is nowhere in sight, kicked under the bed or something. I skirt behind the wide armchair toward the door. I don't want to be in this room when the camerapeople come. I want to be far, far away from here, staring at a nice blank wall instead of Wyatt's face.

"You," he says, grabbing my arm as I try to go past him. "You're not going anywhere."

"Let go of her," Sam says. I must look scared because it's the first time she has ever sounded mad at him. He drops his hand.

"Are you two in love or something?" he says.

"Let her leave. She doesn't need to be a part of this."

"I could make this into something huge, you know, if I wanted to."

If we tried our hardest, Sam and I could take him down and flee. Wyatt has balls, after all, and women aren't afraid to use their teeth when fighting. I would probably go to jail for assault, but it would be worth it because I hate Wyatt. I'm also scared of him, a bit in general but especially now.

"You wouldn't," she says, and she's not even looking at us. She's riffling through her suitcase. She pulls up a floral lilac dress and swings it toward us. "What do you think about this for the date?"

"If I can make this work for us, it's because I'm a genius," Wyatt says to Sam. "I can make this work for all of us, but only because I'm fucking great at my job." He looks me in the eyes. Men can look so angry sometimes. "I'm great at my job. I want you to know that."

"I know that," I say, trying to appease him because I have no idea what he's talking about.

"Get ready," he says, pointing at Sam. "You and I," he says to me, "we need to talk."

Clenching my underwear in my fist, I scamper across the hall, following Wyatt. I expect him to slam Sam's door, his neck veins visibly pulsing, but he doesn't. His eyes track the coffee filter as it drifts from the door jamb to the floor after propping my lock all night.

"You need to send yourself home. Like you needed to do that yesterday if you were going to sleep with her. But you definitely need to do it now. Okay, and we're trading rooms. No sleeping near her. No more talking to her." I want to protest. I can't even remember what the last thing I said to her was. "Sam's going to go on this date today, and afterwards, tonight, you're going to go to Dylan's room with the crew and you're going to tell him you hate God and want to abort every baby you see or something and then say you're going home."

"What about Miranda?" I ask.

"Shit," he says. "Okay, Miranda. Tell Miranda you need to have an honest conversation with Dylan about your values before you can tell him you love him. Tell her you'll drop the three words tonight if the conversation goes well and if you get the reassurance you need. She's desperate for you to win this. It's a bit pathetic, honestly, but that's Miranda for you. She'll take the bait. Then, when you're with him, do the whole 'I hate God' thing and also, while you're at it, say, 'Fuck Denver, I'll never move there.' And let him send you home, immediately. That's most important. If he doesn't, well, I'll think of something. I'm going to tell everyone you're sick today. The doctor on staff will come, take your temp, and look in your ears. Just say you've had diarrhea all night long and need to sleep and drink water. Do you want some Valium? I can drop some off."

"No. No Valium," I say.

Wyatt nods. "I need to go. Cameras are coming to Sam's room."

"You're not going to tell anyone?" I ask as his hand grabs the door handle.

"No," he says. "I remember what a shit show coming out was. I'm not going to make you do it on national television."

And he leaves before I can say, "Wait, what? You're gay?" But that's probably for the best because it seems like that would be offensive. I sit on the bed and stare at the television. There's no remote, no way to turn it on, so I imagine that it plays something so dramatic and tragic that I can forget what happened this morning. Not last night, though; that I don't want to forget. I fantasize about the plot lines *The One* would conjure with the footage of Sam and me sleeping together. I try to remind myself that coming here isn't the most important thing I've ever done. Outside of the show, I graduated from college and made friends, held down a job for a few years and got fired. I was alive. I wasn't hopeless. I don't need the show. In fact, the show needs me more than I could ever need it. Even Miranda hasn't seemed to realize that, but maybe I don't need her as much as I thought I did. The doctor comes and I tell him about my diarrhea. Thirty minutes later, a knock at the door comes. It's a Ziploc of three tiny white pills with a note that reads, "'Imodium' for your stomach. —W." I take the Valium, start to feel drunk, and let myself pass out.

I sleep well into the afternoon, and when I wake up, I stew in the outdoor hot tub until my skin is about to fall off. Then I go to the chapel, dripping in my towel, and pray for an hour. In the feminist meditation that Dr. C made me start doing, there's this line about not judging yourself when your thoughts stray. You're just supposed to recognize that you've gone down the wrong path and return to your breath, in and out. I'm going to be fine. Sam is going to be fine. I will see Sam again away from all of this. No one but Wyatt will know what happened. Well, no one but Wyatt and

Laura will know what happened. I'm going to be fine, in and out, in and out. Water drips from my hair, staining the cement floor around me. I am a good person. Good things will happen to me because I have been good my whole life.

That night, I tell Miranda exactly what Wyatt told me to, dangling my proclamation of love in front of her like a half-dead chipmunk before an owl. He's right that she's easy to dupe, so hungry for what I can offer that she doesn't take time to consider that I could want something independent from her. I can understand why Miranda has done this job season after season. Manipulation is its own kind of high.

Dylan's room is at the topmost floor of the hotel, away from all the women, and surrounded by rooms of handlers and producers so that we could never get to him alone if we tried. It's funny, in a way, that they stored him like a prize all the way up here, while they put Sam and me in the same bed for weeks on end. When he opens the door, he's in a T-shirt and jeans, though it's past midnight.

"I wasn't expecting you," Dylan says. I give him a practiced smile and kiss his cheek. "Is everything okay?" he asks. He takes my hands in his and leads me to a living room area. His suite is enormous with all sorts of gilded furniture strewn about. Out of the camera's view, his hair-makeup-wardrobe station takes up an entire corner of the room.

"Yes," I say, sitting on the couch across from him. I want to ask how his date with Sam was. Maybe they went to a vineyard and crushed grapes between their toes or raked olives down from trees into thinly woven nets or pulled threads of mozzarella into lush white bulbs. Whatever it was must have gone well; otherwise Wyatt wouldn't make me go through with our bargain.

"What's up?" he says. Before I can answer, he leans in to kiss me. "I missed you."

It's barely been twenty-four hours since I've seen him, but I say, "Yeah, I missed you, too. That's why I came here. I know next week is so big, you know, meeting my family. I've never brought someone home to my parents before."

"Stop," he says, kissing me again. His lips feel like sandpaper against my own, though I'm sure that it's half illusion. I don't want him to touch me anymore. "Stop worrying. I get it."

I bat my eyelashes at him because doe-eyed girls get whatever they want. "I'm not sure I can pack up my life right now and move somewhere and start a family. I don't think that's my timeline. I know you want to be married soon. You've always said that. I need to be straightforward with you that that's not where I'm at in my life right now. I wish I knew sooner, but I only realized this morning. I looked down at my ring finger on my left hand during breakfast, and I couldn't imagine it carrying that type of promise yet. I had to tell you."

"This leaves me with a lot to think about," he says. He drops his head against the crook of my neck in partial defeat. It's not a gesture to indicate we're parting ways now, but of a slow collapse, the desperate wheeze of a deflating balloon. Everything he wanted from me, he knows I can't give him. "But I want you to know that I would hate, more than anything, for you to compromise on your values to be with me, Emily."

"Thank you," I say. I look at the ground. I am the most demure woman to ever walk the earth. I may not have been sent home instantly like Wyatt wanted, but Wyatt's going to love my little performance. Almost as much as I hope that Dylan will hate it. I reach across the couch to hug him, no kisses anymore.

When we're out of earshot, Miranda turns to block my path. "What on God's green earth was that, Emily?"

"It just came out," I say. I raise my hands in front of my chest, trying to look apologetic.

"He's in love with you, you know. Did you see his sad puppy face? I thought you were going to tell him you loved him, and instead you pulled that line, that looking-at-your-bare-finger garbage. We had a plan, you and I. We were a team and I looked out for you. You should be thanking me, on the ground kneeling for my forgiveness. I made you and then all I ever get is bullshit." I don't say anything in response. Her face turns red, and for a second, I can picture her striking me across the cheek. She lets out a long sigh, interrupted by the ping of her phone. "I'll handle this. I need to talk to Terry."

The next night, I take my time packing my bags. Nearly every day since coming here, I've crumpled my clothes up and thrown them in my suitcases, confident that six hours later I would return, weighing an additional ounce from the necklace, and have to pull out my pajamas from the recesses of my luggage. Tonight I fold each pair of underwear in half, roll my T-shirts into neat triangles, and lay my jeans flat against one another like Lincoln Logs. They will have to be tucked away like this for another forty-eight hours, until I'm back at Logan Airport, where I'll take the Silver Line to the Red Line to the 86 bus back to my apartment, the apartment that I'll have to move out of in the course of a month; or I could take a Lyft. I'll have my phone again after all, and a bank account flush with what's left of my severance. I leave out a dark green dress, long and scoop-necked, chrome hoop earrings, and metallic heels. I've been saving it as a nice outfit, but I wasn't sure for what occasion. Then, in a carry-on, I pack my pajamas for the hotel tonight. I wonder where they'll take me, somewhere less nice than this hotel I'm sure.

Tonight, for once, there's no waiting. It's the swift slice of the guillotine. The host comes out to say Dylan doesn't need the cocktail party to make his decision. He knows what he needs to do, and without a toast, or any real bit of the usual ceremony at all, we line up in the library. It's the first time I've seen Sam in thirty-six hours, but I can't talk to her. She looks good, though, the Golden Necklace around her neck at last. She could get engaged to Dylan at this point, do that gig for a year or so, amicably part ways, and become rich and famous. Next week, the four remaining women will be shoulder to shoulder, finally fitting into one frame. Laura gets called first. Good for her, less likely she'll tell anyone what she saw, and then Winna next. As silence descends on the room, the last necklace swings on the tree. Dylan picks it up. Three cameras are trained on me, Leigh, and Anna Mae, one for each of us.

Whatever is left of my ego here has metamorphosized now that it's disentangled from the necklaces. I'm happy that either Leigh or Anna Mae will have risen above me in Dylan's rankings. I'll say something nice after he dismisses me, like that I know his future wife is in that room, waiting for forever with him. Wyatt comes to the front. When we catch each other's eye, he doesn't seem mad that I'm still here, but instead looks, like me, determined, comforted by the strictures of a plan.

"There's been a slight change in the proceedings for the evening," he says. Even Dylan seems surprised at the intrusion. Wyatt waves his hand, ushering the host back in. Taking a theatrical tone, the host begins her monologue. It's the most animated she has seemed all season, almost as though she has a real personality.

"Hi, Dylan, ladies. It's been beautiful to see, heartwarming, really, how far you've all come on this journey, and we're so proud of each of you. But the course of true love never did run smooth, and in our biggest twist ever, we can only allow three women to continue forward to hometown dates next week. With how strong each of the connections are, we're taking this seriously and want to give each of you ladies and Dylan as much focused time as possible to solidify your relationship."

"Excuse me, what?" Anna Mae asks, breaking the split second of silence that fell over the room. The pressure in the air cracks. Anna Mae seemed certain that she was going to get the last necklace. She was probably right.

"Terry," Dylan says. He drops the necklace in a tangle on the table. "Did you know about this? We didn't run through this."

"Let's talk in private," Terry says, dodging the question.

"It's my show. It's not his show," Dylan says, pointing to Wyatt. It's like the remaining contestants have stopped existing, and the spotlight finally shines down on the real players: production and the lead, and the twisty dance they're engaged in. "We agreed when I started this, no surprises."

"Wyatt," Miranda says, "what the fuck?" She surges forward from the side of the room and pulls him away, with Andrea trailing behind. Miranda's nails turn white from the pressure on his arm. I wonder if it hurts him.

Before we can hear Wyatt's answer, everyone but two camera-people vacates the room. It's like the snow globe of the show, its perfect world, was shaken too hard until it finally cracked, and the six of us are left to stand in the gelatinous sludge. A production assistant marks the floor where Dylan stood with a chalk *X*.

Winna asks, "Sam, has this ever happened before? Do you know what Wyatt is talking about?"

"No," she says, her voice blank and quiet. "I have no idea."

"Terry didn't even seem to know what was going on," Leigh says. "How can we be expected to?" No one else speaks for a couple of minutes until Dylan returns with the host. He stands in front of us on his marker, and says, "Thank you for that announcement. I'm going to need a couple minutes to think."

I deflate at the obvious pick-up, the false hope of finality, and we're left to wait again. I want this all to be over. Winna sits on the floor, a mess of folded limbs in her tight dress and heels, and one by one, we drop beside her. A production assistant puts the necklace back on the tree, and it swings like a pendulum, a smaller and smaller arc until it moves so little that I could be imagining it.

"You okay?" Sam asks Winna and me at one point, tapping her fingers across each of our bare shoulders. Winna nods and looks to me for my answer. I can tell they're both worried about me and my imminent departure.

"Yeah," I say. I don't know when Sam will touch me again. "I'm fine."

Sam thumbs the necklace between her fingers. She had to know that this was how the night was going to go down, that I would leave for her to stay, that Wyatt wouldn't let her go, not when she had gotten this far. If we were alone, I would assure her of the cosmic rightness of the moment. Everything is slotting into place. Anna Mae cries silently, but Dylan and production take so long that the mood passes over her. Later the host, Dylan, and Terry stride in together again. Terry joins Wyatt, Miranda, and Andrea in their corner. I try to smooth out the wrinkles on my dress. The cameras start to roll. Dylan thanks us for our patience. The host plucks the necklace off the tree with exaggerated solemnity and cups it in her closed hands.

"Dylan, I trust you can take it from here," she says, and leaves the room.

"I know what I need to do," he says with equal gravitas. Wyatt was right to make this happen, the drama in the air is palpable. The viewers will love it. "Sam, I gave you the Golden Necklace because I wanted to meet your family and see where our journey leads. But with these changes, it wouldn't be right to keep you when my feelings for another woman are stronger. I'm sorry, but I need to ask for your necklace back."

After weeks of his boring speeches, this one flashes through my mind faster than I can process. I try to make manic eye contact without moving an inch—with Wyatt, whose face grows paler by the second, his plan disintegrating in two quick sentences, or with Miranda, who watches Wyatt with burgeoning glee. But everyone's eyes are on Sam as she tries to get the necklace off. Dylan reaches over to help her, but she swats him away. He stands there, baffled at her newfound resistance to him, as though he expected throughout all of this for us to remain lovingly at his mercy.

"I've got it," she says. Her voice is shaky. I can't look at her, but I can't look away.

"Turn around," he says. He puts his hands on her shoulders to twist her. When her hands tremble so violently that it becomes clear the only way it's coming off is if she snaps the chain, she turns. She faces us now and her eyes meet mine. "Emily," Dylan says. He's looking at me expectantly with the Golden Necklace outstretched in his hand.

Oh, no. Oh, of course.

I have to keep my face even, like I'm walking out of the limo all over again. I'm watching water boil, paint dry, an ant crawl, traffic still, bread stale, beer ferment, a beginner chess player decide on a move, a plant unfurl a new leaf, wax drip, waves, the ocean, the porch in Madeira.

"I want you to stay," Dylan says, close to my ear, as though he doesn't want the other women to hear it, but loud enough for our mics to pick it up. Dylan spins me around to face them. I'm such a coward that I can only stare at the floor, picturing Sam's bare collarbone. One of his hands moves my hair away; one holds my neck still. His fingers are long and elegant, so familiar now after weeks of doing this. If we were alone, this would be intimate, but nothing is intimate here. The necklace clicks.

The host comes in. "Take a minute to say your goodbyes."

RELEASE

WHEN THINGS DON'T go Miranda's way, when girls start to act out, Miranda gets acupuncture. The first seasons as a senior producer she didn't have an outlet to destress. Three years in a row, she got cracked tooth syndrome and celebrated the end of the seasons nursing root canals. Her husband complained about not being able to go out to eat with her, and when Frank found out, he said she better take care of it before she turned into a toothless wonder. He suggested going to one of those bars where you throw axes to relax. She turned to acupuncture instead. She finds a place in Juneau, where Laura's hometown is taking place. Andrea's her producer, so Miranda gets a few days off. Facedown on the bed, with her head snug in the terry cloth holder, she lets out deep exhales.

The acupuncturist places needles in the nape of her neck, and she can feel the painless slide of steel into her skin. She doesn't want it to hurt, of course; she's not one of those people. It's only that if there's no sensation at all, she can't be sure she's feeling better.

The night Emily pulled her stunt in Dylan's room, Miranda couldn't fall asleep, afraid that the season's reins were slipping from her fingers. She thought that was the worst of it, until Wyatt colluded with Frank for that twist, shilling more drama, higher stakes, never-been-done-before ratings. She laughed when it blew up in his face, quietly enough for it not to get picked up on the mics, Wyatt's top girl getting swapped for Emily. Still, she felt out of control. After the ceremony, she tried to scream into her pillow, picturing Wyatt weaseling into Frank's confidence with ease. It was pathetic. She has turned into a pathetic person, a producer who can't deliver, a wife who likes to be away from her husband, a woman with a mouthful of cracked teeth and sagging skin plumped full with chemicals. Needles poke up from her back like spines sucking up her stress and dissipating it into the ether. As her brain waves slow, she thinks about the shape of the season and the strings she can tighten to make it bow in the right place.

If the viewer starts the season rooting for one woman to become the Wife, it's not a question of how to make them switch their allegiance to a new woman if their pick falls through. It's a matter of making them feel like they never really wanted that first girl to win after all. You want them to think rooting for the new frontrunner was, in fact, their original idea. If she plants the right seeds early in the episodes and highlights the juiciest fragments, she can fix situations that long ago went sour. Each season, the marketing team says the love story is unprecedented, but it's always the same. The couple finds a way to be together, and the villains who stand in their way get their due punishment. No one can wean themselves off love's comforting cycle.

WEEK EIGHT

I HATE DYLAN. It's all I can think about on the plane to Cleveland so that Dylan can meet my parents. Cleveland. After all this, I'm still ending up in Ohio. That's almost the worst part about this. Almost, but not really.

He could have pulled Sam outside to a white painted bench on the terrace of the hotel and sat her down. He could have sent her home gently, releasing her to a black SUV to zip her away into the night. He didn't have to spin her around like a top to face us and take the Golden Necklace from her. He didn't even have the dignity to do it smoothly. His hands fumbled as she stood there with her eyes wide with shock. To be chosen and to have it snatched away. And for what? For me? I can't wait to break his heart. I only hope that he loves me enough to be wrecked over it. I remember the story Micah told me on the date about his old wound from being cheated on. For a second, I regret that he'll never know what I did because I'm sure that would hurt him the worst. I press my face against the double-paned plastic window of the airplane. I'm beginning to feel more and more like a zoo animal, watched for amusement day in and day out. I saw a photo once of a gorilla tragically smushing his face against the glass wall of his cage, staring back at the people who stare at him. Except, here, I'm at fault. Zoo animals don't walk into their cages willingly.

The handler and I get driven to Columbus, only two hours away, but passing the leafless forests in a blur, all familiar again, makes it feel longer. I practice what I'm going to say to Miranda and then I practice what I'm going to say to Dylan. I count the red-tailed hawks in the barren branches, a dozen, two dozen. My mind goes numb. Brown trees, brown grass, cars zipping past us. McDonald's, Burger King, Denny's, Quality Inn, Super 8, McDonald's, like a loop playing in my head replacing the one of Sam being kicked off. At least being on the highway makes me feel like I'm home. If only I were in the driver's seat.

Miranda meets me in my hotel room the next day after traveling from St. Louis for Winna's family date. I hope it went so well. There's a part of me that feels bad for not doing this earlier, for her sake or for Laura's. Miranda watches me get dressed as we chat, camel-colored wool coat, white knit beanie with a fluffy pom-

pom on top, black jeans, ivory cashmere sweater. I look like the other girls in my hometown, so that seems fitting.

"I'm going home," I tell her as I stab my earring posts through my ears, eyeing her in the reflection of the mirror. I'm nervous but resolute.

"I know," she says. "Your parents are so excited. I've gotten them to come around on this whole thing, working my magic, of course."

"No, I'm leaving the show," I say. "I'm breaking up with Dylan."

"After you told him you're not going to marry him and he still picked you, you're going to leave him?" Miranda laughs. "And how do you plan to get out of here? With what wallet, what phone?"

"Miranda, I can't leave here with him."

"Never said you were. You're not a reliable person, Emily. That's what you taught me with your stunt last week. This affects me, too, you know. My job could be on the line for this," she says. It hadn't occurred to me that they could keep me here against my will. I try to think of the contract, but the legal jargon was so dense that I could barely understand what I signed.

"It's your job, but it's my life," I tell her. A flush has crept up her cheeks, and she types on her phone, thumbs whizzing over the letters, but she tamps down her lingering disappointment in me. I don't want her to be mad at me. At the end of all this, I still want to impress her. I've seen her yell at PAs before, people who didn't live up to her standards. She put in so much time trying to make me into something that she thought I wanted, to be the kind of girl who would get engaged after six weeks on a reality show, and to her credit, she almost succeeded. It's hard to fathom how close I was to going through with it, to being Dylan's wife.

"What if I said that my job is my life?" she asks.

"I wouldn't believe you," I say.

She snorts. "Believe me."

"Hey, I'm sure that's not true. You have friends, your husband, other people, hobbies. You told me you had a cat once." I should never have started listing things because it becomes evident I know so little about Miranda's existence outside her role in my time here.

"I don't need your pity," she snaps, looking at me for the first time since breaking the news.

"It's not pity. It was a bit of genuine human emotion."

"Well, I don't need that either."

"Okay," I tell her.

"And besides, I've still got Winna in the game. I know when to cut my losses on a lame horse."

"You're saying it's time to put me down?"

"Yes," she says. For once, I'm happy to be a bad bet, someone you can't count on. "When are you going to break up with him?"

"At my first available convenience," I say. "I don't know. Do you have a preference? I can level with you."

"We're going to need to change the date. I'll need to make calls," she says. "We also need to do a pull-aside, a lot of pull-asides. After last week, I should've guessed this was coming. That's on me. Luckily, America likes to watch heartbreak as much as they like to watch people fall in love. Catharsis, fantasy, it's all the same thing, scratches the same itch." When she returns from a phone call, she tosses the television remote on my bed without a word. That's how I know it's over, that the bubble has finally popped.

An hour later, a conference room in the hotel is decorated with the usual crystal chandeliers, candles, and red curtains. We do an interview about my feelings before the date. Family is so important to me. It wouldn't be right to have him meet them when I'm not sure I can get there emotionally. Miranda keeps telling me to say "If I can't get there with my heart," or that I need to "follow my heart's guidance." I don't want to be in a position where Dylan asks for my dad's blessing when I'm not even sure that I want him to propose. That's a special moment, a man asking the father for the blessing. It should only happen once in a girl's life. It's not the right time for me.

Production begins our date in a park by a highway a few miles away from my house, somewhere I've never been. If I hadn't told Miranda about my plans, I'm sure we would be going somewhere nicer. They seem to have closed the park down, no stray runners or dog-walkers. I break into a jog as I approach Dylan, not wanting to prolong the waving from afar. I have to stop myself from doing our usual routine where I jump into his arms and wrap my legs around him. The greeting kiss, though, is unavoidable. His lips are salty as though he's just been eating potato chips.

"Where's your head at?" he asks me as we sit down on a wooden bench. He must be able to tell something is wrong. Perhaps the delay in our start time tipped him off. For a moment, I feel gratified that he was the one waiting after all those cocktail parties and bus rides when I looked out on the horizon for him, a beacon of my freedom. A cameraperson kneels in front of us, wearing gloves in the cold air. His thighs must be so strong, bearing all that weight constantly. Like a wind-up doll, I begin my rehearsed speech. I practiced all the way from the drive from Cleveland to Columbus. Miranda tweaked the language a bit here and there: "speak my truth" instead of "be honest," "where my spirit has led me" instead of "what I've been thinking about."

"I've been struggling," I say. "It feels like I'm in a dark tunnel. I can't find the walls, I can't hear anything, and I sure as hell can't see anything. I have no idea what's going to happen to me next. It's like, Dylan might be on the other side, but maybe he won't. You were the best guy I ever dated, but I can't be in the tunnel anymore."

"You're using past tense about me," he says. He's always had this edge to him, this astuteness. It only comes out in flashes; the rest of the time he seems like his boyish self. It's the only time I'm able to tell that he was once a key player in this himself. "I put everything on the line for you. Everything."

"I don't feel like I'm at a place, in my heart, where I can marry you," I say.

"We don't have to get engaged next week if you're not ready," he says with an understanding nod. "There's no tunnel. It can be just you and me. Everything can be just us." His arms hang around my neck, hands dangling somewhere behind my head. I wonder what it will take for him to unwrap himself from me. "Just us" is never just us here. Even on this much hyped hometown solo date, we're surrounded by eight people documenting our conversation for future public consumption.

"No. I don't want to marry you ever."

"Why are you saying this?" He looks so puzzled. He throws a look toward Terry behind the camera. I almost feel bad for him, except that I don't. "Is there something wrong with your family? Are you worried about overnights next week? I won't sleep with them. I know what I felt in the Casita. I don't have that with the other women."

"I'm saying it because it's true," I say. "I have to speak my truth to you."

"Are you mad at me?" he asks, like a toddler.

"No," I say, a lie.

"Is this really happening? Are you serious?" He sends a more desperate look toward Terry, but Terry for once doesn't look encouraging behind the camera. Once I leave, he'll have to work to get Dylan to stick it out through the end, but then again, I could be thinking too highly of myself. I don't know if I believe Dylan when he said that if he can't have me, he doesn't want the other girls. I don't even think Dylan believed himself when he said that.

"I'm sorry," I say.

"Emily, you have to tell me why," he says. "You don't understand. I love you."

I didn't realize he was allowed to say he loves me. I thought only the women were allowed to confess that. I nearly laugh at the surprise of it, but laughing in the face of the One during a breakup is sure to make the general public hate me as much as they would for having sex with a woman behind his back, if not more.

"I was so caught up trying to fall in love with you that I was never able to," I say. It's the truth, cold and hard like a bullet. As soon as he can sense that, he turns his attention away from me.

"Can't you talk to her?" he asks Miranda.

"Do you want to propose to someone who needs convincing?" Miranda says.

"You told me it was going to be her," he says. "We all knew it was going to be her. Even with that stupid conversation in my room last week, it's been her. Terry, can't you do something? Did you know about this?"

"Sorry, bud. It's time to say your goodbyes," Terry says, firming his feet behind the camera.

"The only time I've been able to forget I'm on this show is with you," Dylan says as he stands from the bench. "I could picture you as my wife, my real wife."

"Laura and Winna are still here," I say. "You'll be fine."

"I won't."

"Dylan, I can't express to you how fine you will be. You'll get everything you ever wanted."

"I wanted you." My heart races at the words, more powerful to me than when he said he loved me. They shock the cold, dead engine that fuels me. It runs on male validation, not their love but their desire. Everything I wanted is happening to me, but I no longer want it. He looks like he is going to kiss me as I get into the SUV, but instead, he puts his hand on his chest, covering his mic.

With his body pressed against mine, the audio will be even more muffled. He whispers in my ear, "I love you, Emily, and everyone else would have, too. They were rooting for us. Now you'll never have the kind of life I could have given you. I hope you know that."

"Thanks," I say. "I do."

The door closes softly behind me, the latch barely catching. Miranda sits in the passenger seat, craning to look at me. A tripod is attached to the middle hutch, with a camera tracing me. I must look startled. Miranda quirks an eyebrow at me.

"What'd he say to you?"

"That he loved me again," I say. They, them, the viewers, and the world—Sam was right; they existed in the back of his mind, too, powering him forward like a rudimentary animatron. It was never about me. I worry for Winna, who seems to love him without care for the masses. She's special in that way; perhaps her job onstage has taught her when to stop performing. Laura, though, seems to want this life, whatever artifice it may entail. I hope she wins. "What now?" I ask Miranda.

"Now, we get to work," she says. She sends a text. I consider buckling my seat belt in, but that would look stupid on camera. The car rolls slowly away from Dylan. "Can you cry?" she asks me.

"I can try," I say, and I think of onions, a slant tug on a single strand of my hair, the way I can't stop watching myself, constantly trying to be good but never being good enough.

Back at the hotel room, a production assistant hands me a list of my outfits organized by the date I wore them on and asks me to bring some spare shirts. She leads me to a conference room, which now has dark blue curtains behind my bench. I go behind them and change into the outfit I wore to the fake club. The production assistant shows me a screenshot of the video from that day, my hair curled and pinned back, my blush pink and shiny. I try to re-create it, though Winna helped me with it last time. In front of the camera and the studio lights, I sit on the backless bench and straighten my spine.

"What are you most afraid of in this process?" Miranda asks me.

"That the life I want is incompatible with the life Dylan will want," I say.

"Another," Miranda says.

"I'm afraid Dylan and I will have different priorities."

"More. And you look dead bored. Do you want a shot?" Miranda waves her hand at a handler, starting to summon them from the sidelines.

"No, no," I say. It must be before noon. "I can do it." I need to be clearheaded. I slap my cheeks a bit, for color, for life. "I can be slow to open up to people, slow to see where my heart leads me. Dylan could want me to move faster than I'll be able to."

She digs deeper into the sentiments, down to the dregs. Cameras off, I change outfits, my first solo date.

"I don't have her shirt," I say to Miranda, peeking out behind the curtains.

"Whose shirt?" she asks me.

"Sam's. She lent it to me." Miranda looks at the phone that the production assistant holds up to her, another still frame from my date. She riffles through my pile of nondescript tees and throws me one. She warns me that she's going to have to start pushing me. She asks if I can take it. I can.

"Why is today's date important to you?"

"My parents fell in love quickly. I've always wanted that for myself, always compared my relationships to their love. It seems so easy for them. I want it to be easy with Dylan. I don't think I can get engaged if I don't have that. Today will show me how compatible we are, whether we have that click."

Miranda comes over to me, ruffles my hair. She goes behind the curtains, grabs a tube of tinted lip balm, and applies it breezily across my lips, my eyelids, the tops of my cheeks. She orders a production assistant to get a tissue.

"Blot," she directs me, handing me a neatly folded square of toilet paper. "Smudge it a bit." She steps back behind the camera. "How was today's date?"

"Today's date was so amazing. We have great physical chemistry, like fireworks. I love spending time with him."

"What else?"

"I think Dylan and I have the best connection in the group. I can't imagine that the other women here are as far along as I am with Dylan."

"More about the physical connection," she says.

"He's a great kisser," I say. "He takes my breath away. I can't imagine the other women have that powerful physical chemistry either." I fake laugh. "That first night in the Casita, I knew we had something special. Today reaffirmed that. Our feelings for each other are meant to be."

I change into a cocktail dress that I wore at the mansion, jeans and a T-shirt from the day before my solo date, my sweater from Iceland, canvas jacket from Madeira, sundress from Rome. All this was only a few weeks ago, but it feels further in the past as I rehash. I do the math for real, trying to get a handle on the time warp. It has only been fifty days since I entered that LA hotel to sign my contract and get my psych tests. I spin the web that Miranda is constructing, an instant physical connection, a bit of lust but not too much. Being at the front of the group, the other women getting jealous but me not caring; Dylan falling hard for me, my sudden feint, then his heartbreak, heartbreak, heartbreak. I wanted this to work, but it wasn't right for me. I have to do what's best for myself. I get so tired from talking that I'm able to produce the kind of deep racking sobs that make me hiccup. In addition to these new pick-ups, Miranda has hours of footage of me doing her game of truth testing, saying horrible things to see if I believed myself, because I was so far from knowing how I felt about anything or anyone.

"Are you okay?" Miranda asks me. "We can take a break soon."

"No, I'm fine," I assure her. "You asked if I could cry. Voilà."

"People will get mad at you," she warns me. "They'll call you fake and competitive, immature and dramatic, a bitch, whatever."

"I don't care," I say, and I wonder if that's finally true.

It's well past dinner when we finish. The twilight is greenish, lit warmer by the lights of the strip malls around us. I tell a handler that I want to say goodbye to Wyatt, to thank him for everything he's done for me. She leads me to the makeshift hub, where all the screens play the footage from today on loop. I only get a peek of it as she cracks the door to get him, my face everywhere, splices of my audio, my promo photo, up on a bulletin board with the number of the mic pack I use next to it. Laura's and Winna's faces have been circled multiple times in different colored pens.

"Oh, it's you," he says, looking me up and down. He has that producer power, like the driest sand in the world sucking all the watery truth out of me.

"Dylan ruined your plans, not me. I did everything you said."

"You could have been less likable," Wyatt says. It's flippant, like he's not actually mad, but I can never tell with him. He would have needed to give me that advice twenty years ago.

"Give me her number," I say. My voice is stern, though I feel like I'm in an old movie, hauling someone up by the collar and shaking my fist at them.

"God, I wish I could've filmed this," he says. "It would have been the best television this show's gotten in years."

"Thanks for . . ." I pause, not knowing how to finish the sentence. Not outing me to the world, not secretly filming me having sex, saving my life a bit? "You helped me."

"I did it for her," he says. "She deserved better than this place." He stares at the lined wallpaper, then looks me up and down, always sizing me up. I know Sam and Wyatt weren't in love, but the way he looks at me makes me think they fell a bit for each other, hard and fast. I wouldn't blame him for that. I couldn't have escaped her pull even if I had wanted to. "It can break people, you know. I've seen it happen."

"I know," I say. He tells me the ten digits. I sing them in my head again and again, willing myself not to forget.

Back in my hotel room, someone has left a box of everything I gave up to come here on the bed: my bulging black wallet full of loose nickels and dimes, my thin slip of passport, the blissful glass square of my phone holding all its infinite knowledge. I order a car on a rideshare app to take me to the Columbus airport, where the rental car place is still open.

I pay the young-driver fee. I forgo all the insurance, the roadside assistance. They give me the keys to the tiniest car on the lot, no bigger than a golf cart. Inside, it smells like fake evergreens and cigarette smoke. The cupholder is covered in a thick, sticky sludge. I can't figure out how to connect my phone to Bluetooth. The trunk is heavy with my baggage from the last two months, all those dresses I'll never wear again. I can't even figure out how to use the cruise control. I leave a voicemail for my mother. I'm sorry I couldn't come tonight, but there's one last thing I had to do for the show. She doesn't have to worry. I try to imagine the next time I'll see my parents and what I'll say to them. I picture Sam in Dylan's place around our dinner table eking out conversation, like sparks from a bow drill trying to start a fire. My phone, larger in my hand than I remember it, speaks to me.

"Your estimated time of arrival in Chapel Hill, North Carolina, is 5:17 a.m."

My parents will be distressed by my choices, or they won't be, but I don't need to worry about that now. I listen to talk radio from a pastor getting calls from troubled parishioners. I'm in the real world again. Even the air tastes different, windows down on the salt lick highway sprayed white. It's cold, but it keeps me awake. I have to pay for my own gas, relishing the sound of the credit card clicking into place. Read my chip, press my zip code, eat Takis, think of Winna, drink burnt coffee, think of the mansion's machine, listen to NPR, get confused by the news, so much news that I've missed. No one is even talking about the shooting anymore. I eat more Takis and wash them down with the coffee now gone cold. When I sit to pee at a rest stop, half the influencers I follow seem to have broken up or gotten pregnant. I'm happy to see their bronze faces again like old friends at a high school reunion.

I don't even know where Sam lives. I can wait somewhere, anywhere, in a parking lot until morning when she answers my texts. I'm doing the Grand Gesture, what Miranda always wanted from me, the proclamation, the heart beating and bloody on the table in front of someone, ready to be cherished or eaten. That's what people want to see, and now that I'm finally ready to give it, there's no one around to watch. My eyelids begin drooping somewhere in the mountains of West Virginia when I haven't seen anyone else on the road for an hour. I pull over on the side of the highway. There's no signal. Hypothetically, I know it's dangerous, a woman sleeping alone in her car in the middle of nowhere, not even her phone to rely on, God only knows who is out there. But I also know I'm alone after weeks of being surrounded. The siege on my mind has ended. I fall asleep surrounded by trees and blue hills and blue hills, reaching out beyond me until I get to her.

MILK

AT THE SOFT premiere, Miranda doesn't get drunk. She shows up for the beginning, makes the rounds to Wyatt, Andrea, and Terry, congratulates the host on another excellent season, then circles over to Frank. He rubs his knuckles up and down the back of her neck, rattling over the chains of her necklaces, her hair up in a high bun on her head. He tells her she's done a wonderful job, simply spectacular, and that she looks amazing tonight.

"I'm not supposed to say that kind of stuff anymore, though," Frank says. "I hear women don't like to be complimented these days."

"Not me," Miranda says. "I can't seem to get enough."

"You pulled it out, baby. You really did it. I was getting worried we'd have to put you out to pasture soon."

Before the advance episode screening starts, she texts her husband she'll be home late, that he should go to bed without her, and tells her coworkers she needs some quality time with her husband. She goes to the nearest four-star hotel and puts the charge on her personal credit card so her husband will never see the bill. Beneath the plush comforter, she flips her laptop open and streams the video file from the private company drive. Room service arrives with warm cookies and a tall glass of milk laid out on a tray with a sunflower next to it.

The first episode, of course, is perfect, except for a stray Starbucks cup on a side table that ruins one of the shots. She clicks through to the next one, watches it, and clicks on to the next. She licks the cookie crumbs and smear of melted dark chocolate off the plate. The plot of the season winds tighter and tighter around Emily and Dylan, her competitiveness and confidence that grate on the other women. Their warnings to him about making sure his Wife is sincere become increasingly desperate. She watches Emily tell Dylan she's leaving the show, leaving him. It matches with the feminist theme almost, for the man's heart to be broken and patched up by the end. The focus groups went crazy for the ending. That sated bliss is what she wanted for the viewers. The plunging numbers will rise, digit by digit, from the work she did. Friends will tell coworkers that this season, as opposed to the others before it, is worth tuning in to. Frank will give her a bigger bonus this year. She'll have her first pick of the men to produce next season.

Through the open shades of the hotel window, she can see her reflection, illuminated by the glow from the bathroom. The screen pauses on a still of Emily, wiping her fake tears away in the SUV as she's driven to the airport hotel. There are people who have what it takes to walk away and people who have what it takes to stay. She shuts the laptop screen before the engagement episode and swallows the last sip from the glass. Miranda wishes, only for a second, that she was the other type of person. But she has nothing but the show, nothing else to wrangle but the unwieldy, ungrateful creature she has worked so hard to assemble. The silken whole milk, thick with fat for this one night a year, coats her teeth, and for a second, she's worried she'll gag on it.

ACKNOWLEDGMENTS

Thank you to everyone who has ever been nice to me, including, but not limited to, Ashley Bates, Julie Buntin, Gabe Habash, Peter Ho Davies, Janelle Leonard, Anna Majeski, Gaby Mongelli, Claire Messud, Terry Tempest Williams, Laura van den Berg, and Amy Williams.